EVEN BENEATH THE FROZEN ARCTIC
WASTELAND,
THE FLAME OF NAZI EVIL BURNS. . . .

INDIANA JONES—He was given possession of a box by a dying explorer, with the warning to protect its contents at all costs. Now Indy is racing to discover its ancient secret before his old enemies can put him in an early grave.

ULLA TORNAES—A brilliant and beautiful Danish scientist, she joins Indy on his Arctic adventure, only to discover the price of courage and the ruthlessness of Hitler's minions.

EVELYN BRIGGS BALDWIN—He nearly lost his life on a North Pole expedition. Now he must be prepared to put his life on the line again to protect the world's greatest secret.

REINGOLD—He has sworn allegiance to Hitler, and nothing will stand in the way of his mission's success—not even Indy and his friends.

SPARKS—An eccentric radio technician, he sets out on a quest for stolen treasure only to find himself in the middle of a desperate battle whose stakes are nothing less than good and evil . . . and personal survival.

INDIANA JONES™

AND THE

HOLLOW EARTH

MAX McCOY

BANTAM BOOKS
NEW YORK   TORONTO   LONDON   SYDNEY   AUCKLAND

INDIANA JONES AND THE HOLLOW EARTH
A Bantam Book / March 1997

ISBN 0-553-56195-2

Published simultaneously in the United States and Canada

Bantam Books are published by Bantam Books, a division of Bantam
Doubleday Dell Publishing Group, Inc. Its trademark, consisting of
the words "Bantam Books" and the portrayal of a rooster, is Regis-
tered in U.S. Patent and Trademark Office and in other countries.
Marca Registrada. Bantam Books, 1540 Broadway, New York,
New York 10036.

PRINTED IN THE UNITED STATES OF AMERICA

RAD   10   9   8   7   6   5   4   3   2   1

For Don Coldsmith and the Tallgrass Writing Workshop

The ice opens suddenly to the right, and to the left, and we are whirling dizzily, in immense concentric circles, round and round the borders of a gigantic amphitheatre, the summit of whose walls are lost in the darkness and the distance. The circles rapidly grow small—we are plunging madly within the grasp of the whirlpool—and amid a roaring, and bellowing, and thundering of ocean and tempest, the ship is quivering—oh God!—and going down!

—Edgar Allan Poe, "Ms. Found in a Bottle"

AND THE

HOLLOW
EARTH

Prologue

THE CHIMERA OF MEMORY

This is what Indiana Jones remembers:

Cradling the dying Ulla with one arm while pointing the Webley down the tunnel with the other. He can hear the sound of the approaching Nazis, the *tromp-tromp* of their boots and the urgently whispered "Schnell! Schnell!" of the squad leader, but for one long moment they are still hidden by the last bend in the rock-lined passage.

Indy is exhausted, his arm is weak, and his hand is shaking so badly that what he's doing with the heavy revolver can hardly be called aiming. There are only two rounds left in the Webley's cylinder, two shots with which to make a last stand against a half dozen heavily armed SS troops.

Long odds, but Indy and his companions have no choice.

They have reached the end of the Edda Shaft and their backs are literally against the wall: a broad, flat wall of featureless gray rock. There are no more passages to take, no signs to decipher, nothing that would indicate a way around this deadest of ends.

Gunnar has taken off his shirt and is making himself

ready to fight with his bare hands by slapping his own face, hard enough to bring the blood to the corners of his mouth. Sweat gleams from his broad chest, and his flowing red beard and fierce blue eyes conjure images of his berserker ancestors.

Sparks is the youngest and smallest of the group, but has remained the calmest. The seventeen-year-old army radioman is sitting cross-legged, arranging and re-arranging a pile of stones on the floor.

"What color is between red and green in the spectrum?" Sparks asks.

"Yellow!" Indy shouts. "Hurry up! They're almost here."

"I've almost got it," Sparks says.

But Indy can't quite remember why the stones are important or what it is that Sparks almost has.

Then there is Ulla.

The Danish cave explorer has been shot in the chest by a Nazi ricochet. Her khaki blouse is wet with blood and her straight blond hair, where the ends have brushed against her blouse, is stained a strawberry color. Her skin has turned a fishbelly shade of white, and her lips, un-painted and normally a healthy salmon, are tinged with blue. Her breath is ragged and is accompanied by a sick-ening gurgle.

"Jones," she says.

"Sugar, don't try to talk," Indy says as he wipes his eyes with the back of his gun hand. "Save your strength."

"Be a man," she rasps. "And don't call me Sugar."

The heat is unbearable and the thick air feels like molasses in Indy's aching lungs. Then the hair on the back of his neck and along his forearms begins to bristle.

"Do you feel that?" asks Sparks.

"Yeah," Indy says over his shoulder. "What is it?"

"Static electricity. The air has become supercharged. I don't know why."

The Nazis are almost upon them. The rhythm of their boots and the rattle of their equipment has become a cacophony that is about to burst from around the corner.

Gunnar growls.

Then Ulla opens her eyes and looks over Indy's shoulder at the empty wall beyond. Her eyes widen and she wets her blood-flecked lips.

"I must be dead," she says. "The Valkyries are here."

And that is the last that Indy can remember.

What happened next? It is a troublesome but minor mystery, one that continues to tug at the back of Indy's mind but that really doesn't amount to much; after all, it's not as if the fate of worlds turn on his remembering. Oh, he can recall most of the failed expedition down the Edda Shaft—the eventual discovery of the underground river and so forth—but it is here, at the dead end, where his mind goes blank.

It may have been noxious fumes emanating from the superheated rocks, combined with hunger and fatigue, that caused the loss of memory. Or, they could have stumbled into a pocket of bad air, or any one of a half dozen other explanations that would account for the missing time.

Except . . .

Sometimes, in the shadowy world between wakefulness and dreaming that Indy can almost remember, he can almost make sense of it; or during a thunderstorm, when a bolt of lightning hits a little too close and leaves his senses reeling; or even—how curious!—when he spies winged chimeras and gargoyles peeking from the eaves of medieval buildings.

Then Indy goes back to the very beginning, scouring his memory for clues, and like a careful librarian he goes patiently through to the end.

The tale begins in snow and it will end in snow. . . .

1

THE LATE VISITOR

Princeton, New Jersey
Early 1934—Winter

The arctic wind growled like a living beast at the corners of the house, and it was this otherworldly sound—transformed by the imagination into something both frightening and pitiful—that caused Indiana Jones to look up from his reading for the first time since supper.

Having been wrenched from tales of gold and ghosts in the mountains of New Mexico, it took him a moment to gather his senses and correctly place the source of the eerie wail. He marked his place in *Coronado's Children* with a scrap of paper. Then he removed his reading glasses, placed them carefully atop the pile of other books and assorted maps beside his chair, and massaged his tired eyes with his fingertips. His vest was unbuttoned and his favorite bow tie, a gift from Marcus Brody, dangled limply around his neck. Indy glanced at the clock on the fireplace mantel—above the hearth that had grown cold from neglect—and uttered a grunt of disbelief that it was nearing midnight. In a little less than six hours, he would be on a train bound for New Mexico. He should have been asleep hours ago, but he was reluctant to surrender himself to the nightmares.

He couldn't remember exactly when they began—they may have gone as far back as that summer in Utah, when he was thirteen—but there was no doubt that they were becoming more frequent. And more frightening.

The nightmares always followed the same pattern: Indy would come to his senses inside a small, dark box. His arms would be pressed tightly against his sides. Not until the dirt started raining on the lid would he realize that he was in a coffin, and the coffin had been lowered into a grave. He would shout and claw madly at the coffin lid, but to no avail—he was buried alive.

Then came the knock.

Softly, muffled by the crust of snow that clung to the front door and nearly lost in the fury of the winter storm that was turning the New Jersey countryside into something white and alien. Had Indy not been summoned back to the here and now by the shriek of the wind, he might have missed it; even so, he wasn't altogether sure that he hadn't imagined the sound.

Indy unlocked the door and swung it open a few inches, allowing a torrent of snowflakes to swirl and flutter into the living room, and blinked against the numbing cold. A figure in a dark overcoat, with a hat pulled low over his eyes, stood at the bottom of the steps. His right hand gripped the rail, while tucked beneath his left arm was a package about the size of a cigar box.

"Dr. Jones?" the man rasped.

"Yes," Indy said.

"Forgive the inconvenience—" the man began, but he wheezed to a stop in mid-sentence. He closed his eyes, as if in pain, and held up one hand to beg Indy's patience.

Indy grasped the man's elbow.

"We'll be more comfortable talking where it is warm," Indy said as he pulled the man gently into the house and shut the door behind him. He walked him across the room and to the heavily padded chair next to the fireplace.

"Thank you," the man gasped.

The visitor removed his hat, tugged off his gloves, then placed the articles on the arm of the chair. The dark wooden box, however, he kept safely on his lap.

The visitor was at least seventy. His hair and beard were the color of dirty snow, and the skin on the backs of his hands shone like blue-veined alabaster in the light from the electric lamps. There was a nasty scrape on the back of his right hand, and although the cold appeared to have stopped the bleeding, it looked painful. To Indy, the bruise seemed to be in the zigzag pattern of a tire tread.

"Sorry to barge in on you like this," the old man said. "It shows a dreadful lack of manners. But you were the only person I could think of at this hour."

"Don't worry about that," Indy said as he leaned down and looked into the man's unusually alert, steel-gray eyes. "Are you hurt? Or are you sick? Can I ring the doctor for you?"

"I'm quite all right," the old man said with a wave. "Did you lock the door behind me?"

"No, but—"

"Please, humor an old man," the visitor pleaded. "Lock the door."

"Are you sure you're all right?"

"For now. Lock the door."

"If you say so," Indy said as he went to the door and slid home the bolt. Beside the door was his suitcase, packed and ready to go. On top of the suitcase was his fedora.

"A trip?" the old man asked.

"Yes," Indy said. "I'm leaving in the morning for New

Mexico, where I hope to do some limited but potentially rewarding archaeological work in the Guadalupe Mountains."

"Treasure hunting," the old man said. "I am rather cold and would be grateful for something warm to drink. Whiskey, perhaps."

"I'm all out. But I could warm some coffee."

"That will do. Black, with lots of sugar."

Indy went to the kitchen, lit a burner, and placed the pot of three-hour-old coffee over it. While the coffee was heating he knelt at the fireplace and prodded the ashes of the old fire with a poker. Soon he had located a pocket of embers and, by carefully feeding them with paper and kindling, made a cheerful blaze to take the chill from the room.

"Careful," he warned a few minutes later as he handed the visitor a steaming mug. "Don't burn yourself."

"Thank you," the old man said, holding the mug with both hands. Then he eyed Indy curiously. "You don't remember me, do you?"

"No," Indy said.

"I'm not surprised." The old man gently probed the back of his skull with his fingers, then grimaced in pain. "It was years ago. You were a graduate student at the University of Chicago and I was on tour, and our paths crossed one night when you accompanied Abner Ravenwood to one of my lectures at the old civic auditorium. My name is Evelyn Briggs Baldwin."

"Of course!" Indy said. "You lectured on your adventures with Peary in the Arctic and your own dash for the pole in 1902. You built Fort McKinley, discovered Graham Bell Land, and believed that the aurora borealis could be harnessed as a perpetual source of power for humanity. . . . I found the concept quite fascinating, actually."

"It is comforting to know that someone remembers me after all these years," Baldwin said. "I certainly remember you. You were so full of questions after the lecture, so brimming with enthusiasm. You impressed me that night, and afterward I made a point of following your career in the papers. You have been no saint, Dr. Jones. You seem to have had more than your share of what in simpler times used to be called scrapes."

"Well . . ."

"No matter," Baldwin said. "It shows that you have spirit, that you aren't afraid to challenge convention for the sake of the greater good. It is the reason that I am here tonight. I obtained your home address, with the intent of mailing you this chest."

Baldwin tapped the box with his forefinger. It was made of some kind of dark exotic wood, had brass hinges and a sturdy thumb latch, and resembled a tiny treasure chest. It had obviously held some type of medical or scientific instrument, but that must have been long ago; there were many gouges and scratches on its exterior, the corners had been beaten down, and the gold-scripted name of the manufacturer, Burroughs Wellcome & Co., was badly cracked and faded. A heavy piece of twine had been tied around the chest to discourage anyone from trying to open it.

"Why me?" Indy asked.

"Because there is no one else I can trust," Baldwin wheezed. "I have been forgotten by the world, condemned to old age and a series of meaningless clerking jobs with various government departments. I never married. All of my friends are dead. I have a niece who lives in Kansas, but we are hardly close. And the secret which I am about to entrust to you requires someone with your degree of resourcefulness."

The old man paused. So much talk had clearly exhausted

him, and he needed a last bit of strength. He leaned back, rested his head against the back of the chair, and draped his hands over the box in his lap. A drop of blood glistened from the interior of his right ear.

"I'm calling the doctor," Indy said.

"No," Baldwin said.

"I am no longer asking."

"But I have more that you must know."

"Then you can tell me while the doctor is on his way," Indy said. He hurried to the telephone, jiggled the switch hook, but his ear was met with silence.

"It's dead," he said as he replaced the receiver. "The storm must have knocked down the lines. I'm surprised that we still have electricity."

"Not the storm," Baldwin said. "It is the *Schutzstaffel*, and they have followed me here. Do you own a gun?"

"Of course," Indy said. He glanced at the suitcase, where his .38-caliber Webley revolver and a box of cartridges were nestled amid the socks and underwear. "But who are these people and why would we need to defend ourselves?"

"You know them better as the SS," Baldwin said.

"Nazis," Indy said. "Stormtroopers."

"This is a special squad," Baldwin said. "Agents of the Luminous Lodge of the Vril, also known as the Thule Society, the seed from which the German National Socialist party grew. This group of fanatics has been trailing me for months. Finally, earlier tonight, on the streets of Washington, they ran me down with a motorcar in an attempt to kill me and take my secrets. I escaped only because an alert cabbie saw me go down and stopped to help. . . . Get your gun."

"You're delirious," Indy said as he took his winter coat from the hook next to the door. "You rest here quietly. I'm going to bring a doctor back with me."

"No," Baldwin said. "There is no time."

"You're right," Indy said as he buttoned the coat and patted down his pockets for the keys to his Ford coupe. "We've got to get you to a hospital. Come on, I'll help you to the car."

"No." The old explorer grasped Indy's sleeve. "I beg you," he said. "Listen to me."

Indy paused.

"Grant me five minutes, then I will go."

Indy hesitated, then nodded.

"All right, Captain," he said. "Five minutes. Then we're off to the hospital."

"Agreed." Baldwin nodded. "Do you remember, so long ago in Chicago, the one question in particular you asked which took me aback, one that nobody had ever asked me before. Do you remember it?"

"Yes," Indy said. "It was a silly, graduate-student sort of question—I asked if any artifacts from an advanced, ancient civilization had ever been found in the high Arctic. Of course, you said no."

"I lied," Baldwin said.

He shoved the box into Indy's hands.

"There is no one else I can trust," Baldwin wheezed. "The Nazis have finally killed me, but they do not have the prize they seek. Protect the contents of this box at all costs. . . . There are some things that mankind is not yet ready to know."

"You're not going to die," Indy said forcefully.

"Everybody dies," Baldwin said. He rested his head against the back of the chair. "And I have lived more than my allotted time on the earth—I am beginning to feel positively biblical. Time to make room for somebody else, wouldn't you say?"

"No," Indy replied, "I would not."

"Dr. Jones," Baldwin said. "Have you ever pondered what is beneath our feet?"

"As an archaeologist, that's about all I ponder."

"No," Baldwin said. "I don't mean a few feet. I mean miles beneath our feet—hundreds of miles, in fact."

"Past the crust."

"There are nearly two hundred million square miles on the surface of the earth," Baldwin said, "and less than one third of that is land. But beneath the surface, there are two hundred and sixty-eight *billion* cubic miles, and nearly all of it is unexplored."

"Are you trying to say the earth is hollow?" Indy asked. "If so, I've heard these arguments before, and they have failed to convince me."

"Not hollow, not like an empty sphere or some type of geode spinning in space," Baldwin said. "More like a nearly solid body that is shot through with veins and fissures. If only one tenth of one percent of the earth's volume is in these habitable spaces—and that is a conservative estimate, given what we know of how spinning solids form—then it would mean that the greatest voyages of exploration lie within the earth, and not on it."

"Habitable spaces," Indy repeated. "Don't you mean traversable spaces?"

"No, Dr. Jones, I do not," Baldwin said.

"You can't be suggesting that there are places within the earth that are peopled," Indy said. "One of the surest tenets of modern science is that the energy for all living things comes ultimately from our sun. Nothing can survive in the depths of the earth, shut away from the sun's warmth and light, not even simple organisms—to say nothing of the complexity that is mankind."

Baldwin smiled.

"I said habitable. I didn't say human."

"You are ill," Indy said. "I don't mean to be unkind, but—"

Baldwin held up a frail hand.

"I have seen things that others have spied only in their reveries—or nightmares," he said. "A fantastic world, beyond the comprehension of our infant sciences. It has been called by many names, but there is truth in the old, old stories. You are familiar with the legend of the Kingdom of Agartha?"

"The ancient Buddhist myth about the race of supermen at the center of the earth."

Baldwin nodded.

"But what are the Nazis after?" Indy asked.

"Vril!" Baldwin gasped. "The vital element of this underground world. Matter itself yields to it. With it, one becomes godlike. All but immortal. Pass through solid rock, heal wounds, build cities in a single day—or destroy them. To possess Vril is to be invincible."

Indy was silent.

"I did not think that you would believe me," Baldwin said. "But the sum of my experience is contained in that box you hold, and it is testament enough. I have been terrified of the implications of unleashing this material upon the world, so I have shared it with no one. You must swear to protect these secrets, Dr. Jones. And if the loss of the contents of the box appears imminent, you must promise to destroy them."

"But—"

"Don't argue. Swear, damn you."

"Captain—"

"Swear!"

"I promise," Indy said finally.

"Good," Baldwin said weakly. "I know that you are a man of your word."

"Captain . . ." Indy placed the box aside and frantically

grasped his hand. "Stay with me now. We're going to get you some help."

"It is too late, Dr. Jones," Baldwin said. "Nothing can be done. And I am no longer the captain of anything, including this old wreck of a body. . . ."

Baldwin's voice trailed off. Then his eyes became cloudy and his head slumped to one side. The hand in Indy's grasp went limp.

"Captain!" Indy shouted.

Outside, the wind reached a crescendo. There was the earsplitting sound of a tree limb breaking free, and then the buzz and crackle of power lines separating.

The lights flickered and then went out.

By the glow of the fireplace, he pulled the old man from the chair and slung him over one shoulder. He remembered, however, to take the box with him.

2

THE THULE STONE

Indy watched in silence as the plain wooden coffin containing the body of Evelyn Briggs Baldwin was loaded onto the Penn Railway baggage car. His hands were thrust deep into the pockets of his leather jacket, his fedora was pushed back on the crown of his head, and his suitcase was at his feet. The mysterious box from the night before was tucked safely in the satchel that was slung, beneath his coat, over one shoulder.

The railway agent stood beside Indy with a clipboard, stamping his feet in a vain attempt to keep warm.

"Relative?" the agent asked.

"Only in spirit," Indy said.

The handlers placed the casket on the floor of the car with a thump that made Indy wince. Because the rest of the baggage and freight had already been loaded, they slid the door of the car shut. The outside latch fell into place with a sharp metallic clang.

"You'll have to change trains twice, but don't worry about the casket," the agent said as he snapped the tickets from the clipboard and handed them to Indy. "It will be switched automatically, and we've never lost one yet."

"That's good to know," Indy acknowledged. "And thanks for helping with the last-minute change in the intinerary."

"No trouble, Dr. Jones," the agent said. "Actually, I was expecting your call, since someone had inquired about your schedule just a few minutes before you called."

"Oh?"

"Yes," the agent said. "A gentleman from the university phoned and asked if you had changed your schedule yet. I told him no. I thought it was rather odd—that is, until you did ring me up and explain."

"Did you tell this gentleman anything else?"

"No," the agent answered. "Well, he asked if you were still bound for Chicago tomorrow. I corrected him and said that you were on your way to New Mexico today."

"Did this gentleman give his name?"

"No," the agent said. "But he spoke with an accent— German, I believe—and he seemed to know you quite well. Does that ring any bells?"

"Yes," Indy said. "Thanks."

Then he heard someone call his name, and when he turned he saw Marcus Brody waving and attempting to thread his way through the crowd jamming the Princeton Station platform. Indy said good-bye to the agent, picked up the suitcase, and met Brody halfway.

"Indiana," Brody began, "where have you been? I waited for nearly an hour. It is so unlike you to miss an appointment that I decided to come looking. . . . You look rather raw. Haven't you slept?"

"No," Indy said. "There was no time, considering the circumstances. I'm sorry that I missed our breakfast at the university club, but I've had some pressing business to take care of."

"Are you all right?" Brody asked. From the expression and the tone of his voice, his concern was evident.

"I'm fine," Indy said reassuringly as they made their

way to a half-empty bench. "But I'm afraid I can't say the same for the visitor I had last night. Have you read that newspaper you have tucked in your overcoat pocket? Is there anything on Evelyn Briggs Baldwin?"

As they sat down a tall blond man in a black trench coat near the platform's news kiosk lowered the *Saturday Evening Post* magazine he was pretending to read just enough to watch as Indy slid the suitcase beneath the bench, where it would be out of the way of the passing crowd. As soon as Indy's hand had left the suitcase, the man in the trench coat abandoned his spot near the newsstand and began to serpentine his way through the crowd toward the back of the bench where Indy and Brody sat.

"Baldwin?" Brody took his reading glasses from his pocket and unfolded the morning's copy of *The New York Times*. After thumbing through several pages, Brody found a six-inch story on the back of the first section, sandwiched between an article about two thousand Italian marriages performed simultaneously to inaugurate the twelfth year of fascism and a wireless item from La Paz about new fighting over the Chaco region.

E. B. BALDWIN DIES IN HIT-AND-RUN

71-Year-Old Explorer Is Struck on Icy Street

Special to *The New York Times*

PRINCETON, N.J.—Evelyn Briggs Baldwin, polar explorer, died here early today of a fractured skull after having been struck by an automobile on an ice-covered thoroughfare.

He was pronounced dead on arrival at the hospital, where he was brought by private car.

Mr. Baldwin accompanied Robert E. Peary on his

north Greenland expedition in 1893–94 as a meteorologist. In 1898–99 he was second in command
of Walter Wellman's polar expedition of Franz Josef
Land. He built and named Fort McKinley, discovered
and explored Graham Bell Land, and organized and
commanded the Baldwin-Ziegler polar expedition
in 1901–02, which ended in near disaster. His life's
ambition was thwarted in 1909 when Peary discovered
the Pole.

"Were you involved?" Brody asked as he removed his
glasses.

"I didn't run him down with my car, if that's what you
mean," Indy said, rubbing his hands together to keep them
warm. "Marcus, he came to my house after the accident.
He claimed that the Nazis were behind it, and that they
had been tracking him for months to steal some kind of
polar secret from him."

"What kind of secret?" Brody asked.

"Something called Vril."

"Never heard of it," Brody said. "Did you know this
Baldwin well?"

"I knew him not at all," Indy said. "We met once, years
ago when I was a graduate student and he was on the lecture circuit showing some of the motion pictures he had
taken in the Arctic. But our paths never crossed again, at
least not until last night. When the police inspected his
belongings at the hospital morgue, they found funeral
instructions neatly typed out and folded into his wallet. A
plot and a stone awaits him in his hometown in Kansas."

"Remarkable," Brody marveled. "What a gentleman."

"He may also have been a crackpot," Indy said. "Or he
may have been delusional as a result of his injuries. In
either event, he said some pretty fantastic things last night.

He said his secrets were contained in this little wooden box he gave me to protect. He made me swear."

Indy withdrew the little treasure-chest-shaped box from the satchel.

Brody took it, turned it over while examining it with an experienced eye, then ran his finger along the gold script. "Burroughs Wellcome," he read. "Indy, this is the kind of medicine chest that explorers carried at the turn of the century. Stanley, as I remember, had one of these things in Africa. It would make sense for Baldwin to have carried it to the Arctic."

He tugged at the string.

"Don't," Indy warned.

"Why not?" Brody asked. "Is there something dangerous inside?"

"That's the thing, Marcus," Indy said. "I don't know. Baldwin made me swear to protect whatever is inside, but he died before he could tell me whether he actually wanted me to open it or not."

"Something of a conundrum," Brody muttered as he returned the box.

"That's a good word for it," Indy said as he stowed the box back in the satchel. "I don't know what I'm going to do. I am bound to respect Baldwin's wishes—if only I knew what they were. But then, my curiosity has been piqued."

"I'll say," Brody said. "If it were me, I'm afraid I would have already had the contents cataloged. But you operate differently, Indy. I'm sure that given some time, you will discover the right thing to do."

The man in the black trench coat, who was now standing behind their bench with the magazine again covering his face, hooked his foot around a corner of Indy's suitcase and was slowly easing it away. The sound of the suitcase scraping against the ground was hidden by the din of the crowd.

Indy lowered his voice.

"Marcus, it would be a great help to me if you could ring some of your pals in Washington. See what they know about an organization called the Thule Society," he said. "It could merely be the ravings of a tired old man, but my instinct tells me there is something more to it."

"Such feelings would be understandable," Marcus acknowledged, "considering the circumstances. It is not every day that one has a guest die on them."

"Maybe," Indy said. "But I could almost swear that I have been followed since leaving the hospital early this morning."

"I will make some inquiries," Brody promised.

The suitcase was now clear of the bench and resting beside the man in the trench coat's right foot. With practiced nonchalance he closed the *Post*, picked up the suitcase, and disappeared into the crowd.

"You had better take this before I forget," Brody said as he reached into his jacket pocket. He drew out a small, flat package wrapped in brown paper and tied with string. "After all, it *is* the reason I agreed to meet you this morning."

"Ah," Indy said. "You found it."

"It wasn't easy," Brody admitted. "Despite the scanty information you gave me, I managed to locate this in a collection at Mexico City. Apparently it is the document you read about in *Coronada's Children*. The parchment which was first discovered in the basement of the palace at Sante Fe. It tells of a Capitán de Gavilán, who discovered a rich gold deposit in the Guadalupes. The document survived the Pueblo uprising of 1680, but de Gavilán—and every other Spaniard who did not flee New Mexico—did not. When you have a chance to examine it, you will note that a crude map has been drawn on the back."

"Marcus, I could kiss you."

"I'd consider it a personal favor if you wouldn't," Brody said. "And do be careful with it, since the parchment is in rather bad shape. I promised the curator we would have it back to him within the month. We will, won't we?"

"Of course," Indy said as he placed the two-hundred-fifty-year-old document into his satchel. Then, when he saw the worried look on Brody's face, he placed a hand on his friend's shoulder and asked, "Have you ever known me to lose anything?"

Brody smiled wanly.

"It's not that, Indy."

"Then, what?"

"It's the sudden taste you have developed for gold," Brody said. "It is unlike you to go after a treasure trove simply for the sake of wealth. I could understand it better if you were seeking an important piece for the museum, that just incidentally was worth a fortune."

"Believe me," Indy said, "I have my reasons."

"This has something to do with the Crystal Skull, doesn't it?"

Indy was silent, but his jaw muscles quivered.

"Tell me," Brody urged. "Perhaps I can help."

"It's better if you remain out of this," Indy said. "It could get ugly, and I don't want you or the museum mixed up in it more than you already are."

Brody looked hurt.

Indy placed a hand on his shoulder.

"But thank you, Marcus. Your offer is truly appreciated."

"I hope you know what you're doing," Brody said.

At that moment the conductor called, "All aboard."

"Well, I had better go," Indy said. "Thanks for your help. I'll contact you when I get a chance."

Brody was the curator of special collections at the American Museum of Natural History in New York. Indy had acquired many outstanding pieces for the museum through the years, and Brody had learned never to question him too closely about the methods he employed. Although the older man knew that Indy would invariably make the right decision when faced with an ethical choice—even when he had to go with the more difficult option—some of the means that he applied toward that end were likely to make a curator's head swim.

"You'd better hurry," Brody said. "Or you'll miss your train."

They shook hands, then Indy reached beneath the bench for his luggage. "Marcus," he said with a puzzled look, "where's my suitcase?"

The man in the black trench coat walked unhurriedly across the platform, Indy's suitcase swinging lazily by his side, a smile tugging at the corners of his cold blue eyes. Beneath his ordinary-looking business suit, on a heavy cord around his neck, swung a perforated zinc disk that identified him as a captain—a *Hauptsturmführer*—in the Leibstandarte SS, Adolf Hitler's personal guard. The disk carried other encoded information, such as his service number and blood type, but this last was a bit of redundancy; the type—A—was also tattooed beneath his right arm.

The man was six-foot one-inch tall, the minimum height for the Leibstandarte (but two inches greater than that required for the regular SS). His steps had the energy and grace of a natural athlete, and even now, at thirty, he prided himself that not even a filled tooth marred his physical perfection. He did not consider the scar tissue that ran like a lightning bolt down his right cheek as a mark of imperfection; but rather, like the young officers of the Great War and their saber scars, he wore it as a badge of honor. He considered the wound a testament to his

patriotic actions in the series of street battles with degen-
erates that culminated in the Reichstag fire, and the instal-
lation of Adolf Hitler as chancellor of Germany.

His name was Rudolf Reingold and six months earlier
he had been called away from his most recent assignment,
as an adviser for some of the grimmer construction details
of a new kind of *Konzentrationslager* at Dachau. Now
Reingold had an even more important task, one that had
been conferred upon him one heady Sunday afternoon in
the mountains at the Eagle's Nest. The memory of that
sunlit moment was with him even on this dreary winter's
day in New Jersey.

As the conductor continued his call to board, Reingold
walked leisurely into the unoccupied men's room. During
his stroll across the platform, three similarly dressed companions had fallen into step beside him, and they now
crowded around as he placed the suitcase on the wash
counter. While one of the trio stood watch at the door,
Reingold thumbed open the latches. He rummaged through
the clothes and books without success and finally picked
up a bullwhip and regarded it with disdain.

"Curious," he said as he threw the whip back into the
suitcase. "These Americans have such a fascination with
primitive weapons. Unfortunately, the box we seek is not
here. Jones must be carrying it on his person."

"Herr Captain," the man at the door, an SS assassin
named Jaekal, said in alarm. "The train is pulling away."
His hand was already inside his jacket, his fingers touching the butt of the 9mm Luger Parabellum semiautomatic
pistol that nestled in a shoulder holster there. "We hesitated at the opportunity to kill him last night, but we could
kill him *now*."

"Stating the obvious is an unthinking response," Reingold said as he carelessly tossed an undershirt into a
wastebasket. "We need something better. Now."

The two other men—whose names were Dortmuller and Liebel—were somewhat younger than the assassin, and they both fell miserably silent at this reprimand.

"Come, come," Reingold taunted. "We have only seconds before the train is out of the station and Jones is beyond our grasp, at least for a time. Can you think of nothing?"

Inspiration caused Dortmuller's face to brighten. He was the youngest of the squad, and as he pushed his glasses up on the bridge of his nose, he resembled a boy anxious to impress his schoolmaster.

"He will be looking for his suitcase, no?" Dortmuller asked in German. "Then you will return it. Explain that you have taken it by mistake. Apologize, offer to buy him a meal. That way, you can get close—"

"Yes, yes!" Reingold said as he hurriedly stuffed the clothes back into the suitcase and latched it. "But this is a one-person assignment. More would arouse suspicion."

"Should we follow?" Jaekal asked.

"Not immediately," Reingold said as he made for the door. "But if you do not receive word from me by the end of the day, then we will rendezvous in Kansas."

"Javolt."

The assassin started to make a Nazi salute.

"Not here, you idiot," Reingold hissed.

With the suitcase in his right hand and his left holding the hat on top of his head, Reingold began to run for the closest passenger car. As he neared the tracks he collided with Marcus Brody, who was stepping idly backward while he watched the train leave the platform.

Brody landed on his rump.

"I beg your pardon," was the strongest thing that he could bring himself to say.

"Sorry old chap," Reingold shouted in a near-flawless

English accent, but without stopping. "I was too long in the water closet and I have very nearly missed my train."

He grasped the railing with his left hand and lithely swung up onto the steps of the vestibule. Then he turned back toward Brody and threw him an impromptu salute by touching his forefinger to the brim of his hat.

"I beg your pardon," the pleasant-sounding voice with the English accent inquired, "but is this seat taken?"

Indy stirred beneath the fedora. He had slumped against the window and placed the hat over his eyes the moment the train had left the station, thankful that no one was in the next seat to disturb his slumber. But the question had been asked so politely that he felt compelled to sit up and respond in kind.

"Excuse me," Indy said as he removed his leather coat and satchel from the vacant seat. "Please, sit."

"Thank you," Reingold said as he slid into the seat. He had a black trench coat draped over a suitcase that Indy wished he could get a better look at. "I've had some rather rotten luck so far today."

"Oh?" Indy asked.

"Rather," the tall blond man said. "I seem to have grabbed someone else's suitcase this morning on the platform. I had placed my bag down for a moment in order to turn the pages of my magazine, and I must have taken this one by mistake."

"Could I take a look?" Indy asked.

"Sorry?"

"The suitcase. Do you mind if I take a look?"

"Please do," Reingold said as he removed the trench coat. Indy picked up the case, turned it over on his lap, and smiled.

"It seems my luck is improving," he said. "This case is mine. I lost it on the platform this morning."

"Really? Outstanding!"

"What a coincidence," Indy said appreciatively.

"You didn't happen to pick up *my* bag, did you?"

"I'm sorry, no," Indy said. "Actually, I saw no other bag."

"Ahem," Reingold said nervously. "I hope you don't mind my saying so, old boy, but perhaps this is too much of a coincidence. There's no name on the outside of the case. I know, because I looked desperately for one. Tell me, how should I know that it's yours?"

Indy smiled.

"I can describe what's inside," he said. "Did you open it?"

"No."

"Well, on top of my clean shirts is a carefully coiled bull-whip, which I imagine you would think is a trifle odd," Indy said. "There are also a half-dozen books on the geology and archaeology of New Mexico. Open it up and have a look."

The man paused.

"I'm sorry," he said, and looked away. "I will not participate in a charade. I did open it, but I was only looking for some identification. I hope you can forgive me."

"Understandable," Indy said, although his voice conveyed the opposite message.

"I can see that we're off to a bad start." The man gathered his coat as he spoke. "It would be best, I think, if I sought a seat elsewhere."

Indy hesitated.

"Wait," he said. "There's no harm done. If you say that you were merely looking for identification in order to return the case, then I can take your word for it. Please, sit down."

"You're certain?" the man asked.

"Of course," Indy said.

"Rudolph Hyde-Smith, formerly of London, currently

of Boston," Reingold said, holding out his hand. "You may call me Rudy. All of my friends do. Perhaps I could buy you lunch to make up for the horrible inconvenience my carelessness has caused you."

"That won't be necessary," Indy said as he shook hands. "My name is Jones. Indiana Jones."

"Now, there's a name!" Reingold exclaimed. "You colorful Americans. Is Indiana your given name or is it simply a nickname?"

"Just something that stuck," Indy said absently. "It was a long time ago. I took the name of—well, somebody I was very close to as a child."

Reingold smiled. He pulled a shining metal cigarette case from his pocket, opened it, and offered it toward Indy.

"I don't smoke," Indy said.

"As you wish." Reingold nodded and took a cigarette from the case, then snapped it shut. The lid was inscribed, but he had returned the case too quickly to his jacket pocket for Indy to read the inscription.

Reingold tapped the end of the cigarette on the crystal of his watch, then with a flourish brought out a windproof lighter. He thumbed a flame. His cheeks hollowed as he sucked flame into the cigarette. He closed the lighter by slapping it against his thigh, then leaned back in the seat and, with a contented look on his face, shoved it back into his trouser pocket.

"Foreign?" Indy asked, his nostrils twitching against the strong, stale smell of the tobacco.

"Not to me," Reingold said. "English."

"Of course," Indy said.

"Does the smoke bother you?" Reingold asked, suddenly concerned. "I will put it out."

"Thanks," Indy said.

Reingold snubbed the cigarette out on the heel of a well-shined shoe then dropped the butt in a nearby ashtray.

Indy turned his face to the snow-covered New Jersey landscape, which was rolling by at a steady pace. He was already regretting his decision to be amiable.

"Beautiful, isn't it?" Reingold commented, motioning to the window.

"Um," Indy grunted.

"The vastness of this country never ceases to amaze me," Reingold went on. "It all seems so fresh, so new. An unspoiled paradise. No wonder you Americans have such a sense of freedom and individuality."

"I'm not so sure that's how we all feel right now," Indy said. "The breadlines tend to remind us that we're in the same boat as the rest of the world."

"Quite right," Reingold said. "It *is* difficult to make a living, is it not? I'm in sales. Hister Industries. We make kitchen appliances. Ovens, mainly. Gas, not wood. If you don't mind my asking, what is it that you do?"

"I'm a college professor," Indy replied.

"Splendid," Reingold said. "What area?"

"I'm with the department of art and archaeology at Princeton."

"That explains those serious-looking books in your suitcase. Your work sounds fascinating. Buried treasure, lost cities, and all that. I'll wager you've had your share of adventure, eh?"

"Actually, it can be rather dull." Indy settled back and clasped his hands over his stomach. "But every so often I am allowed out of the classroom."

Indy was thankful for the silence that followed. He closed his eyes and let the gentle swaying of the car guide him toward sleep. He began to feel warm all over, despite the cold that seeped from the window, and the stress of the night before began to fade away.

Then Reingold asked, "But what about the whip?"

Indy sat up.

"What about it?" he asked testily.

"It seems odd," Reingold said cautiously. He knew he was risking early alienation of his quarry, but he could not resist the fun of testing this overaccommodating American's patience. "I have been sitting here trying to think of what use a professor of archaeology could possibly have with a bullwhip, and my mind has drawn a blank. Surely you wouldn't use it on your students. When I was a lad, the headmaster at my boarding school frequently used a riding crop, with painful results. But a whip of this size is out of the question. You could bloody well kill somebody."

Indy sighed.

"You have a vivid imagination," he said. "The whip is just another one of my tools, like a pick and shovel. I find it more useful than a simple coil of rope, because it is ready at—well, the drop of a hat."

"And yet, Dr. Jones, the whip is a formidable weapon," Reingold said. "Come now, you are with a friend. Do you mean to tell me that it has never tasted human flesh?"

"Only in self-defense."

"Ah, I knew it."

"Look," Indy said, pushing his hat back on the crown of his head with one hand and shaking the index finger of his other at Reingold. "You are damned curious for a simple kitchen-appliance salesman. If you want to believe that I am some sort of whip-wielding monster, then fine. But just leave me alone. All I want is some shut-eye."

"Dr. Jones," Reingold said apologetically. "I never meant to imply that you were a monster. But you *are* something more than a simple college professor, no?"

Indy tried to ignore him.

"I crave excitement," Reingold continued. "My life, it is so mundane. There is no passion. And here you are, the brash American with the colorful name and a bullwhip in his luggage. And I can only guess as to what you have in that satchel of yours that is slung beneath your coat. Can you understand my curiosity? Can you forgive a rather envious man a few moments of vicarious pleasure?"

Indy softened.

"Please, Mr. Smith—"

"Hyde-Smith," Reingold corrected. "But call me Rudy. All my friends do."

Before Indy could continue, the conductor appeared in the doorway with a hole punch in his hands. He asked for their tickets.

Reingold handed over the ticket he had expertly lifted from the vest pocket of a businessman he passed in the aisle after boarding the train. The conductor looked at it, then punched a diamond-shaped hole in it, and handed it back.

Indy gave the conductor his ticket. After punching it, the conductor told him that he would be changing trains at the next stop, which was coming up in about an hour. Indy glanced at his watch. He couldn't believe that he and the man he knew as Hyde-Smith had been talking for so long.

"Rudy," Indy said when the conductor was gone. "I am awfully tired and I'm going to nap until it's time for me to change trains."

"Of course," Reingold said.

"Thanks," Indy said.

"Go on to sleep. I'll wake you just before you need to change trains."

Indy eyed him suspiciously.

"You're sure?"

"Certainly," Reingold said. He retrieved a well-thumbed copy of an outdoor magazine that had been shoved between the seats by a previous passenger. "I'll just sit and quietly read. You won't even know I'm here."

• • •

The train came to a stop amid the squeal of brakes, the whoosh of steam, and a series of jerks that shook Indy awake. He yawned and looked at his watch, then turned to ask the man he thought was Hyde-Smith why he hadn't nudged him awake before they reached the station.

The seat was empty, except for the copy of *Sports Afield*. The magazine was open to an article on snaring the arctic fox.

Indy stood. He watched in disbelief as the leather strap that had held the satchel securely to his body snaked to the floor. The ends of the strap had been cut with near-surgical precision, and the satchel, of course, was gone.

Indy pressed his face to the window. Outside, he could see Reingold strolling across the platform, the satchel tucked beneath his arm. A cigarette dangled from his mouth. The ghost of a smile played across his lips and tugged at the corners of his sparkling blue eyes.

Indy dug the whip out of the suitcase, then made a dash out of the compartment and down the aisle to the end of the car. He bounded down the steps to the platform, slid across a patch of ice like a drunken figure skater, then regained his balance and raced after Reingold.

"Slow down!" the conductor yelled from the other end of the car.

The shout alerted Reingold, who turned to see Indy barreling through the crowd toward him. He feinted for the exit, then made a run back for the train and ducked beneath a passenger car. As Indy followed he could hear the conductor yell for them to stop, and the prediction that they were going to be killed—it was a busy yard.

On his hands and knees beneath the tangle of machinery on the underside of the car, the road bit into Indy's palms and dug at his knees. He jumped involuntarily when the train lurched as another string of cars was added. His head banged against a fitting that he could not identify, except on a hardness scale. The blow put a rather unfashionable dent on one side of his fedora that, he hoped, did not continue into the skull beneath.

When he emerged on the other side of the train, he nearly stepped into the path of a switch engine that was industriously chugging away on the nearest set of tracks. When the engine had passed, Indy spotted Reingold wading through the snow toward a high chain-link fence at the far end of the yard. The closer he got to the fence, the deeper the snow drift became, and the slower and higher his legs were forced to pump.

Then Reingold's fingers hooked the fence and he pulled himself up out of the snow. Quickly, he began to climb, then paused as he balanced astride the top bar to switch the satchel to his right hand. With his left hand—his gun hand—he drew a 7.65mm Walther, a small but deadly handgun that had been hidden in a jacket pocket.

Indy was still fifteen feet away, but his whip was now uncoiled. As Reingold pointed the Walther at his chest Indy lashed out. The end of the whip bit into Reingold's wrist and snaked around his arm like a living thing. He cried out as he dropped the Walther, which fell into the snowdrift below. Then Indy tugged on the whip, toppling Reingold from his perch.

"I told you it comes in handy," Indy said.

The big blond man disappeared in the drift, then found his footing and shook the whip loose from his bloody forearm. As he dug madly in the waist-deep snow for his gun, Indy lunged forward and grabbed the satchel, which Reingold had dropped in his fall from the fence. Then Reingold's frozen fingers found the butt of the gun, and with both hands, he pulled it up out of the snow and thrust it toward Indy.

Indy froze.

"I wouldn't pull that trigger," he said.

"Shut up," Reingold said. "Hand over the bag."

"Your barrel is packed with snow," Indy said.

Reingold hesitated.

"If you fire," Indy said, "your nasty little pistol is going to blow up in your face. The firing pin will probably bury itself right between those blue eyes."

"You could be lying."

"Could," Indy said as he drew in the bullwhip. "But there's only one way to find out. Shoot me."

Reingold was trying hard to appear confident, but ever so slightly, his hands began to tremble. He tightened the grip on the Walther.

"Who are you?" Indy asked as he slung the whip over his shoulder.

"Names do not matter. What matters is that you give me the box, or I will kill you and take it."

"You must be part of the gang that ran down Baldwin," Indy said. "The poor guy was seventy-one years old. Why murder an old man? What could this wooden box possibly contain?"

Indy opened the satchel and reached inside. Reingold expected his hand to emerge with the box, but instead it came out holding the Webley revolver.

"Too bad you didn't have time to look inside," Indy said.

Reingold cursed, in German.

"You men! Stop where you are!"

A trio of burly track workers, led by a detective carrying an ax handle in his left hand, had passed between two of the passenger cars and were making their way toward them.

Reingold hesitated.

"Put those guns down," the railway detective shouted. He shook the ax handle at them. "The conductor said there was some trouble in the yard. I see that he was right."

"Back away," Reingold said. "Or I will kill you as well."

The detective laughed.

"Am I supposed to be scared?" he asked, advancing, the ax handle at the ready. "You may kill one of us, but you can't get us all."

"No?" Reingold said. "I have a full clip. I could kill all of you in short order, and have enough ammunition left over for target practice."

The other men stopped. They had not yet reached the middle set of tracks.

"What's wrong with you?" the detective asked. "Are you going to let a pipsqueak with a popgun get the best of you?"

"Mac," the track foreman said, "you know I'm not scared of any man. But a bullet is different. I'm not getting paid to let folks target-practice with me."

At the far end of the yard, a freight train began to chug toward them, amid a couple of short whistle blasts and the clanging of the brass bell atop the locomotive.

Indy and Reingold still had their guns pointed at each other.

"Well"—Reingold sighed—"it looks like what we have here is a Mexican standoff. Assuming, of course, that there is no snow plugging the end of my gun barrel. That was a clever bit of playacting, Dr. Jones. I congratulate you."

"Coming from you," Indy said, "that is high praise indeed."

"Both of you had better stop jawing and put down those guns," the detective said, "because both of you are headed to jail. I don't let anybody run around my yard trying to shoot each other." The freight had gained some speed now. As it approached, the three track workers stepped out of the way. Reingold bolted toward the moving train.

"Stop!" Indy shouted, and pointed the Webley at the retreating figure. He cocked the weapon and drew a bead on Reingold's back, but he could not bring himself to squeeze the trigger.

Reingold grabbed a rung of a ladder at the corner of a boxcar and swung up, the tips of his boots now free of the roadbed and scrambling against the wooden side of the car. Then he found his footing, leaned away from the ladder, and threw a salute in Indy's direction.

Indy lowered the revolver.

"*Auf Wiedersehen*, Dr. Jones!" Reingold shouted. "I knew you wouldn't shoot me in the back, at least not when the prize was no longer in danger. That's the difference, my friend, between—" The scream of the train whistle drowned out the rest of his words.

Two days and what seemed a century later, Indy stepped from another train—this one carrying a string of Missouri, Kansas, and Texas passenger cars—onto the depot at Oswego, in southeast Kansas. Besides the railway crew, only one other person was on the platform: a well-dressed young woman whose face was all but hidden by a fur hat, a muffler, and a smoldering cigarette in an absurdly long holder.

Indy walked over to her and put down his suitcase.

"At least there's no snow," he said.

"I beg your pardon?" the woman mumbled.

"No snow on the ground. Back east is covered in a blanket of the stuff. But the sky does look like rain. . . . Pardon me, but I am assuming that you are Zoë Baldwin?" He extended his hand. "I'm Indiana Jones."

"You'll forgive me if I don't," she said. "There may be no snow, but it still seems dismally cold to me, and I would rather not remove my glove. My word. What happened to your face?"

"This?" Indy asked, rubbing the purple bruise on the right side of his chin where the left-handed detective had clobbered him after Reingold's escape. "A railway detective didn't like the way I conducted business in his yard."

"Oh dear," she said.

"I'm sorry we had to meet under these circumstances," Indy said.

"Don't be," Zoë snapped. "We weren't that close. I'm sorry he's gone, but I hadn't seen or heard from Uncle in years. He never married, you know. By the way, what was your connection to him?"

"Brief," Indy said. "Very brief."

"Hmmph." Zoë shifted the cigarette holder to the other side of her mouth.

"I take it that you are not familiar with your uncle's work?"

"Not really," she said. "When I was in high school I tried to read that book he wrote—*Under the North Star* or something like that—but it bored me to tears."

"Oh?" Indy was surprised. "I found it rather fascinating."

"It was all such a long time ago," Zoë said, "and none of it matters now, does it? Say, I hate to be forward, but Uncle did not leave anything resembling a will, did he?"

"A legacy, perhaps," Indy said.

"What does that mean?"

"Could we discuss this elsewhere?" Indy asked. "It is rather colder than I expected here on the platform."

From the plate-glass window of the Burgess Café— located on the ground floor of the Hotel Burgess—Indy watched as freezing rain began to pelt downtown Oswego. He savored the sensation of being inside the warm, steamy café while the weather did its worst outside.

Zoë Baldwin had removed her fur hat, her muffler, and her gloves, and placed these articles carefully on top of her coat in the chair beside her. Her car, a ten-year-old roadster, was parked at the curb.

Her dark hair was cut short in a style made popular in the Roaring Twenties. She was not an unattractive woman, Indy decided, but she seemed spoiled and her hairstyle looked somewhat dated on a woman in her mid-twenties. She looked like a flapper in search of a party that had long since ended.

The waitress brought two steaming mugs of coffee, and after Indy had taken a sip or two of his, he asked, "What is it that you do?"

The question seemed to take Zoë by surprise.

"What do you mean?"

"Well, I'm guessing that you're not a housewife," Indy said.

"No, Dr. Jones, I'm not a housewife." She smirked. "And I don't work, at least not in the usual sense of the word. If you ask most people in this town, I suppose they would tell you that I live off what is left of my family's money, and that's not going to last much longer. Does that answer your question?"

"I didn't mean—"

She held up her hand.

"It's all right," she said. "I'm just bored, and I have been for years. It's not your fault."

"Maybe you should get a hobby."

"I have hobbies," she said. "Unfortunately, most of them are married."

Indy nearly spilled his coffee.

"You say that you hardly knew your uncle. . . ." he began.

"No. He was already globe-trotting by the time I was born," she said. "Oh, he used to come home once in a while, but he never stayed for long. Then the trips back got fewer and fewer, and eventually he never came back at all."

"So he wouldn't have discussed anything with you recently."

"Like I said, it has been years since I heard from him."

"But you are his closest surviving relative?"

"That's right, for all the good it does me," she said.

"So you never heard your uncle talk about his arctic experiences, or something called the Vril, or anything that would strike you as out of the ordinary?"

"I never heard him talk about his explorations at all, except when he was lecturing," Zoë said. "Say, you told me that you didn't know him very well. Why are you asking so many questions?"

"Because I'm trying to solve a puzzle that your uncle left to me," Indy said.

After briefly recounting the last hour of Baldwin's life, and the promise he had elicited from Indy to protect the secret of the box, he removed the box from his satchel and placed it on the table.

"So you think he may have been murdered for this?"

"There's a strong possibility," Indy said.

Zoë picked up the dark box.

"What do you think is in it?" she asked.

"I don't know. But whatever it is meant a great deal to him."

"It's cute," she said. "It looks like a little treasure chest. What do you suppose the chances are that there's money inside?"

"Slim," Indy said.

"Damn." Zoë placed the box back on the table.

"Actually, it's a medicine chest," Indy informed her. "Baldwin probably carried it with him on expedition."

"Why haven't you opened it yet?"

"Because he didn't give me clear instructions about that," Indy said. "He just told me to protect it. And I wanted to get your advice . . . as his next of kin."

"Let's open it," she suggested. "Whatever's inside you can keep, unless it is something valuable."

"Define *valuable*."

"Something you can quickly turn into cash," was her immediate response.

"But with no historic or scientific value," Indy added.

"Agreed," she said.

Indy untied the knot and unraveled the twine from around the box. Then he placed the chest squarely in front of him on the table, thumbed open the latch, and lifted the lid. It contained no medicines, no bandages. Instead, there was a thick ledger book whose cardboard covers were held together by a rubber band. Beside the book glittered a chunk of some smoky crystal. A leather thong hung from one end.

"A diamond!" Zoë exclaimed.

The rest of the café turned to look.

"Sorry," Indy said, and grinned apologetically. Then, to Zoë: "It's not a gemstone, at least not a precious one." He picked up the rock and held it toward the light. "Icelandic spar, I'd guess, from the double refraction. Beautiful, but somewhat common."

Indy handed it to her.

"Oh ..," Zoë frowned, peering through the crystal. "Why would he save something like this? And why is it on a strap? What are you supposed to do with it?"

"I don't know," Indy said. "Maybe it had sentimental value, and he wore it around his neck."

Indy removed the rubber band and opened the book.

"This is Baldwin's journal for the 1902 expedition, or at least a portion of it." He began to scan the pages. Some of the entries were accompanied by sketches: sledges, dogs, the flagship *America*. "Page after page of daily log entries. Position, weather, supplies."

"How dreadfully dull," Zoë commented, throwing the

piece of quartz back into the chest. "The old man was obviously daft. There's nothing here that could possibly be of use to anybody. Why do you suppose he carried it around all these years?"

"I'm sure he had a reason."

"Stop," Zoë said. "Go back. That one drawing."

"This?" Indy asked.

It was a sketch of a slender finger of rock, sticking up out of the snow, covered with strange markings. It was difficult for Indy to tell because of the size of the sketch, but the markings resembled Norse runes. The caption beneath the drawing said simply, *The Thule Stone*.

"Yes," Zoë said. "That's the piece of rock that Uncle had sent back here when I was just a baby."

"Really?" Indy asked. "Where is it now?"

"Where it always has been," Zoë said. "At the cemetery, waiting for Uncle to be planted beneath it. You'll see it tomorrow, if you're planning to stay for the funeral."

"Actually, I wasn't," Indy said apologetically. "My train leaves rather early in the morning. I hope your uncle would understand."

"Wait a minute," Zoë said. "Why are you so interested in that old rock? Is it worth anything?"

Armed with a few yards of newsprint and a charcoal stick purchased at the drugstore down the street, Indy hailed a cab and set out for the cemetery, at the edge of town.

"I'd appreciate it if you'd wait here," he told the driver. "This shouldn't take long."

"Don't matter to me," the driver said. "It's your nickel."

The grave wasn't hard to find: it was the only plot marked by a slender, three-sided stone.

Squatting next to the stone was a disheveled, middle-aged man with wild black hair and bloodshot eyes. Despite the intermittent freezing rain, he was arranging a stack of firewood as casually as one might for a living-room fire-place. A can of gasoline was within arm's reach.

"I'm the gravedigger," the man said. "What are you?"

"Indiana Jones. I'm an archaeologist."

"Ha!" the man cried triumphantly. "I plant 'em and you dig 'em up."

The gravedigger pulled a pint bottle of whiskey from his back pocket, plucked an unlit cigar from his mouth, and took a long swig. Then he wiped the bottle with a dirty sleeve, replaced the cigar, and offered a drink to Indy.

"None for me, thanks," Indy said.

"Wise man," the gravedigger said. "What do you want, anyway?"

"I want to make a rubbing of this stone, if you wouldn't mind holding off on that fire for a few minutes," Indy said. "Baldwin sent it back from the Arctic, so it does have some historical significance."

"Suit yourself." The digger shrugged. "But your buddies have already been here to take pictures of it."

"Buddies?"

"Yeah, a couple of tall good-looking fellows with one of those newfangled German cameras. It was small, about the size of a pack of cigarettes."

"Terrific," Indy said as he unrolled the paper and went to work. The stone was a reddish, fine-grained granite, about a foot around at the base and narrowing to per-haps half of that near the tip. All three sides had been smoothed, and the runes were large but cut with skill. The designs were familiar, but of a period—obviously Norse, before 900 A.D.—that Indy had difficulty reading. The stone was badly weathered and the edges of some of the characters had been worn away.

"You know, in the old days they had to wait for a thaw to put their dead in the ground," the gravedigger announced as he sloshed gasoline over the jumble of logs, then stamped his foot on the frozen cemetery plot for emphasis.

"The dead are in no hurry," Indy said.

"Maybe not," the digger said. "But can you imagine waiting a week or two with gramps lying stiff as a board in the shed out back?"

"That would be unpleasant."

"Oh, that's not the worst of it," the digger continued as he searched his pockets for his matches. "You hear all sorts of horrible tales in this business. Why, they knocked open one old grave over in Cherokee County while they were digging next to it, and you know what? The poor devil had been buried alive. He was in his casket, like this"—he twisted his face up and turned his hands into hooks—"trying to claw his way out."

"Maybe there was a postmortem explanation," Indy suggested. "The effects of nature can sometimes put corpses into some awfully frightening positions."

"Nope," the gravedigger said. "Because you know what they found stuck on the inside of the coffin lid? *His fingernails.*"

I've seen worse, Indy thought.

"Can you imagine what that must have felt like?"

Indy hoped the question was rhetorical. He had finished the third and last side. He rolled up the paper and slipped a rubber band over the tube.

"Thanks," he said.

"Don't mention it."

The gravedigger struck a match. He held it cupped in his hand for a moment, then tossed it onto the gasoline-soaked logs, which ignited with a *whoosh* and a bright orange ball of flame.

"I'll let it burn for the rest of the morning, then spread out the ashes," he said. "It will be ready for digging by this afternoon."

"These men," Indy said. "Did they do anything besides make some photographs?"

"No," the digger replied. "Oh, they asked me some rather strange questions. They seemed morbidly interested in Baldwin's body. Had I seen it, and so forth. Then they asked me directions to the funeral home."

3

BURIED ALIVE

Indy returned to the hotel and checked into a room on the second floor. He took the suitcase from the bellhop, pressed a dime into the boy's hand, and locked and chained the door behind him. The lock was predictably cheap and the chain equally insubstantial, so Indy took the straight-backed chair from the room's writing desk and wedged it beneath the knob. Then he went to the window and made sure it was latched.

Outside, the late-afternoon sun glinted from the ice-covered street. All along the street, shopkeepers were closing up. Next door to the hotel was the Nu-Day Theater, and its neon marquee—which was at about eye level to Indy's room—suddenly buzzed to life. Lionel Barrymore was starring in *Stronnger's Return*, followed by *House on 56th Street* with Kay Francis. Also, as an added bonus, Professor Rand's Vaudeville Canine Review and Dog Circus, direct from Harlem for one night only, would perform.

Indy sat on the edge of the bed and took the piece of quartz from the box. He held it in his hands for a few seconds, testing its weight, looking around the room for a place to hide it. He didn't know the rock's intended use, but he had promised Baldwin to protect it. There didn't seem to be any good hiding places around the room, so finally he slipped the thong over his head and placed the rock beneath his shirt.

Indy kicked off his shoes and swung his legs up on the bed. He fluffed the pillow, then tucked the Webley beneath it. He took Baldwin's arctic log from the satchel, which hung from a post at the head of the bed. The damaged strap had been repaired at a shoe shop while he waited to change trains in Chicago.

He opened the logbook and began to skim the entries.

March 20, 1902: at Camp Ziegler, on the coast of Franz Josef Land, eighty-two degrees N. The sunless arctic winter has passed and we have emerged into spring, at least as reckoned by the calendar; although one would not know it from the daily meteorological reports (we have averaged thirty-two degrees F below zero, much colder than usual, but it is now minus twenty-four—something of a heat wave!). The health and spirits of the forty-two men in my command remain good, and our diet has been augmented by fresh polar bear. Nearly eight long months have passed since we sailed from Norway, and I am anxious for summer to arrive and to proceed with the business at hand, the dash to the Pole! Strange that the word dash should have become synonymous with any attempt at the Pole; it implies a mad rush, when the truth is that no other activity on earth requires as much careful planning. Our preparations have been as thorough as humanly possible, and we have established three supply depots along a northern line as bases for our final thrust. Three more of these caches have been established along the coast of Greenland, to ease our return. I am confident that, come summer, the Stars and

Stripes will be the first flag to wave at the Top of the World. . . .

May 2, 1902: The spring thaw has not arrived as expected. We remain locked here in the ice, and I fear our flagship the America *has sustained irreparable damage to her hull. But the spirits of the men remain good and our two smaller vessels and most of our four hundred dogs have survived— with luck, and the expected resupply ship, we should be able to reach the Pole by our goal of July 4.*

May 17, 1902: The resupply ship has not arrived.

June 1, 1902: The situation is becoming quite serious, and all hope of reaching the Pole this year is gone. Half of our dogs have died, many of the sledges are wrecked, and our food is running dangerously low. Morale is deteriorating and more than one fight has broken out among the men. It is our dwindling supply of coal, however, that is our most pressing problem. We have stayed on here in the belief that a resupply ship must surely be on the way, and we have made liberal use of our coal for cooking and heating. The supply is now nearly exhausted. Not only do we not have enough to fire our boilers for the return trip, we will freeze to death if we remain here. Today I am sending up a balloon asking for an emergency shipment of coal.

June 25, 1902: No response yet to any of the fifteen balloons we have sent aloft asking for emergency supplies. I have been forced to place the last of the dogs under an armed guard, or risk having them eaten too soon . . . hunger, cold, and despair are our everlasting companions . . . the horror of the situation has affected the minds and the morale of the men, who waste energy fighting constantly among themselves. . . .

June 26, 1902: The horror. I awoke this morning to find that three more of the men had died during the night, and that at least one of the poor devils had been partially canni-balized. . . . I will mete out an appropriate punishment should I discover the man responsible for this outrage. The last dog has been boiled and eaten.

June 27, 1902: I am forced to make an unpleasant deci-sion. We must conclude that even if a resupply ship is en route, it will not reach us in time to help the thirty-four souls who remain here. Therefore, I will set out with a small party aboard the Pluto *to seek help. We shall make use of wind and current when we can, and of anything that will burn when we can't. Another group will set out in the* Proserpina, *to double our rather slim chances of success. May God have mercy on our souls. . . .*

Sometime later Indy shivered. It was cold, and for a moment he did not know if he was awake or merely dreaming he was freezing to death. He reached for the covers, was annoyed to find himself lying on top of them, then opened his eyes. He was fully dressed except for his shoes, with Baldwin's open logbook lying across his chest. With the exception of the surreal neon glow of the theater marquee shining through the open window, the room was dark.

Indy pushed the logbook aside and sat up. He rubbed his eyes, stumbled across the floor, and brought the win-dow down with a bang. Then he yawned, scratched the small of his back, turned toward the bed, and froze—he saw the glint of neon along a six-inch blade.

"You should not be so careless, Dr. Jones," a voice with a heavy German accent came from the darkness. "You will catch your death."

"Rudy?"

"No." There was a slight hesitation, as if the speaker were considering the odds of Indy living long enough to identify him to the authorities. "My name is Jaekal. My friends call me the assassin."

"What do your enemies call you?"

Indy could feel the smile in the darkness.

"They never get the opportunity," came the reply.

"Well, that's encouraging."

"There is a desk lamp to your right. Switch it on, please. Do it slowly."

Indy reached out carefully with his right hand until he found the lamp, then the switch. He blinked against the light. Jaekal was sitting in the chair, his back to the door. The knife was a wicked-looking switchblade with bone handles.

Indy's eyes flitted to the satchel hung from the bedpost.

"Not to bother," Jaekal said. "I have removed the bullets from your revolver and placed them neatly on the desk. Actually, I am rather disappointed in you. Why do you carry that clumsy piece? It is much too heavy."

"Maybe," Indy said. "But I like to throw it at people."

Jaekal laughed.

"How did you get in?"

"Your room is not too high, and a simple flick of the blade—" Jaekal made a graceful motion with the knife— "opens the window latch."

"What do you want?"

"You know what I'm here for," Jaekal said.

"The logbook is on the bed."

"There is something more, is there not?" Jaekal asked. "The *lapis exilis*, a smoke-colored stone. It was in the chest. What have you done with it?"

"You seem to know so much about it," Indy said. "You find it."

"We wouldn't be having this conversation," Jaekal said,

"if I had not already searched the room and found nothing. The stone could be on your person, but I did not want to risk killing you without first making sure. If you have hidden it elsewhere, then I must keep you alive long enough for you to tell me."

"How do you know so much about this stone?" Indy asked.

"Don't be stupid," Jaekal spat. "It is you who will give me answers, and not the other way around."

The assassin got up from the chair and walked to the bed, all the while being careful not to turn his back on Indy. He held the switchblade casually in one hand while he picked up the logbook with the other. He slipped the book inside his leather jacket.

Then Jaekal took a length of rope from his pocket.

"Sit in the chair, please."

"No," Indy said.

"Do not be tiresome, Dr. Jones." Jaekal walked over and put a hand on his shoulder. "You *will* sit in the chair."

Before Indy could move away, Jaekal's thumb found a pressure point along the collarbone. Indy dropped to his knees, unable even to cry out. Waves of pain radiated down his arm.

"There is no point in resisting," Jaekal informed him. "I am in control. I can make you move this way, or go that way—" Directed by the pressure of Jaekal's thumb, Indy lurched like a puppet toward the right, then to the left. "Remarkable, no? It is something I learned in the Orient, and it never ceases to delight and amaze my friends."

Jaekal kneed him in the solar plexus, then released him. Indy fell to the floor, coughing, unable to catch his breath for a few agonizing moments.

"In the chair, please. You have wasted enough time."

Still coughing, Indy held up his hand to signal his compliance. Then he crawled over to the chair, grasped the seat, and pulled himself to his knees. He rested his forearms on the chair and said he could go no farther.

"I am growing impatient," Jaekal barked.

"I can't—"

"Schnell."

Jaekal reached out to grasp Indy by the collarbone once again, but he was unprepared for the speed at which Indy sprang at him with the chair, which burst into pieces as it came down on his head and shoulders. He dropped the knife and staggered back, instinctively lifting his hands to his face to protect his head.

Indy kicked the knife under the bed.

"Now, you sadistic sack of—" Indy said as he punched Jaekal squarely in the chest, driving him backward into the window. The pane shattered as Jaekal sailed through the window. He hung for a moment in the window frame, largely unhurt because of his leather jacket, a bloody grin on his face.

"No!" Indy shouted as he remembered the logbook. But it was too late: Jaekal was slipping out of the window even as Indy was reaching for him.

Indy stuck his head gingerly through the broken window. The would-be assassin had snagged a drain pipe, scrambled along a narrow ledge of bricks, and was now making his way onto the marquee of the Nu-Day Theater.

Indy looked longingly at his shoes, uttered a mild curse, and followed the assassin through the broken window. The bricks were hard and cold against his stocking feet. From the porchlike marquee, Jaekal was kicking his way through a locked door. It took him several blows to force the latch, and Indy had nearly caught up with him by the time he entered the theater building.

They found themselves in a deserted projection room, but the theater was not closed. From the stage they could hear the excited yapping of dogs, followed by applause from the audience. Jaekal kicked wildly at Indy and missed. Indy countered with a classic combination, a left jab and a right cross that sent the Nazi stumbling backward.

Jaekal collided with the projector.

The machine fell over with a crash and a flash of bluish-white light as the power shorted out. But before the flickering light died, Indy could see that the logbook had fallen from the assassin's jacket.

The last reel of *Stronnger's Return* had been knocked from the projector and now balanced mysteriously on the sill of the projection window, seeming to defy the laws of physics. Then gravity reasserted itself and the reel dropped from the window, bounced across the balcony, and rolled beneath the railing. Film stock billowed out behind it as it fell, and as it rolled down the aisle toward the stage.

Jaekal burst from the projection room.

"Hey!" shouted a man working the arc light. The spot meandered away from Professor Rand and his star performer, a dachshund named Toby who was more or less howling *Yankee Doodle*. "What is going on?"

Indy, who had paused at the door of the projection room after picking up the logbook, could hear the audience gasp. The theater was packed, but the light from the stage was so brilliant that it was difficult to see anything else.

Jaekal jumped onto the balcony railing. For a moment he tottered precariously, then regained his balance and stood upright. Instinctively, the arc-light operator turned the beam upon him.

"*Heil Hitler!*" Jaekal shouted, and threw a Nazi salute.

"I beg your pardon," a strong, clear female voice called from below, "but *this* is America."

Then, as he stood there squinting against the glare of the spot, he began to realize that all of the upturned faces were black.

• • •

"We had the sawbones check him over. He's all right, except for some cuts and bruises and a dog bite on his rump," the sheriff said. He was holding the logbook, slipping it from palm to palm, weighing it. "Now, *that* must have hurt. But he hasn't said a word to us. Are you sure he can speak at all?"

The sheriff shrugged and propped his boots up on the corner of the desk. Roy Dickerson was a lanky, red-faced man in a brown uniform who could shrug with perfect condescension.

"Look, Sheriff," Indy said. "He spoke plenty, and in English, while he was trying to kill me in my hotel room."

"I know that's what you said."

"You don't believe me?"

"There was no identification on him," the sheriff said. "No money. No weapon, not even a pocketknife. I think he might be a lunatic escaped from an asylum. Who else would jump up and salute Hitler in a theater full of—" The sheriff used an unfortunately common derogatory term.

"I dislike that word," Indy said. "Don't use it again."

The shrug again.

"You found the knife," Indy said. "You know he attacked me. You *are* going to charge him, aren't you?"

Another shrug.

"We also found a whip and a revolver in your room," the sheriff said. "Maybe you assaulted *him*. Or are you going to tell me that you're a lion tamer? Then you chased him out the window and over to the theater, where you continued the fight."

"I told you how it happened."

"Right," the sheriff said. "He's a Nazi assassin who broke into your room to steal this thirty-year-old notebook, which his buddies already killed this Baldwin guy for, and

which may contain the secret to a lost civilization underneath the North Pole. Is that about it?"

"Well, when you say it like that—"

The sheriff sat up and leaned across the desk, his face
just inches from Indy's. His cheeks were even redder than
before.

"You know what I think, Jones? I think you are both
crazy. Escaped lunatics."

"I told you who I am."

"How come I've never heard of you?"

Indy feigned surprise. "You're not a reader?"

"Shut up!" The sheriff pounded the logbook on the
table. "You are going to stay put until I get that phone call
from New York City. Who is this Brody character, anyway?
Your doctor at the asylum?"

As if on cue, the telephone rang.

Dickerson snatched up the handset, then turned away
as he barked some questions. Gradually he quieted down,
and after a couple of minutes of uninterrupted listening,
he handed the receiver over to Indy.

"He wants to talk to you," he said.

"Probably has a new prescription," Indy mumbled.

"Indy?" Brody asked. His voice sounded tinny and very
far away. "I hear you've had some trouble. Are you all
right?"

"I'm perfect," Indy said. "Except for some cuts on my
feet."

"Well, I think I have managed to convince the sheriff
that you are not normally a threat to yourself or others,"
Brody said. "Do you think the fellow who attacked you last
night is a member of this Thule organization?"

"That would be my guess," Indy said.

"And an educated one at that," Brody commented. "Do
be careful. I contacted our friends at army intelligence and
asked them about the Thule Society."

"And?"

"The members of *Thule Gesselschaft*, as it is called in German, tend toward a belief in such things as ritual magic, mind control, and lost civilizations. It is named, of course, for the mythical island in the far north from which their master race is reputed to have sprung. Their philosophy is a hodgepodge of Norse mythology, Atlantis theories, and nineteenth-century spiritualism."

"What's the Nazi connection?"

"Well, the society was apparently organized shortly after the Great War by members of upper-crust Bavarian society as a sort of occult study group," Brody said. "But the group's devotion to the old Norse myths inspired a brand of nationalism that soon began to appeal to a broader audience. Not all Thule members were occultists, but the founding core certainly was, and in the 1920s the group served as a kind of nucleus around which the Nazi party formed."

"That's what Baldwin said."

"There's more," Brody said. "The man credited with being the spiritual founder of the Nazis was an expert on Norse mythology named Dietrich Eckhart. He was also a satanist and dope addict. It's unclear whether Eckhart was actually a member of the Thule Society or just an adviser, but in either case he was highly regarded by Hitler—so highly regarded, in fact, that Hitler ends *Mein Kampf* with a dedication to Eckhart."

"Sounds like a prince of a guy."

"The Luminous Lodge of the Vril is a part of the Thule group—sort of the most secret of societies, if you will. It was inspired by a book, *The Coming Race*, which told of a group of supermen who live at the center of the earth in a perfect, ordered society—"

"What?" Indy asked. "Why did you stop?"

"Indy, the fellows at army intelligence are unsure what

the connection with the Arctic means. They have asked—
since you already seem to be up to your neck in the
thing—if you would be interested in helping them keep
track of the Germans."

"Help them?" Indy asked. "Who's going to help *me*?"

"You seem to have a knack for taking care of yourself,"
Brody said. "They offered to provide you with air trans-
portation and other support should you need it."

"Marcus, do you remember the last time I tried to help
these guys out?" Indy asked. "I nearly got thrown out of a
dirigible somewhere over the Atlantic, the fascists used
me for target practice across half of Europe, and I almost
became part of the desert. Tell them 'Thanks, but no
thanks.'"

"You're quite right."

"Besides, I have a schedule to keep. New Mexico,
remember?"

"Of course," Brody said.

"You tell them no."

"Certainly."

"Good," Indy concluded. After a brief good-bye, he
hung up.

The sheriff jumped as Indy slammed the receiver down.

"What are you looking at?" Indy growled.

"Judging from the half of the conversation I heard,"
Dickerson said, "I'm not quite sure. The Nazis are chasing
you here and the fascists nearly got you in Europe?"

"It's a long story."

"I'll bet," Dickerson said. He held out the logbook, then
snatched it away just before Indy could take it. "Look, Dr.
Jones, I'm going to release you, but will you promise me
one thing? Get out of my county just as soon as possible."

"Love to."

Dickerson handed over the logbook.

●   ●   ●

Indy left the sheriff's office and limped back through the snow to the hotel. The theater and the café were dark now. As he passed the desk he waved to the night clerk, but the man was asleep behind the sports section of that evening's *Kansas City Star*.

Indy walked upstairs to his room and unlocked the door. It was freezing inside. The curtains were billowing inward from the broken window, and snow blanketed the floor. He shook his head, because he had forgotten the window had been shattered in the fight. He gathered up his things, went back down the stairs, and woke the night clerk.

"I need another room," he stated.

"Huh?"

"The window's broken."

"Yep," the clerk said.

"Well," Indy asked. "Do you have another room?"

The clerk looked over his shoulder at the rows of keys hanging on the wall. He methodically selected one from the bottom row, made a note of it in the register, and handed it over.

"Thanks," Indy said. "Oh, and you might want to do something about that window—it's like an icebox in there."

"Yep," the clerk said.

Once inside his new room, Indy chained and bolted the door. He was still cold, so he turned up the radiator. Then he took Baldwin's logbook and stood in the middle of the room, searching for a place to hide it.

There was a knock at the door.

"What is it?" Indy barked.

"It's me," a female voice said. It took him a moment to place the voice as Zoë's. "I heard you had some trouble. The clerk told me you had changed rooms."

"News travels fast around here."

"It *is* a small town, dear," Zoë said.

Indy dropped the logbook on the desk, then went to the door and put his hand on the chain. He hesitated. He put his ear to the wood, trying to hear if there was anyone besides Zoë on the other side.

"Are you alone?" he asked.

"Of course. Why?"

"Just checking," Indy said as he swung open the door.

"Why, you wicked thing," Zoë drawled as she drifted lazily into the room, smoke trailing from the cigarette in the absurd holder.

"Do you mind putting that thing out?" Indy asked.

"What's wrong?" she asked as she threw her coat on the bed.

"It stinks," Indy said. "And the smoke hurts my eyes."

"Well, if you're going to be such a baby about it." Zoë ground out the cigarette in the ashtray on the desk. Then she turned and draped her arms around his neck.

"What do you want?" Indy asked.

"That should be obvious," she said, "even to an old gravedigger like you. Wouldn't you like to examine these bones? Render a professional opinion, perhaps? You might learn something that could benefit . . . mankind."

"I'm flattered." Indy gently pushed her away. "But it's very late and I'm not in the mood, even if I am turning my back on the Rosetta stone of Romance."

Zoë frowned.

"I just came by to see if you're hurt."

"I'm not."

"Or if you needed anything."

"I don't."

"If you're going to be that way—"

"I am."

She looked at him with hurt eyes.

"I'm not too old, am I?" she asked.

"Of course not," Indy said. "Zoë, I don't really deserve

all this attention. I'm glad you came by to check on me and all of that, but I'm really okay and all I need is some sleep."

"Oh, all right." She sighed and grabbed her coat.

Indy glanced at the logbook on the desk.

"Zoë," he said suddenly. "There is one thing you can do for me."

"What would that be?" she asked tiredly. "Quit breathing?"

Indy held up the logbook.

"You want me to hide it for you?" she asked.

"I don't know," he said. "Maybe it's not such a good idea."

"What do you mean by that?" she asked, taking the book. "I can do this. I've hidden lots of stuff in my time."

"This is what those thugs were after earlier tonight," Indy said, "and I would feel safer if it wasn't in the hotel. But I would hate to think what might happen to you if they knew you had it."

"I thought there was only one thug, and he was in jail."

"They run in packs," Indy said. "Like wolves."

"I can take care of myself," Zoë told him as she put on her coat. "See you in the morning."

"Hey, wait a minute," Indy said. "Where're you going—"

She placed a finger to his lips.

"Shush," she said. "Either you trust me or you don't. When you want it back, just ask."

"All right," Indy said. "I'm too tired to argue. Wait. There's something else."

He took the crystal from around his neck and gave it to her. She put it on.

"Does this mean we're engaged?" she asked.

"Be very careful, Zoë."

She waved him off.

"Piece of cake, Doc," she said, and shut the door.

Indy rubbed his eyes, wondering if he had done the right thing by letting her take the logbook and the crystal.

His gut told him, however, that the book was safer with her, at least for the time being. Then he locked the door and undressed, uncharacteristically letting his clothes spill across the floor. He took a pair of long underwear from his suitcase and pulled them on. Then, after he had slipped beneath the covers, he realized he was still wearing his hat. He removed the fedora and tossed it on a bedpost.

An hour later Indy had a vivid nightmare that someone was trying to strangle him by shoving a handful of ripe persimmons down his throat. He woke to find Reingold holding an ether-soaked rag over his mouth and nose.

Indy struggled, but his hands and feet were tied.

"Anesthesia," he heard Reingold say, "has been described as dying in degrees. What do *you* think, Dr. Jones?"

Indy's curses were muffled by the rag.

"Oh, I'm sorry," Reingold said. "How rude of me."

He removed the rag for a moment, and instead of screaming, Indy found that all he could do was gasp for air. When he had filled his lungs, Reingold clamped the rag down again.

"Becoming faint, are we?" the Nazi asked. "Things growing dim? It will get blacker and blacker, you know, until you finally lose all consciousness. Can you imagine what we will do to you then?"

Indy's eyes narrowed in defiance.

"All you have to do is give us what we want," Reingold continued. "Then we will leave you alone. It's that simple. Do you understand?"

Indy nodded.

Things were very dark now.

"Good," Reingold said. "No tricks, now, or I'll be forced to shoot you."

He removed the rag.

Indy gulped in air, nodding, while Reingold hovered over him anxiously.

"I'm never staying at this hotel again," Indy muttered.

"Enough of your bravado," Reingold snapped. "Where is the journal?"

"I don't have it," Indy said.

Reingold shook his head.

"I am sorry to hear that," he said. He produced a bottle from his pocket, removed the stopper, and doused the rag again. "We have a very nasty surprise for you if you disappoint us. Now, once again: where is the journal?"

"I told you," Indy said. "I don't have it."

"Can you tell us where to find it?"

Indy was silent.

"Ah, I was afraid it would come to this," Reingold said, feigning sadness. "And it is such a waste, Dr. Jones. Why die for a few dozen pages of scribbles?"

Silence.

"This is your last chance," Reingold said. "Once I administer this final dose, you won't be coming round again—at least not on this side of the grave."

Indy swallowed.

"Maybe we could work something out," he suggested.

"Go on," Reingold said.

"Okay," Indy said quickly, trying to buy time. "Let's say, just for the sake of argument, that I tell you where Baldwin's journal is."

"Yes."

"How do I know," Indy said, "that you'll let me go?"

Reingold laughed.

"You don't," he said.

"Terrific," Indy said.

"Enough stalling, Dr. Jones. This is your last chance. Are you going to tell me where to find the journal?"

"Yeah, I'll tell you where to look for it," Indy said. "You can start by *going straight to*—"

Indy's shout was silenced by the rag in his mouth.

"By the way," his tormentor crooned. "My name is Reingold. Just thought you might like to know. Pity you won't get a chance to share this knowledge with anyone."

At first, Indy thought he had gone blind. The only times he had experienced such numbing darkness had been in caves and other underground places.

Or in dreams.

Then, of course, he thought the nightmare had returned. He was in some kind of tightly closed box, as usual, with barely enough room to wiggle his shoulders. He could hear voices, and the droning of what sounded like a minister's voice, but the words were strangely muted.

The peculiar thing was that his head ached. And it was cold. But it wasn't until he ran his hands along the inside lid and sides of the coffin, and jammed a splinter into the tip of his right index finger in the process, that he realized that this was no nightmare.

He truly had been buried alive.

Then he heard the preacher quite clearly:

". . . ashes to ashes, dust to dust . . ."

A handful of soil sprinkled down on the lid of the coffin with the gentleness of a light rain. Indy tried to scream, but his throat was so dry from the anesthesia that all he could manage was a hoarse, painful whisper. He tried beating his fists against the lid, but there wasn't enough room to get much of a swing; if anyone heard the resulting sound, they did not show it.

Slowly, the sounds of the crowd moved away.

All was quiet for a few minutes.

Then the first shovelful of dirt splattered down with the finality of a death sentence. Indy rocked back and forth and clawed at the lid, but it did not stop the torrent of dirt that followed. He could hear the gravedigger humming to himself as he worked.

Indy fought down his panic. He closed his eyes and concentrated on working up enough saliva for one long, loud scream.

"Help!"

The avalanche of dirt ceased.

Indy could hear the gravedigger grumbling to himself.

The tip of the shovel scraped away some dirt, then thumped twice on the lid.

Indy thumped back.

"Get me out of here," Indy pleaded hoarsely.

"I'll be damned," he heard the gravedigger say as he clambered down into the grave. On his hands and knees, he put his head close to the coffin. "You alive in there?"

"I hope so," Indy managed.

"What do you mean by that?"

"I mean we wouldn't be having this conversation if I weren't," Indy said. "Come on, get me out of here."

He heard a couple of other voices urging the gravedigger to get him out as well. One of them belonged to Zoë, but he couldn't place the male voice.

A few minutes later the gravedigger had pried the lid off the coffin and Indy crawled out onto the snow-covered ground. He lay on his back in the snow, looking up at the Thule Stone framed by the winter sky.

He was still in his red long johns.

"You're not my uncle," Zoë said.

She was standing over him with her arms crossed. Next to her was a middle-aged man in an expensive suit.

"I never thought I'd be so glad," Indy said, "to be seen in public in my underwear."

The gravedigger rubbed his neck. Then he pulled the pint bottle from the back pocket of his overalls. He pulled out the cork and held it high in a toast.

"Now I've seen everything," he announced.

The man in the suit held out his hand.

"I'm glad that I stayed behind to say good-bye to Captain Baldwin in my own way," he said.

"Well, you're wasting your time," Indy said. "He's not at home."

"So I gather," the man said. "Forgive my manners. I'm Lincoln Ellsworth."

"American millionaire and arctic explorer," Indy said.

"The very one," Ellsworth said. "And you are the infamous rogue scholar Indiana Jones. I had rather hoped that I would meet you here. Although, I must confess, I never expected such a dramatic entrance."

Ellsworth removed his overcoat, draped it around Indy's shoulders, and helped him to his feet.

"Thanks," Indy said.

"He's getting a real reputation around here," Zoë said. "You should have seen what he did to the movie theater last night. I'm sure the sheriff will be thrilled to hear about this."

"Tell me," Ellsworth said. "May we presume that Captain Baldwin's body is missing?"

"You presume right," Indy said. "That's his coffin I was in—I know because I brought it with me from Princeton—but I don't know where the old boy is now. I was drugged when they stuffed me in that thing at the funeral home."

"Lucky they held up the funeral for two hours waiting for my arrival," Ellsworth said, "or else you would have come to with six feet of soil on top of you. But who would do something like this?"

"The same Nazi thugs that have been trying to steal Baldwin's journal since I left New Jersey," Indy said.

"Nazis in Kansas," Ellsworth remarked. "How very strange."

Indy waited for Ellsworth to ask why they were after the journal. When he didn't, Indy suspected that he already knew the answer.

The millionaire put his hand out and touched the Thule Stone reverently.

"Dr. Jones," he said. "Forgive my rudeness, considering your ordeal, but have you been able to decipher this?"

"Not exactly," Indy admitted.

"Let me give you a hint," Ellsworth said. "The stone tells the story of Ultima Thule, the mythical land where the gods live at the top of the world."

"A fairy tale," Indy said.

"A legend," Ellsworth said. "And some legends ring true. The name first cropped up as long ago as 330 B.C., when the navigator Pytheas of Massalia was commissioned to find a new trade route to the amber markets of Northern Europe. According to Pytheas, who found the place when he was blown off course, Thule lay far north of Britain—a sunless land in winter, where volcanoes erupted under glaciers, the sea turned to jelly, and beneath which the gods lived. The Venerable Bede applied the name to Iceland, but I think he was in error. . . ."

"So this is what brought you here?" Indy asked as he picked the splinters out of his palm.

"I came here to pay my respects to Captain Baldwin," Ellsworth said indignantly. Then, he added, somewhat less defensively, "And I am highly interested in the area where Baldwin was lost in 1902. You see, that is the same area in which my friend Roald Amundsen disappeared during an airplane flight some years ago."

"Amundsen was on a rescue mission," Indy said.

"Yes," Ellsworth said sadly. "Roald was fifty-six and considered himself retired from polar exploration. He had been the first to reach the South Pole, you know, and then flew over the North. I had the privilege of accompanying him on that expedition, and it was an extraordinary experience. He undertook one last air expedition in 1928, to search for his colleague Nobile and the airship *Italia*."

"I remember that!" the gravedigger exclaimed, and took another swig while the others tried to ignore him.

"Nobile was eventually found alive," Ellsworth continued, "but Amundsen—and his hydroplane, and the magnificent airship *Italia*—were lost to the frozen wastes."

Indy could not suppress a shiver.

"Dr. Jones," Ellsworth said. "Do you have the *lapis exilis*? Did Baldwin give you the stone?"

"You mean this old thing?" Zoë asked. She reached inside her blouse and brought out the smoky crystal. "The doc here already told me it wasn't worth much."

"Worthless, and yet priceless," Ellsworth said.

"You want to buy it?" Zoë asked.

She slipped the thong from her neck and held out the stone.

"It's not for sale," Indy growled, and snatched the stone away.

"Hey!" she protested.

"I'm not offering to buy it," Ellsworth said. "I am not that crude. My interest is in the stone's connection to Ultima Thule."

"So you don't want to buy the stone?" Zoë asked.

"I'm afraid not, my dear."

Zoë rolled her eyes.

"Do I have anything else you're interested in? There's this journal—"

"Zoë!" Indy snapped.

"Don't worry, Doc," she said. "It's safe. I hid it under the front seat of my car."

"And it's still there?" Indy asked incredulously.

"Sure," she said. Then she took Ellsworth's arm. "And if you're not interested in that, maybe I could just show you around town. I promise you'll have a good time."

"I'm sorry," Ellsworth said as he gracefully disentangled

himself. "As charming as you are, I'm afraid that I'm simply not in the market—for anything."

"Tell me something," Indy said as he draped the stone around his own neck. "How is it that you know so much about Captain Baldwin and all this stuff about a mythical land in the far north?"

"After his patron quit him, the good captain approached a number of wealthy men looking for support," Ellsworth said. "He came to me and said he had the secret which would unlock the power of the aurora borealis, the northern lights, and provide an inexhaustible source of power for mankind. He shared with me a portion of his story of being lost in the wasteland in 1902—just enough, mind you, to whet my interest. But it just sounded too fantastic at the time, so I declined to finance an expedition; I did not think of it again until my friend Amundsen was lost in the same area."

Indy's teeth began to chatter.

"I'm freezing," he said. "Do you mind if we go someplace a little warmer?"

"I'm afraid that I must be going," Ellsworth said. "Business demands, you know. But I would be keenly interested in following your progress in this matter."

He produced a business card and handed it to Indy.

"Please give me a call, at any time."

"I'll keep you in mind," Indy said.

Ellsworth hesitated.

"Ah, Dr. Jones—this is somewhat awkward, but may I have my coat?"

Zoë dropped Indy off in the alley behind the hotel.

"Wait," she said, and handed him the journal.

"Thanks," Indy said.

"See you around, Doc," Zoë said. "Good luck."

Indy slipped into the hotel through the service

entrance. A somewhat astonished maid let him back into his room. After a warm bath and donning fresh clothes, he packed his bags and went downstairs to the desk.

"Dr. Jones," the clerk said. "I'm surprised to find you still here."

"Not as surprised as I was," Indy said. "Look, I missed my train to New Mexico this morning. Can you call the depot and find out when the next one is?"

"Of course," the clerk said. "I'll be happy to make the arrangements. Do you have any preferences?"

"I don't care what line or what the accommodations are. And anywhere in southeastern New Mexico will do. I'll ride in a cattle car if I have to."

"You may have to."

"Thanks," Indy said. "I'll be in the café."

Indy sat down at a window table. By the time the waitress had brought his coffee, the clerk had told him that he was booked on a train leaving at one that afternoon.

Indy looked at his watch. He had more than an hour to wait.

"Thanks," he said. "What do I owe you for the rooms?"

"Including the damages?" the clerk asked.

"Well, it wasn't exactly my fault."

"Yes, but you are responsible for the window and the broken furniture."

Indy sighed. He took out his wallet and shelled out three twenty-dollar bills.

The clerk made a noise deep in his throat.

Indy added another bill to the stack.

"Ah," the clerk said, and scooped up the money.

Indy regarded the contents of his wallet. He had barely enough money to order lunch and pay his way to New Mexico. He didn't exactly know how he would finance the trip back. He hated to wire Marcus Brody for money. It seemed as if he was always calling on Brody to get him out of one jam or another.

"Adventure is expensive." He sighed.

"Beg your pardon?" the waitress asked as she refilled his cup. She seemed barely out of high school. Her brown hair was pulled back into a tight bun, and her blue eyes sparkled when she looked at him.

"Sorry," Indy said. "Just talking to myself. What's your cheapest lunch special?"

"That would be the ham and eggs."

"That's breakfast," Indy said.

"It's cheap," she said.

Indy nodded.

As he waited for his food he took out Baldwin's journal. He skimmed through it until he found the place where he had left off the day before. In the last entry he had read, Baldwin and his men had been stranded and were facing certain death because the resupply ship had failed to arrive at their base camp. So Baldwin had set out aboard the *Pluto* to seek help.

June 28, 1902: Miserable weather and rough seas. Compass headings are next to useless this far north, and we haven't seen enough of the sky to be able to fix our position. I have set a course for Ellesmere Island by dead reckoning, but this is mere guesswork. Rations are running low. A ferocious storm is brewing.

June 28, addendum: The storm has struck and the Pluto *has taken a terrible beating. The mast has been torn away and we are shipping water. Two of the men have been swept overboard, leaving the four of us to bail water—and to pray. Reynolds, I'm afraid, has gone mad.*

June 29, 1902: Lost at sea. We have patched up our little boat as best we can, and now our fate is entirely in the hands of Providence. We drift with the current. Reynolds, the poor devil, has been reduced to a babbling idiot. We have been obliged to bind him hand and foot to keep him from doing harm to himself or the rest of us.

July 1, 1902: Curiously, the speed of the current has increased. We have passed a number of ice floes. The sky still has not cleared sufficiently, however, to take our position. Reynolds gnawed through his bonds, slipped over the side, and drowned himself before we realized that he had set himself free. May God have mercy on his soul.

July 2, 1902: We are flowing along with the current at what could almost be called a clip, and we are encountering more and more ice. We have managed to augment our diet with a little fish. Also, every so often we spot a bird or two—gulls, perhaps—decidedly unusual for this climate. Surely we will make landfall if only our little Pluto *can hold out.*

July 3, 1902: Still we proceed with the current. There is a dark smudge on the horizon—it could be terra firma, or a bank of low clouds. Without sunlight, it is impossible to tell. The climate is surprisingly temperate, although the thick cover still obscures our view of the sky.

July 4, 1902: Independence Day. We are nearing land. The curious tide is sweeping us into a bay protected by black volcanic cliffs. It is a coastline that I do not recognize. It is not Ellesmere Island or Franz Josef Land. It resembles the rocky coast of Iceland, but we could not have possibly traveled so far in so short a time. And unlike the true polar regions, which are merely huge masses of ice floating on a near-frozen sea, the coast we now see is firmly attached to the crust of the earth. Could this be the Pole? Or an as-yet-undiscovered—dare I say it—continent? We will soon have a chance to explore this mysterious region at close quarters. We are drawn inexorably toward the treacherous-looking rocks that stud the bay.

July 5, 1902: Our boat has been dashed to pieces upon the rocks, with the loss of all on board—except one. Would God that it were not so, that I had perished instead with my crew. Providence, however, has deemed that I must suffer yet a little longer. I am marooned upon a bleak and craggy unknown shore, unlike anything I have encountered before in the Arctic. From the wreck I have managed to salvage one rifle, half a box of cartridges, some clothes, and a knife. I have no choice but to abandon this barren coast and trek inland in search of food. A river empties into the bay—or, I should say, astonishingly flows inland from the bay—and like the explorers of old, it will be my path. Addendum: Evidence that I am not the first to visit these shores. I have found a yellowed human skeleton slumped against a curious stone obelisk. From the shield and ax lying close by the remains, I presume that this ancient explorer was Viking. Around his bony neck I found a double-terminated crystal of Icelandic spar hanging from a rotting piece of cord. I slipped the curious thing in my pocket. The obelisk itself is approximately one meter in height, and along with a runic description of the mythical land called Thule carries a warning in Anglo-Saxon: I am all colors and I am none. Circle me backward and you are undone. *I have no idea what the warning means, but could the description of Thule be an indication that I am in some remote part of Iceland? Viking superstitions aside, I have little choice but to continue my inland journey.*

July 6, 1902: Success! Shot a polar bear today and ate bloody chunks of it raw. Although I have flint and steel, there was no fuel with which to make a fire. Beefsteak never tasted so good. It's been said that polar-bear meat is dangerous for civilized men to eat, but I will risk illness rather than certain starvation. But the shooting of the bear has done more than fill my stomach: it has confirmed my suspicions that I have landed not in Iceland, but somewhere in the Far North.

July 9, 1902: The sky has cleared with dramatic results, allowing the aurora borealis to burst forth with all the dazzle of a fireworks display. The stars are clear, but unfortunately the tools I need to fix my position (the sextant and the star tables) were lost with the wreck of the Pluto. *The only clue I have is Polaris, around which the rest of the sky revolves. If not for my aching limbs and the blisters on my feet, I would seriously suspect that I had passed from the land of the living. How can the very laws of nature be abrogated here? The mysterious river continues to flow inward through this hellish landscape, drawing me closer to the most prominent of the volcanic peaks on the horizon. A dull reddish glow envelopes the summit. Curiously, I have discovered that the crystal taken from my Norse predecessor glows curiously when pointed in the direction of the peak.*

The waitress brought Indy's food. He thanked her, took a few bites, then glanced out the window. The sun was out and the snow was turning to slush. Indy could hear the yapping of dogs. In front of the theater, Professor Rand was herding his performers into their bus for the trip to their next engagement. Across the street from the café, a black Pontiac plowed through the mess and pulled up at the bank. When a pair of men in dark suits got out, Indy noticed that the taller one had an overcoat draped over his left arm. Indy smiled. The tall man was cursing because he had stepped in a hole and filled his shoes with ice water.

July 15, 1902: I have either gone mad or am witnessing the greatest wonder of the natural world. As impossible as it seems, the river now appears to be flowing uphill, toward the smoldering peak. Also, it seems as if the aurora borealis is being sucked down from the sky, a glittering celestial river that likewise disappears into the cone. What could be the meaning of this amazing confluence?

July 17, 1902: Having spent the better part of the past forty-eight hours climbing, I am exhausted and ailing but have nearly attained the summit. The Viking crystal fairly sparkles with some kind of energy. I am convinced that I will perish in this barren and beautiful place, but my curiosity drives me on. I want to bathe in the glow of the celestial waterfall before I die.

July 19, 1902: The Top of the World. Within the cone is a maelstrom of swirling water and atmospheric energy leading down into the bowels of the earth. The wind howls relentlessly. Lightning pops and cracks inside the storm like sparks from a giant Catherine wheel. And most amazing of all, there appears to be a man-made path leading down into the heart of the maelstrom.

"I wonder what's going on across the street," the waitress said. Her left hand was on her hip and her right held a steaming pot of coffee.

Reluctantly Indy glanced up from the journal.

"Sorry?"

"At the bank," she said. "That guy is acting awfully peculiar."

Indy looked across the street. The taller of the two men he saw get out of the Pontiac was standing nervously on the top step of the bank, the overcoat still over his arm. Down the street, a beat cop was making his rounds.

"Don't know," Indy said.

"Maybe they're robbing it," the waitress joked. "That would be okay with me, as long as they give me some of the money. Say, handsome, is there anything wrong with your food?"

"Pardon?"

"Your food," the waitress repeated. "You've hardly touched it. Is there anything wrong with it?"

"No, no," Indy said. "It's fine."

"How about some coffee?" she asked. "Do you want a refill?"

"Sure," Indy said distractedly.

My strength is failing, but I shall try to continue. How ironic that the scientific discovery of the age might be lost with my own death . . .

Suddenly the sound of gunfire brought an abrupt end to Indy's reading. The tall man standing on the top step of the bank had thrown back the overcoat to reveal a Thompson submachine gun with a drum magazine. His companion had just emerged from the bank, a bagful of cash in one hand and a smoking revolver in the other.

The waitress dropped the pot of coffee on Indy's leg.

"That's hot!" Indy cried, shoving away from the table.

"Oh my gosh," the waitress screamed. "It's Wilbur Underhill!"

The beat cop was crawling beneath the rear axle of a farm truck. The tall gangster trained the Thompson on the truck and the gun began to chatter. The vehicle rocked back and forth as if it were some kind of mechanical beast shaking itself free of glass and chrome. A bullet skipped like a stone from the pavement beneath the truck, ricocheted from a light pole, and shattered the window of the café.

A large dagger of broken glass hung for a moment at the top of the frame, and then dropped as if in slow motion. Indy turned his head just in time to avoid decapitation, but not quickly enough to keep the tip of his left ear from being nicked.

"Who's Wilbur Underhill?" he asked as he pulled the waitress beneath the table with him.

"Just the most notorious bank robber ever," she said.

"How come I've never heard of him?" Indy asked. He was probing his ear with his fingers, making sure that it was still attached and mostly intact.

"You're not from around here, are you?"

Indy reached up to snatch the journal from the top of the table just as a stray slug punched a hole in the napkin dispenser, followed by another stray that entered the café with a buzz-saw whine and shattered a stack of dinner plates along the back counter.

"They call him the Tristate Terror."

"Must be because of his aim," Indy said as he examined the blood on his fingertips.

"This is exciting, isn't it?" she asked.

Before Indy could answer, she grabbed the lapels of his coat and kissed him full on the lips. His eyes bulged in surprise and for an instant he forgot about the flying lead above them.

Indy pulled back and wiped the lipstick away with his cuff.

"You don't get out much, do you?" he asked.

Outside, there was a deafening crash.

The gangsters had made it to their Pontiac, but in their haste to escape had collided with the bus carrying Professor Rand's Vaudeville Canine Review and Dog Circus, direct from Harlem for one night only. The bus had overturned. The front fenders of the Pontiac were so badly crushed that the wheels wouldn't turn. The gangster with the revolver was slumped over the wheel. The Pontiac's horn was blaring.

Professor Rand, dazed but unhurt, crawled through the

shattered windshield of the bus. The tall man with the machine gun kicked open the passenger's door of the Pontiac and regarded the overturned bus with rage.

Inside, the dogs were whining anxiously.

"This is what I think of your stupid mutts," the gangster shouted. He put the Thompson to his shoulder and took aim at the bus.

"Oh no," the waitress said. "He's going to shoot the dogs."

"No, please," Professor Rand pleaded.

"Shut up," the gangster said.

The professor put his face in his hands.

There was an impotent *click* as the gangster pulled the trigger. The gun had misfired.

"That does it," Indy said as he climbed out from beneath the table and jumped through the vacant window frame onto the sidewalk.

"Uh-oh," the waitress said.

The gangster regarded the jammed Thompson with disbelief as Indy strode across the street, dusting shards of glass from his clothes.

"Are you the heat?" the gangster asked.

"Worse," Indy said. "I'm a dog lover."

The gangster grasped the gun by the barrel and swung it like a baseball bat. Indy deftly caught the Thomspon and wrenched it away.

"You could hurt somebody with this," he commented.

Then he dropped the gun and hit the gangster squarely on the chin with his best haymaker. The gangster sprawled backward on the pavement, unconscious.

From the café, the waitress clapped. Then she ran out and peered at the gangster from behind Indy's shoulder.

"That's not Wilbur Underhill," she said. "I knew it wasn't all along. Wilbur would never try to kill an animal, you know. Just people."

"A real humanitarian," Indy said. "But who is *this* guy?"

"Oh, that's just Wilbur's cousin. *Wally* Underhill."

The policeman who had hidden beneath the farm truck had crawled out by now and was handcuffing the stunned gangster that had been behind the wheel of the Pontiac. Professor Rand had released the dogs from the bus and was sitting in the middle of the street while they swarmed around him.

"Looks like a happy ending," the waitress said as she and Indy walked back to the café.

"Not quite," Indy said as he searched the table where he had been sitting when the trouble began.

Baldwin's journal was gone.

4

APACHE GOLD

The Guadalupe Mountains
New Mexico-Texas Border

In the twilight before dawn, near the summit of Guadalupe Pass, the old bus ground to a stop in front of the Pine Springs Café. The door swung open. The driver, who had grunted noncommittally for the last seventy miles while Indy had attempted conversation, uttered the one word that so far had escaped unbidden from his lips:

"*Out.*"

Indy gathered his gear and stepped down, then turned and touched a finger to the brim of his hat. "Nice chatting with you," he said.

"You easterners talk too much," the driver said.

Then he closed the door and the bus was rolling and bouncing again, down the same trail that the old Butterfield Stage had used, before the Civil War.

Indy's feet still ached from his late night chase, but at least his ear had stopped bleeding. He shouldered his pack and regarded the café. Judging from its cracking paint and generally aged appearance, the building might have served as one of the original stops on the Butterfield line. The screen door made a sound like a dying cat as he swung it open. Indy peered cautiously into the darkness inside, unsure of whether the place was open.

"Don't just stand there like an idiot," a woman barked from the inside. "You might let the critters in."

"Sorry," Indy said, and quickly closed the door behind him. "Didn't know you had an insect problem."

"Good Lord, I'm not talking about bugs," the woman said. "I'm talking about rattlers. We've got some big ones up here. The *herp-ah-tologists* say there ain't no such thing, but I've seen some ten- and twelve-footers. They're generally dormant this time of year, but they love to crawl up onto anything that's warm."

"I'll remember that," Indy promised.

The woman struck a match and lit a kerosene lantern on the countertop, then replaced the smoky globe and turned up the wick. The warm light revealed an ample woman in her fifties.

"You're up with the chickens," she said. "Want some breakfast?"

Indy nodded.

"You betcha," the woman said. "Best place to eat in Pine Springs. *Only* place to eat in Pine Springs, actually." She wiped her palm on her apron and stuck out her hand. "My name's Bertha. What's yours, honey?"

"Jones."

"Please to meet you, Jones," Bertha said. "What'll be your pleasure? We have eggs and then we have more eggs."

"Scrambled would be just fine," Indy said.

"What brings you out to the middle of nowhere, Jones?" Bertha poured Indy a cup of coffee before he could ask for one, then began to break eggs into a bowl.

"Well, I—"

"I hope you're not one of those treasure hunters we get through here every so often. The dummies. You know, Geronimo said that all the gold the Apaches ever had come from these here mountains—but I've never seen so much as a nugget of it."

"Actually, I'm an archaeologist."

"Good," she said. "I don't suffer fools lightly, and that's what those treasure hunters are." She added some milk and sugar and began to beat the eggs with a whisk.

"You must be with that Danish spelunker woman who came through here a couple of days ago. What's her name? Funny sounding. Tornado or something like that."

"I'm alone."

Bertha poured the eggs into a waiting skillet. Water that had dripped from the rim of the bowl sputtered and popped in the hot grease.

"She was cordial enough," Bertha said. "But cold, you know? Like a man. What do you think of her?"

"I really can't say. Don't know her."

"Well, who could know a cold fish like that?"

The screen door squawled again. A deputy sheriff came in and sat on a stool two spaces down from Indy. The deputy took off his cowboy hat, smoothed his hair with the palm of his hand, and placed the hat on the stool between him and Indy.

"Breakfast?" Bertha asked.

"No," the deputy said, and rubbed his eyes. "Just coffee."

"Buster, you look beat. They have you working all night again?"

"Found another one last night," Buster said. "West, at the edge of the salt flats."

"You're kidding," Bertha said.

"I wish," Buster said.

Bertha poured coffee, then placed her elbows on the counter and leaned close to the deputy.

"Did they find the head?" she asked.

"Nope."

"Just like all the others," Bertha said reverently. She went to a blank space on the wall beneath the calendar, took the stub of a pencil from behind her ear, and added another slash and the date to the six already there.

Indy scratched his jaw.

"Look, I hope you don't mind me butting in," he said. "But exactly what was found last night?"

"A corpse," the deputy said. "The seventh one in the five years that Bertha's been counting. We don't know who they are, and we haven't found any of their skulls."

"But you know who's doing it," Bertha added.

"We do not," the deputy added quickly.

"Of course they do," Bertha told Indy. "They are just too stubborn to admit it because they can't deal with it."

"Deal with what?" Indy asked.

"The revenge of John Seven Oaks," Bertha said. "Or his ghost."

"Hush up," the deputy said. "You're going to start a panic."

"Buster, how many people live in Pine Springs?" she asked. "Thirty? That's not panic—that's anxiety."

The deputy shook his head.

Indy sipped his coffee.

"Tell me about it," Indy said.

"You betcha," Bertha said. "It all started when a baby was—"

"Now, wait a minute." Buster held up his hand. "For a stranger, you seem awfully interested in all this gruesome stuff. Just who are you?"

"My interest is academic," Indy said. "I teach at Princeton. My name is Jones."

Buster reluctantly shook the hand that was offered.

"Princeton, eh? You don't look much like a college professor. I had a brother who went to the state teachers' college up in Kansas for a couple of terms. He always wore this ratty-looking raccoon-skin coat."

"It *was* the rage."

"Seriously, Dr. Jones," the deputy said. "I hope you don't put too much store in what Bertha here has to say. She's the closest thing we have to a town gossip and mother confessor, all rolled into one."

Bertha waved him off. She turned, stirred the eggs, and refilled Indy's cup.

"John Seven Oaks was abandoned when he was a baby," she said. "He was found in the outhouse right behind this here café, nearly twenty years ago. Nobody knew where he came from, or what his real name was. Down near Juniper Springs there lived an old Apache couple, Juan and Maria Seven Oaks. They had tried for years to have a child, and finally they just got too old and gave up. They considered the finding of the child a miracle, and they agreed to take the baby in."

"And they called him John," Indy said.

"The Seven Oakses were kind of a mysterious couple," she said. "Very traditional Apache. They minded their own business and expected others to do likewise."

"Sound like good neighbors," Indy remarked.

"They must have been," she said. "Only, some people claimed the old man was *brujo*, a wizard or some kind of medicine man, and that he could turn himself into a snake."

"Why am I not surprised?" Indy asked.

"You betcha," Bertha said. "There's things we'll never know about these Apaches."

"What about John?"

"He was a wonderful child. He loved his foster parents

and he was right at home in the mountains. He seemed to have a special understanding with animals. Isn't that right, Buster?"

"It was before my time," Buster said. "But that's what they say."

"Well, everything was just as happy as could be for the Seven Oaks family," Bertha said. "Until one day when John was nine years old. Two riders approached the homestead. They were cowboys from a nearby ranch, and they were drunk. They demanded whiskey, and when old Juan told them they had none, one of the cowboys shot him—just like that, without any more thought than you or I would kill a snake. When Maria came out and saw what they had done, they shot her, too. Then they burned the cabin to the ground."

"Who were these cowboys?" Indy asked.

"Their names were Jake and Jesse Cruz," the deputy said. "They were brothers."

"What happened to John Seven Oaks?"

"That's the spooky part," Bertha said. "Although everybody believed that he must have been murdered, too, and thrown into the fire, they never found his body."

"Tell him about the bullet in the throat. And the cross."

"That's right," she said. "One of the cowboys told a bunk partner about the killing, and he said the other fellow had shot little John in the throat after he attacked them after seeing what they did to his parents. He said they left John for dead."

"And the cross?" Indy asked.

"Months before this horrible thing happened, the father had whittled a little wooden cross out of cedar for his adopted son. John wore it everywhere, and was wearing it on the day his parents were killed."

Indy nodded.

"The sheriff investigated the killing of the Seven Oakses,"

the deputy said. "Although there was talk that the Cruz brothers were involved, there just wasn't enough evidence to prosecute. You can't go to trial on gossip, you know."

"I have a feeling there is more to the story."

"Right," Bertha said. "Three or four years after this happened, the bodies of the Cruz brothers were found in the desert. Their heads were missing."

She turned, scooped up the eggs, and threw some toast and potatoes on the plate.

"Their bodies were found impaled on some fence posts down by Juniper Springs, all shriveled and hideous looking," she said. She put the plate in front of Indy. "Want some ketchup with that?"

"Pass," Indy said.

"Every so often somebody comes in and says they've seen a naked wild man running up and down the mountains," Bertha said. "It has to be John Seven Oaks."

"How can you be so sure?" Indy asked.

"Because he's wearing a little wooden cross on his bare chest," she said. "And because he's got this horrible scar on his throat. He can't talk because of it."

"And this latest body?" Indy asked. "If John Seven Oaks has already avenged the death of his parents, then why would he keep on killing?"

The deputy shrugged.

"We don't know that it's him," he said. "We haven't even identified the victim. All we know is that we have the fresh remains of an unidentified male, minus the head. For all we know, this poor guy could have died of natural causes out there and his head was carried off by animals."

"Buster, you don't believe that," Bertha said.

"It makes more sense than your story," the deputy snorted.

"Not a chance."

"Dr. Jones is right," he said. "Why would Seven Oaks keep killing people?"

"Maybe he's out there taking care of folks and seeing that justice is done," Bertha said.

"Bertha," the deputy said, "you listen to too much radio."

"Jones, do me a favor," Bertha said. "While you're out there in the desert poking around for rocks or pot shards or whatever else it is that you came out here for, keep your eyes open for a wild naked man. If you spot him, ask him to stand still long enough for a picture. I'll put it right there on the wall next to my head count."

"I'll be on the lookout," Indy said.

"Don't get too worked up," Buster said. "It's just a story."

Indy smiled.

"I'll try not to lose my head over it," he said.

Indy paused beneath a tall agave plant at the edge of a rocky arroyo so that his silhouette would be broken. He didn't think he was being followed, but for hours now he had hiked with the uncomfortable feeling that someone was watching.

He plucked a spine from the stalk of the agave and tested the tip with his finger. He winced. The Apaches used the point for sewing, and various other parts of the plant could be eaten raw or cooked, woven into mats, or fermented to produce tequila or even more potent liquors. Indy himself had relied on the agave on more than one occasion for makeshift repairs, and out of habit he stuck the spine in the brim of his hat.

Indy sat on his heels.

Below him was a spring that fed a small pond. Beyond the pond, above the rim of yet another ridge, was the shoulder of El Capitán, the peak whose craggy outlines stood like a Gibraltar over the desert. Beyond the peak a dark bank of storm clouds was gathered on the horizon.

He unslung his pack, retrieved the map that Marcus Brody had given him before boarding the train at Princeton, and slid the fragile document from its thick envelope. Then he blinked, hard. Sweat had trickled into his right eye. He wiped his eyes with the sleeve of his leather jacket. Then he compared the terrain in front of him with the markings that had been made so long ago on the parchment.

"There's the spring, and the peak," Indy said. "This has to be the place, although *X* doesn't exactly mark the spot."

What did mark the spot on the map Indy did not like: it was a coiled serpent, which in southwestern folklore meant "dig here for treasure."

The spot in real topography was a crevice at the side of the arroyo on the other side of the spring, a slit that looked barely big enough for a man to squeeze through. Indy rubbed his stubbled chin as he looked over the terrain one last time and compared it with the map.

There was no mistaking it.

Indy folded the map, replaced it in the envelope, and returned it to the pack. Then he untied a small shovel from the bottom of the pack and started down the arroyo.

As he crossed near the spring, at the bottom of the little valley that was sheltered by small hills, he still had the feeling of being watched. But then, he always had that feeling when he was about to dig.

The crevice was hidden in shadow. Rocks had fallen from the cliff above to fill the entrance in a classic rubble pile, one that looked as if it had not been disturbed for decades, if not more.

Standing at the bottom of the cliff, Indy looked up and regarded the height from which the rocks fell. He removed his hat, placed a stick in the pile of rocks, and hung the fedora on the makeshift hatrack. Then he donned the hard hat that he had brought along, and slung a coil of rope over his shoulder.

As Indy began to shovel away the loose rocks, he remembered what Bertha back at the café had said about the size of the local rattlesnakes. He hoped he wouldn't get a chance to confirm her observations.

In the distance, a bolt of lightning flashed to the ground. The thunder came seven seconds later, reverberating from the rocky walls of the cliffs. The storm was moving in, and Indy knew it would soon begin to rain.

He began to work faster.

In a few minutes Indy had cleared the entrance, at least enough so that he could squeeze his shoulders inside while holding a carbide lamp in front of him. The crevice opened on a narrow passage that led far back into the limestone cliff.

"Looks like Rattler City to me," Indy muttered.

Despite his anxiety, he could not see—or more importantly, hear—a single snake. With a grunt and a groan he squeezed his torso through the opening, then slid awkwardly down the pile of rocks on the other side. He dusted himself off, then reached back and pulled his pack in after him.

He held the carbide lamp aloft and inspected the walls of the passage. On the right-hand side was the carving of a turtle, its head pointing into the darkness.

"Please," Indy said, "let this be an easy one."

There was enough room to stand upright, but the passage quickly narrowed so that before Indy had gone the length of a city block, he was on his hands and knees, and then was crawling on his stomach. The floor was curiously ridged and bit into his flesh. The grooves were man-made, but for what purpose Indy couldn't guess. As he dragged himself along the floor the toes of his shoes drummed across the ridges with a *thu-thu-thu-thump* sound.

Indy was pushing the carbide lamp ahead of him. There wasn't enough room to sling the pack, so he had looped it around one ankle and was dragging it behind him. Every twenty yards or so he found another turtle symbol, its head pointing deeper into the mountain.

Just when he thought that the passage had gotten too narrow to continue, it began to widen. Soon he was able to rise to his hands and knees, then he was crouching, and finally he was standing. He heard falling water in the distance. With each breath Indy sampled the familiar, metallic taste of air that had long been in the earth.

Indy slung the pack over his shoulder and clipped the lamp to his hard hat. The ground here was smooth. On the right-hand wall he saw another reassuring turtle symbol, but on the left he noticed something new: a stick figure walking back down the passage, toward the entrance. Only, the stick figure had snakes poking out of its eyes.

"Terrific," Indy said.

He proceeded with renewed caution.

In a few more yards he came to a fork in the passage. On the left-hand wall was the turtle symbol, while the right-hand wall was blank. Following the sign, which had so far been reliable enough, he took the left fork. The passage rose up for a few yards and then ended in a smooth wall.

Crumpled on the floor, next to the wall, was a pile of bones and rags and a grinning skull. Indy examined the gruesome jumble in the hissing light of the carbide lamp. The corpse was dressed in rotting Levi's and a checkered shirt, and around its waist was a gun belt, cracked and brittle with age. The holster was empty, and a .45 Colt six-gun lay rusting on the floor next to the spindly bones of the right hand. One of the skeleton's legs was broken, several of the ribs were cracked, and there was a neat, nearly half-inch hole in the side of the skull.

Indy picked up the revolver. He tried opening the cylinder, but it was stuck. He tapped the gun against the rock wall. Scales of rust fell away and he managed to force the cylinder open. As he expected, the gun was fully loaded except for the chamber that had been beneath the hammer.

"Used that bullet on yourself, didn't you?" Indy asked. "I can't say that I blame you, as busted up as you were. Brother, I wish you could tell me what happened to you."

He returned the gun to the skeletal hand, then backed away carefully, not wanting to discover what deadfall or other trap had crushed the cowboy and left him for dead.

Indy traced his way back down the passage to the fork and took the right-hand path, which led downward.

The sound of falling water grew louder.

The path ended on a ledge overlooking a huge cavern—at least Indy believed it to be huge, judging from the thundering echo of the waterfall. Although the beam of the carbide lamp could penetrate only a few dozens yards into the darkness, he could see the reflected flicker of the light in the surface of a pool of water far below.

Indy sighed.

He unslung the rope, then took a rock hammer from the pack and drove a piton into the ledge. He threaded the end of the rope through the eye of the piton, made it fast, and threw the coil into the darkness.

He wasn't surprised when he heard the splash.

Indy slid down the rope to confirm what he already suspected: there was no solid ground in range of the lamplight. The end of the rope dangled in a subterranean lake, probably fed by the same spring that created the little pond in the valley; in fact, the underground lake and the pond were probably at the same elevation, but the lake was tucked inside a mountain.

As Indy started back up he heard a growl and felt the

rope twitch. Then there was another snarl and the rope
not only twitched, it bounced.

Indy looked up.

Reflected in the flickering beam of the lamp were the
luminous, tapered pupils of a mountain lion. The eyes
belonged to the biggest cat he had ever seen.

The mountain lion snarled again, reached a paw over
the ledge, and batted the rope. Indy bounced satisfacto-
rily. Amused, the big cat reached both paws over the side
and slapped furiously at the rope—which, after a minute
or so of this, began to fray.

Indy unholstered the Webley.

"Cougar," Indy muttered to himself. "That's not so bad.
Just a great big cat, and I *like* cats. I just need to scare him
away before he drops me into the lake."

He pointed the gun toward the ceiling, then reconsid-
ered. The bullet might ricochet around the cavern and
come back to strike *him*. So he pointed the gun down, at a
right angle to the water, instead. Then he closed his
eyes—which seemed, somehow, to help brace him against
the sound—and pulled the trigger. As loud as the gunshot was, it was nothing compared with the cacophony
that followed.

The mountain lion gave a horrific scream and took off
down the passage toward the outside. At the same time the
cavern was filled with the sound of bats. Thousands took
flight in the darkness, squealing in alarm. Several flew
blindly into Indy. The collision extinguished the flame of
the carbide lamp, and Indy grabbed his helmet to keep it
from falling. Hanging in the darkness, he could occasionally feel their leathery wings beating against his face as
they swarmed past.

"Bats," Indy muttered. "Still not so bad. I can handle
bats. Just mice with wings. Maybe I shouldn't have scared
the cougar away."

Ten minutes later the commotion in the cavern had died down enough for him to attempt to relight the flame of the carbide lamp. He unclipped the bulky brass lamp from his helmet, thumbed the flint wheel, and a shower of sparks ignited the oxyacetylene gas with a satisfying *pop*.

"Good," Indy said as he returned the light to his helmet.

He shimmied up the rope, scrambled onto the ledge, and after making sure the mountain lion really was gone, cut the rope below the frayed portion. Then he hauled in the wet rope and, as he slung it over his shoulder, noted that it was both heavier and colder than before.

He returned to the fork in the passage and took the left branch again. This time, when he reached the literal dead end where the cowboy lay, he inspected the area more carefully.

There were no marks or other unusual features on the smooth expanse in front of him, or on either wall. The floor was the same as the rest of the path. Then he looked up. He was at the bottom of a narrow chimney that led up into darkness.

"Pardner," Indy said consolingly to the dead cowboy, "you fell."

Indy turned his pack around so that it rode against his chest, and readjusted the coil of rope. Carefully, he straddled the remains of the cowboy. He put his back against one wall and his feet against the other and began to inch his way up the chimney. The walls were smooth and, in places, slick, so he had to proceed very cautiously. Also, the higher he rose in the chimney, the farther apart the walls were. What had begun as a rather snug and easy climb had become an uncomfortable and dangerous test of flexibility and coordination. A false move could result in a twenty-foot plunge.

Just when he thought the walls were too far apart for him to go any farther, Indy found a handhold chiseled into the rock behind him. He searched for another, higher, and found it. Carefully he turned around, jammed his fingers in the holes, and began to climb even higher.

Forty feet above his starting point, the chimney ended in another lateral passage. Indy threw the pack up over the lip of the chimney into the passage, then pulled himself up. A turtle was carved into the floor, its head pointing deeper into the mountain.

"Okay," Indy said as he stood up and brushed the dirt from his pants and the elbows of his jacket. "I've made it this far. I'm still game."

He slung the pack, by one strap, over his shoulder, but just as he was about to take a step he froze. In the dust that had collected on the floor of the passage, at the edge of the shaft, he could discern the outline of a bare, left human foot. The toes were pointed toward him.

Indy glanced back at the mouth of the shaft, then down the passage toward the beckoning darkness. He crouched down and dabbed a finger into the dust, then rubbed the red sandlike stuff between his thumb and index finger.

"It could be a thousand years old," he said to himself, "or it could have been made this morning. Which is it?"

He brushed his fingers and stood up.

"There's only one way to find out," he muttered.

There was little dust and no footprints as he went deeper into the passage, and his only guide was the occasional turtle sign urging him to go on. From the lip of the shaft he had been counting his steps, and although he had traversed less than the length of a football field, the oppressive atmosphere made it feel as if he had journeyed to the very center of the mountain. Again, the sound of water was growing louder.

On his ninety-seventh stride, Indy stopped.

The passage opened into a small natural cavern and then appeared to end in a shimmering waterfall cascading *upward.* The torrent emerged, geyserlike, from a pool in the floor and appeared to be swallowed by the ceiling.

For a moment Indy was dumbfounded.

Then he extended his hand toward the water and his fingers met cold, translucent calcite. Over the ages the mineral had followed the course of the water to form the elaborate drapes and folds of a real waterfall. Beyond his fingertips, beneath the veneer of calcite, the water still flowed, but because of a steady stream of air bubbles appeared to surge upward. The water was falling in the direction dictated by gravity, but the air in the water was coursing upward as demanded by physics.

Indy guessed that the water had passed through so many layers of finely porous limestone that it had become charged with air, like the mechanically pumped water in an aquarium.

Indy searched the formation for a passage through or around it, and his expectations were realized when he found, behind one of the calcite folds, a small opening at the base.

He got down on his hands and knees and examined the opening, but he had to hold the lamp at such an odd angle that he could tell little. He pushed the lamp ahead of him and squeezed his head and shoulders into the opening, then had to twist his hips around to accommodate his legs.

The sides of the passage were cold and damp.

It had started fairly straight, but soon began to meander at crazy angles through the rock. In negotiating one particularly sharp curve, Indy's pack became wedged between his back and the wall, and became stuck even tighter when he attempted to pull it free.

Indy grumbled, shifted the position of the Webley on his hip, and laboriously turned over. The pack came free, but he now found himself on his back. He continued for a few more yards, then began to hear the blood rushing in his ears, and it occurred to him that his head was suddenly lower than his feet. The farther he went, the steeper the angle became.

Indy's stomach sank—or did it rise?—with the realization that he could no longer back up. He attempted to wiggle his way back up, but the angle was too steep, and he was going in the wrong direction.

For a moment he had a vision of the next generation of explorers finding his skeleton jammed in the narrow passage. The wisest of the cavers would inspect the rotting leather jacket, the rusted gun, and the frayed bullwhip, then shake his head sadly and comment to the others: "Poor devil didn't know he was in trouble until it was too late."

Indy wiggled harder.

It was the wrong thing to do.

The hard hat—with the attached carbide light—fell from his head. Indy tried to grab it, but could not free his arms. The hard hat slid down the passage, illuminating successive portions like the headlight of a locomotive passing through a tunnel before winking out of sight about thirty yards away.

Indy forced himself to stay calm.

He had no choice but to go forward.

He inched his way along on his elbows and knees. As the angle became even steeper he began to slide. He used his feet against the side of the passage to slow his descent. When he reached the place where the hard hat had disappeared, he suddenly discovered why: the passage turned down and became another chimney, and Indy plunged headfirst into it.

He broke the ten-foot fall with his forearms, landing next to the hat in a bed of red clay. It was upside down but the carbide lamp was still burning, and what Indy saw by its flickering light took his breath away.

The chamber was heaped with gold.

Along the rock ledge against the wall were mounds of gleaming nuggets, some the size of walnuts. Here and there were piles of quartz, and even at a distance Indy could see the thick veins of gold that ran through the crystals. There were stacks of ingots as well, cast by the conquistadores shortly after their arrival in—and plundering of—the New World. There were piles of Spanish armor, mostly helmets and breastplates, and a couple of heavy swords. There were three Wells Fargo strongboxes, a golden communion cup studded with jewels, and a long chain made of golden links.

In the center of the chamber was a massive calcite formation that nature had shaped into something resembling a sacrificial altar. On top of the altar was a carefully constructed ring of human skulls encircling a pile of jewelry and old gold coins. Poking its diamond-shaped head from the center of this pile was a world-record rattlesnake—obviously stuffed, Indy noticed with relief.

The snake and the skulls glittered curiously in the light. They had been sprinkled with gold dust.

He counted thirteen skulls, and although most were yellow and brittle with age, a few were chillingly white. One was whiter than all the rest, the black crust on it undoubtedly dried blood.

Indy turned slowly as he surveyed the room, mesmerized by the amount of wealth and half expecting to see a naked wild man swinging a sword at his head.

There was more wealth in the chamber than could have possibly come from the Guadalupes. Every period of the last five hundred years of the history of the Americas was represented in some fashion.

Indy felt light-headed.

It wasn't the value of the objects that made him dizzy, but the untold history behind them. How many lives had been lost in the struggle for so much wealth, and how many chapters in the history books would have to be rewritten to accommodate this one magnificent room? Indy had an urge to take out his pencil and notebook and make a quick survey of the chamber, to take the first step in the long road to understanding, but he knew that was forbidden. He was an interloper here, a mercenary, a thief; it was justifiable thievery, perhaps, but thievery nonetheless. The chamber had to remain secret for now. It wasn't just that Indy did not want people asking questions about this particular expedition; he wanted to protect the chamber as well. He suspected it was still actively used as a storage area by the Apaches—or at the very least, judging from the most recent addition to the calcite altar, it was being actively guarded. In ages to come, the chamber might belong to history, but for the present Indy knew it must belong only to the Apaches.

His price for keeping the secret was three bars of gold.

He took them from the nearest stack of Spanish ingots. From their markings Indy knew the bars had originally been minted far away, and that would make them difficult to trace back to this chamber in the Guadalupes.

Then he searched for a way out.

The answer, of course, was in the footprints in the clay floor. They matched the one he had discovered earlier on the floor of the passage. They threaded their way through the treasure trove, around the calcite altar, and to a doorway on the other side.

Indy paused and took one last look at the chamber of gold, as if to imprint it in his memory. He was still looking back over his shoulder as he stepped through the doorway. As soon as his foot fell on the ancient wooden panel set in the floor, and he felt the sickening *click!* of its mechanism engaging, he knew he should have been looking down instead.

Indy plummeted through the darkness in a torrent of dust and debris that threatened to choke him. Then he struck the surface of the subterranean lake with a tremendous splash.

At the shock of the cold water, Indy reflexively sucked air into his lungs just before his head disappeared beneath the surface. The gold bars, as heavy as lead weights, were dragging him to the bottom. Indy fought against the straps as he sank, and the helmet with the extinguished carbide lamp fell away, but he had other problems to worry about. As he managed to squirm his left shoulder out of the pack, he felt his knees touch the rocky bottom. Now that he was no longer tumbling through the water, it was easier to deal with the potentially deadly burden. He slid the pack down his right arm, but did not release it to the keeping of the dark water. Holding tightly to one of the straps with his right hand, he found the end of the coil of rope with his left. He brought his hands together, threaded the rope through the strap, then tied it. His lungs were beginning to ache, but Indy told himself that he had come too far to leave the gold behind now; he took the time to find the other end of the rope and loop it beneath his belt. Then he took the Webley from its holster and shoved it blindly in the pack before kicking hard for the surface.

From the relatively mild water pressure on his ears, Indy knew the lake was less than twenty feet deep, but the swim to the surface against the drag of the rope made it seem like a hundred and twenty. He broke the water and instinctively threw his head back to clear the water from his eyes, but without light there was nothing to see in the cavern. Indy chose a direction and began swimming, hoping that he had not picked the long way across the lake.

Soon his shins were scraping on a rocky bottom, and he stood in the shallow water. By touch, he hauled in the heavy pack as he coiled the rope. He slipped the rope and the pack over his shoulder, then felt for the bullwhip at his side. It was still there.

He searched his pockets for something, anything, which would make light. But Indy did not have so much as a cigarette lighter; because he didn't smoke, he had never gotten into the habit of carrying one. He didn't need one for the carbide light, because it had its own striker. He *had* tucked some matches in the pack, but of course they had since been drenched. And, Indy thought, that probably wasn't the only thing the water had ruined.

"Fudge," Indy said. He would ordinarily have uttered a stronger expletive, but dire circumstances always made him a little more careful with his language, just in case it mattered. Somehow, Indy knew that it did.

"What am I going to tell Marcus?" he wondered aloud. Then: "Well, that's assuming I get the chance to tell Marcus *anything*. If I don't get out of here, I won't have to worry about it, but that seems a rather extreme way to avoid telling a friend some bad news."

Indy hesitated.

Talking to himself was a way of easing tension. It was also a good way of gauging his level of anxiety, because he had learned never to readily admit—not even to himself— his own misgivings, especially when a situation demanded action instead of reflection. He knew that the more he talked to himself, the more worried he became.

Indy took a couple of steps forward, then stumbled.

He sat for a moment in the water, looking blankly around him, not willing yet to concede that his eyes had been rendered useless.

He shouted: *"Hey!"*

The sound of his own voice echoed harshly back to him from half a dozen directions, but none offered a clue as to which one he should take.

He listened harder.

Somewhere, just at the edge of his hearing, Indy was able to catch the whisper of rain falling. Then, more distinctly, the rumble of thunder.

He closed his eyes and turned his head from side to side like an owl as he attempted to locate the source of the familiar sound. He was concentrating so intently that the sound seemed to exist in the middle of his head, a three-dimensional thing that had color and form: the rain was blue and mistlike, while the thunder was streaks of orange. When he turned his head to the left, the sound dimmed, but as he turned back the sound and color grew until reaching their maximum when his nose was pointed at a forty-five-degree angle to the right.

His eyes still shut, Indy stood and began to make his way cautiously toward the sound of the rain. He did not hurry, for fear of stumbling over a rock and breaking his leg, and he tested each step before he placed his foot down, for fear of plunging down a chasm to his death. But he kept the image of the rain clearly fixed in his mind's eye.

Indy crept along in this fashion for another fifty yards or so, every so often bruising his shin against an unseen boulder. Then he would stop for a moment, let the pain subside, and again take his bearings. Although it was a painful and slow process, at the end of every repetition of the cycle, the sound of the rain grew more distinct.

An hour later he came up against a wall.

Indy was certain he had been on a correct heading, and that the obstacle was not a solid expanse, but perhaps a ledge. He could not, however, reach the top of it with his outstretched fingers.

He uncoiled the bullwhip and flicked it upward, testing the barrier. The whip hung suspended for a moment before its own weight pulled it lazily down, looping over his head and shoulder.

"Ah," he said with satisfaction.

He used a couple of practice strokes to pay out the length of the whip behind him, then put his back into it as he cracked the whip up into the darkness. The tip lashed itself around the base of a stalagmite.

Indy tested his weight against the makeshift grappling hook a couple of times, then pulled himself up the ten-foot drop hand over hand. The leather whip creaked and groaned in protest, but held firm. When he finally scrambled onto the ledge, he was rewarded by the sight of a pinpoint of light shimmering at the far end of the tunnel. The sound of the rain was louder here, and it was more than just the sound of rain; it had become the sound of rushing water.

Indy drew in the bullwhip and rested on his knees for a moment, staring at the light.

"Good thing it's still daylight out," he said.

The pinpoint of light seemed to dance, however, swinging from side to side and then zooming up before floating back down.

Indy shook his head and looked again.

Still, the light seemed to move.

"Autokinesis," Indy told himself. "A visual phenomenon in which a stationary light seems to move of its own volition. That's what it has to be."

Indy gathered up his things, struggled to his feet, and began to advance cautiously down the tunnel toward the light—which still seemed to sway as if it were a lantern carried in front of someone.

"Hallo!" a voice echoed down the corridor. "Mr. Jones, are you in here?"

Indy stopped dead.

"Yes!" he said. "Right here!"

"Are you unhurt?"

"Yes!"

"Then come quickly toward me," the voice called. "There is much danger."

"I have no light," Indy called.

"There is no time. Do your best."

Indy began to step quickly along, feeling his way as best he could. He had approached close enough to the light that he could make out the floor and sides of the tunnel in its beam, and the hazy shadow of a figure standing at its end.

Then he bumped his head on the low ceiling and, at the same time, lost his footing and fell up to his armpits in a hole in the floor. He tried to pull himself out, but his right arm was wedged too tightly against his body.

"I'm stuck," he called.

"Hang on," the voice called.

The light began bobbing urgently toward him.

Soon the figure had set the lantern down and a pair of strong, suntanned arms reached down and grasped the straps of his pack. In one motion Indy was pulled free from the hole and set on his feet.

"Thanks," he said.

Then as the lantern was picked up and the beam played briefly over his rescuer, Indy saw a shock of blond hair and a figure that, although clad in denim and flannel, was unmistakably feminine.

"You're a woman," Indy blurted.

"No time for talk," she said.

There was a great rushing and rumbling sound, as if someone had suddenly pulled the chain on a gigantic toilet. Behind him, he could hear boulders crashing against the sides of the corridor as they were driven by the force of the water.

The woman grasped Indy by the hand and together they made their way back down the corridor. At a spot that he could hardly distinguish from the rest of the passage, she found a high opening and pulled him up after her.

Below them, a torrent of water, mud, and gravel thundered past.

"Flash flood," the woman told him.

"You saved my life," Indy said.

"Nonsense," she replied, brushing some wild strands of hair from her blue eyes. "You saved yourself. I just showed you the way."

"But who are you?" Indy asked. "How do you know my name? And how did you know I was in here?"

"You Americans," the woman scoffed. "Always asking rude questions. And we are not out of the woods quite yet, as your countrymen say."

"You're the Danish spelunker," Indy said, finally making the connection. "Bertha mentioned you, back at the café."

"Please, I prefer to be described as a caver," she said. "Spelunker has such a grotesque ring to it, don't you think? Like some kind of freak that lives underground. Here, I believe this belongs to you."

From beneath her belt she took his fedora. It had obviously been soaked with rain, and it had been crushed mercilessly by the pressure of the belt.

"I found it on the stick outside," she explained. "I have been searching for you since. My name is Ulla Tornaes. By the name inside your hat, I know that yours is Jones. That *is* your last name, correct?"

"Correct," Indy said as he unfolded the hat and tried to put some shape back into it. Then he stuck it on his head. "Thanks a lot."

"Come," she said, stooping down as the passage narrowed. "We have one more challenge before we are free. The Apaches say these caves are guarded by the rattlesnakes who live in the rocks. Now I am inclined to agree with them. Just how much treasure did you take, Mr. Jones?"

"It's Dr. Jones," Indy said testily.

"A medical doctor?"

"No. A professor. And how—"

"That knapsack of yours seems unusually heavy," she explained. "And, you have obviously refused to release it even when it could have meant your life. Is wealth that precious to you?"

"No," Indy said. He was crawling along behind her. "At least, not wealth for wealth's sake. I took only what I needed."

"Your needs must be quite exorbitant," she said. "The Apaches say that if your heart is pure, you will pass the test. Is your heart pure, Mr. Jones?"

They had reached the point where the grooves were cut into the floor of the passage. Except this time there was something strange about their feel to Indy—warm and dry and occasionally *moving*.

"Shine the lantern back for a second," Indy told her. "There's something strange here."

"Better to keep on going, Mr. Jones," she said. "We must go forward. We cannot go back."

Indy kept crawling.

When the passage opened wider again, and Indy emerged, the woman shone the lantern back. Dozens of reptilian eyes reflected the light, accompanied by a chorus of telltale rattles.

"Snakes," Indy whispered. He could barely get the word out.

"Congratulations," the woman said. "You passed the test. I rather thought you wouldn't."

"You believe in those old superstitions?" Indy asked, trying to appear brave.

She shone the lantern in his face.

"Then you explain it," she said.

Then she scrambled up the rubble pile, wiggled through the opening, and stretched in the open air like a cat. Indy followed. It was still raining, but the worst of the storm had passed.

From within the cave they could hear rumbling and the crashing of rocks.

"I would say that's the end of the treasure cave," the woman said. "Or at least of the entrance which you found."

"Just as well, I suppose." Indy sighed in exhaustion.

"If I hadn't stumbled on your hat—and realized that you had foolishly entered the cave system despite the threat of storm and flash flood—you might still be in there. A permanent resident, in fact, like the skeletons and the snakes."

She paused and regarded him with a practised, professional detachment.

"Say," she ventured. "You're not the famous archaeologist Indianapolis Jones?"

"No," Indy said. "My name's—"

"Quite right," she said. "My mistake. You're just a common fortune hunter."

5

GHOST STORIES

"Look here," Indy said. "My name is *Indiana* Jones, not Indianapolis."

"Of course," she said. "What do your friends call you?"

"Indy," he said. "But you can call me Dr. Jones."

"I would prefer that," she said, walking away. Over her shoulder she called: "If, as you say, you are indeed a doctor. Do you have any proof?"

"I'm not in the habit of carrying my diplomas with me."

"Pity," she said. "In that case, it's still *Mister* Jones."

The woman led the way on an arduous three-mile hike across rugged terrain to a mesa above Bell Canyon. As they reached the modest camp—consisting of a single canvas wall tent, some simple cooking utensils, and a stone circle for a fire—a shaft of sunlight broke from the clouds and the landscape glimmered, as if diamonds instead of raindrops had drenched the little valley.

"Amazing," the woman said, "how quickly these storms pass."

"And how wet they can leave things," Indy said as he sat down on a rock and examined his fedora. He massaged the misshapen mass with his fingers. "Do you think this will ever regain its shape?"

"You're lucky to be alive," she asked incredulously, "and you're worried about your hat?"

"It was a nice hat," Indy said sadly. Then: "I'm sorry. I'm really very grateful for your climbing down into the hole and pulling me out by the scruff of my neck. Thanks."

"It was an interesting problem," the woman said as she began unlacing her boots. "I didn't know if I could find you in time." She paused. "I mean, you're welcome. Besides, you seemed like you were doing a pretty good job of saving yourself when I found you."

Indy put the hat down.

"Where are you from?"

"Copenhagen."

"What has brought you to the American southwest?"

"The karst," she said, and indicated with a boot the rugged landscape around them. "This magnificent, exposed karst is the mother to a network of caves that reaches from here to Kentucky."

"How do you know that?" Indy asked.

She smiled at his schoolboy question.

"Mr. Jones," she chided. "We tag the cave fish."

"Right," Indy said. "So you are a scientist?"

"No," Ulla said with a wry smile. "I am an adventurer, Mr. Jones. An explorer. But instead of the predictable topography of the earth's surface, I am interested in the unknown, the land beneath our feet."

"Right," Indy said.

"You sound incredulous."

"It is rare that I meet such a rugged, strong-minded woman," Indy confessed.

"Oh?" Ulla brushed her blond hair from her eyes and then tugged off a wet sock with a satisfying *slock*! "I would imagine that it is rare that you meet anyone, male or female, who is as strong, confident, and capable as I am."

"Well, yes," Indy admitted. "Not to mention modest."

"Do you feel threatened, Mr. Jones?"

Indy laughed.

"Too bad," she said as she unbuckled her belt. "I would have rather hoped that you would feel just a little threatened. After all, my friends in Denmark often say that my apparent lack of modesty reminds them of that famous archaeologist Indianapolis Jones that we read about in the papers."

"You mean me," he said, jerking a thumb at his chest. "Indiana Jones."

She regarded him with cold detachment.

"I suppose I should be flattered," Indy grumbled.

"I'll let you know," she said, "when you should reach that happy state of mind."

She took off her belt and her mud-stained denim pants fell, revealing the tails of her man's flannel work shirt.

"What are you doing?" he asked.

"Getting out of these wet things, of course," she said as she stepped out of the jeans. "Oh, I keep forgetting how prudish you Americans can be about such things."

"Sorry," Indy said. He looked away, but could not help but notice how tanned and athletic her legs were. "It's just that I'm—"

"Don't apologize." She sighed as she gathered the wet jeans around her and made for the tent. She paused at the flap. "I am a naturist, so I really don't think twice about such things. But I can see how it might make you uncomfortable, so I will honor your provincial wishes. When in Rome, as they say."

The tent flap snapped shut.

"I've been in Rome," Indy commented, "and nobody there acts like you."

The flap snapped open again.

Ulla threw a blanket at him.

"Instead of putting your energy into wisecracks," she suggested, "you might want to find some dry branches with which to make a fire. You will need to dry your clothes, and I wouldn't mind some coffee. You'll find everything you need in the mess kit."

Indy stared at her.

"You do know how to make coffee, don't you?" she inquired archly.

As the sun disappeared in the west Indy drew the blanket around his shoulders and sipped coffee from a tin cup. The modest meal of beans and jerky had mellowed him somewhat, but he still was rankled at Ulla's refusal to believe that he was indeed Indiana Jones; the *real* Jones, she said, would never be so thickheaded as to become lost in a cave.

Ulla sat a few feet away, brushing her blond hair and humming contentedly to herself. She paused, then pointed the brush at the horizon around them.

"All of this," she said, "was once underwater."

"I know," Indy said.

"During the Permian period of our geologic past, this area was covered by a vast tropical sea, and the mountains here were a huge limestone reef system not unlike the Florida Keys," she said. "This canyon was once an underwater canyon, and the formations we see here were carved by the waves over the course of millions of years."

"Later," Indy said, picking up the story, "the water receded and the entire plain was thrust upward by earthquakes. Ironically, the forests that remain at the highest elevations in the Guadalupes were created during the Pleistocene Ice Age, and remain today much as they were then."

"Ironic," Ulla mused. "All of this is part of a giant jigsaw puzzle, the edges of which we are just now beginning to discern. Nobody knows the true extent of these vast cave networks. The link between places like the Guadalupes and Kentucky may only be a small part. For all we know, the entire inner earth may be honeycombed by such interconnected passages."

Indy smiled.

"You think I'm mad, don't you?"

"No," Indy said. "I think you are a fantasist."

"The earth is a living being, Mr. Jones." Ulla leaned forward and placed her palms on the ground. "The rock beneath seems dead to us only because of our inconsequential life spans and our equally limited imaginations. But there is life surging beneath my hands, even though it may be a thousand years between heartbeats. The rain that drenched us today is the lifeblood of the planet. The limestone continues to be dissolved by rainwater, which becomes mildly acidic during its journey through the earth's atmosphere, and it eats away at the karst and gradually forms new arteries and veins—which we call caves and sinkholes. They are designed for a purpose, to carry the water which the ground cannot absorb. That is why it was so dangerous for you to go stumbling into the caves before the storm."

"I thought I could beat the storm," Indy said defensively. "If I had waited, it might have been days—if ever— before I could penetrate the cave."

"What difference could a day or a week make?" she asked. "For that matter, what difference would a year make? Are you in that much of a hurry to be rich—or dead?"

Indy dragged the knapsack over to him and removed one of the bars of gold. He held it toward the fire, studying the mint marks.

"This was worth risking your life for?" she asked.

"No," Indy said. "But what it represents may be."

"And what is that?"

"Look." He pointed to the line of stamps and marks. "You call me a thief, but this gold was stolen originally by the Spanish, probably from the Incas in Peru. The Incas may have ripped it from the earth themselves, but more probably they took it from other tribes, either as spoils of war or as tribute. Only God knows how many irreplaceable works of pre-Columbian art were melted down to make this one bar. From this mark, we can tell the Spanish cast the ingots in Mexico City in the sixteenth century. Here is the name of the captain who was entrusted with hauling the gold from Mexico City to Spain—Don Pedro Juan Garcia. Somewhere along the line he failed, either losing his charge to bandits or helping himself to a little of the loot and taking off. And here is a little warning added by the church that the gold is the property of God and King, and nobody but a Catholic who has recently made confession should carry it, and that the fires of hell await any pagan whose hands it should fall into."

"Are you a pagan?"

"No."

"Damn," Ulla said. "I would have thought you were."

"Are you?" Indy asked.

"Of course," she said. "I worship the sun. And, on some days of the week, the Aesir."

"The old ones," Indy translated. "The Norse gods."

"Exactly. I don't actually believe they hear me," she continued. "But it makes as much sense to me as being a Protestant or a Catholic or a Muslim. At least I'm not out killing people who don't agree with me."

"It wouldn't be much of a leap," Indy grumbled.

"Go on with your story," she said. "How did the gold get here, in the mountains?"

"Only the gold knows that," Indy said. "It was stolen,

and stolen again. Eventually it came into the hands of the Apaches, who stored it here to keep it out of the hands of the Europeans."

"And it has been stolen yet once again," Ulla observed. "And what will you do with your wealth, Mr. Jones? What is your heart's desire? A big house? An estate, perhaps? With dozens of servants that make you coffee and say, 'Yes, Mr. Jones, right away, Mr. Jones'?"

"What, do you want a cut?"

"Absolutely not." She looked shocked at the very idea. "It is tainted, and I will have no part of it. Only a fool would believe that it could bring him happiness."

"Then I am a fool," Indy admitted, "who is trying to buy a miracle."

"What do you mean?"

"I don't want to talk about it," Indy said as he replaced the ingot in the knapsack.

"Why not?"

"I'm used to risk," Indy said. "Most of the time it is for a shining bit of history that I can hold in my hand and then stick in a museum so other people might get the same feeling of awe that I had when I first saw it."

"What is different now?"

"This time it's personal," he explained. "I have brought myself down to the level of the Belloqs of the world."

"What is a Belloq?"

"A special sort of little monster," Indy said. "Except that what he does for money, I'm doing for love."

"I don't understand."

"I said I didn't want to talk about it."

"Please."

"It's a long story, and I'm not sure I would even tell a friend about it. You seem not to like me very much."

She moved closer to him and placed a hand on his arm.

"I am not sure that we could be friends," she said, "but I

am disliking you a little less now that I am hearing your story. Please, if you feel any small debt of gratitude toward me for pulling you out of that hole, then tell me the rest of your tale. The world has so few great love stories that you shouldn't keep this one hidden."

Indy cleared his throat.

"How do you know it is so great?" he asked. "Love found and lost—that is rather a common tale, don't you think? It happens to kings and paupers with the same unremarkable regularity."

"Trust me," she said. "And keep talking."

Indy closed his eyes. He felt as if he were about to pull his beating heart from his chest for Ulla to see. He told her about how, deep in the jungles of British Honduras, in the lost city of Cozán, he had found a skull made of quartz crystal.

"It was patterned after a female skull, and of the purest quartz rock, beautifully articulated, a cult object that some lost generation must have revered as both inspiring and terrifying. But there was a curse, as there usually is with such treasures. But this one was a little more diabolical than most: that the finder of the skull would not die, but would kill what he loves most."

"And what is it that you love most?"

"Not what, but whom," Indy corrected. "Her name is Alecia Dunstin. Red hair, blue eyes. Clairvoyant. She was the sister of an alchemist the fascists captured in the hopes of turning lead into gold."

"She died?"

"She lived, but no thanks to me," Indy said. "I was bad for her health."

"She became ill?"

"I was nearly the death of her," Indy said. "Peculiar things would happen when we were together, usually involving somebody attempting murder. The closer we became, the worse it got. In the end the plot to turn lead into gold failed. Her brother died, as did many others. She survived, but narrowly. It was too much for both of us. I have not seen her in some time."

"Where is she now?"

"I don't know," Indy said. "England still, I suppose. We no longer speak."

"And the skull?" Ulla asked.

"Lost," Indy said. "After being stolen from me, it passed through several hands, then went down aboard a Nazi submarine. But it's in a waterproof canister which may have bobbed to the surface and drifted away at sea."

"Nobody knows where it is?"

"Someone does," Indy said.

"And this somebody who claims to know where it is—they will tell you, but for a price," Ulla guessed. "So the gold is to pay for this information so you can locate the skull and return it to the jungle in hopes of lifting the curse?"

"Yes," Indy said.

"But if they know where the skull is, why don't they just recover it themselves?" she asked.

"Because that would be double-crossing the Nazis, who have already paid him for it once," Indy said. "It's safer for him to sell the information to me, and then let me risk my neck."

Ulla was silent for a moment.

"It sounds rather unbelievable. . . ."

"Believe what you want," Indy said.

The flames of the campfire danced in Ulla's eyes as she struggled with Indy's story.

"This Englishwoman," she said softly. "Did you ever . . ."

"Did we ever make love?" Indy asked. "No. It may sound irrational, but I think that is the only thing that kept her alive."

"That is sad," Ulla said. "But your problem is not unique. Sex and death have often been associated in mythology as well as in mental illness."

"You think I'm crazy?"

"No," she answered carefully, "but many people who have had similar problems have responded well to therapy."

"I don't need a psychiatrist," Indy said.

"Of course not," Ulla said. "And you don't have a problem with reality, either. You are the famous Indianapolis Jones, who between discovering lost cities and fighting fascism has labored under a curse that threatens to kill your true love."

"When you put it like that," Indy said, "of course it sounds crazy."

"So what's your point, Mr. Jones?"

"The least you can do is refer to me as Dr. Jones!"

"Exactly," Ulla said.

Indy sprang to his feet.

"I've had enough of this," he said as he tied the blanket around his waist and began to gather his still-wet clothes from where they hung from sticks on the opposite side of the fire. "Thanks for saving my life, sister, but if I stay here another minute I *will* be nuts."

"Sit down," Ulla said evenly.

"No," Indy said. "I can only take so much."

"Sit down, Mr. Jones," she repeated. "Can't you see that we aren't alone?"

Indy froze.

At the edge of the firelight was a man with a gun. The man was tall and broad-shouldered, with a mop of black hair, and most of his face was hidden by a beard that was as dense and tangled as a blackberry thicket. The gun was an old single-shot rifle, the kind a farmer would keep to shoot varmints, and its barrel was marred and pitted.

"A lovers' quarrel?" the man growled.

"How long have you been out there?" Indy asked.

"Long enough to hear what I needed to," the man rasped. "Long enough to hear you talk about gold. Now, keep your hands where I can see them."

"Gold?" Indy asked.

"Don't lie," Ulla said. "It's unbecoming. Besides, he obviously knows the truth. You may be prepared to die for your precious gold, but I'm not."

Indy's shoulders slumped.

"Keep 'em up," the man warned. "She's right. I'm liable to kill you both."

"Who are you, mister?" Indy asked. "You don't look like the killing kind."

"You're wrong," the man ranted. "I've crossed some kind of line in my head, like I'm no longer human but some kind of animal. That's what life is about, ain't it? It's taken me forty-three years to learn it, but the name of the game is eat or be eaten."

"Things can't be that bad," Indy ventured. "Surely we can work something out."

"You city fellers are always wanting to work out some kind of deal, ain't ya?" the man asked with disgust in his voice. "I'm just a man who lost his farm to the dust and to the bank. My wife run off with the city feller who served the papers on me. So I said to hell with it, I'm going west. So I spent my last dime on a sorry excuse for a car in Tulsa from a city feller who swore it would take me to California. It quit me three days later in New Mexico. The transmission was filled with sawdust to keep the busted gears quiet until I got out of the state. Since then I've been drifting, and every town I come to the city fellers tell me they have laws against vagrants. So I've been living off the land since then, and this is not exactly the kind of land that'll make you fat. Now, what kind of deal are you going to offer me, city feller?"

"You've had some bad luck, all right," Indy told him, his hands still in the air. "But why don't you put down that squirrel gun, have something to eat, and we'll discuss the situation?"

"I ain't discussin' squat," the man said. He lowered the gun a bit as he looked around at the darkness. "Besides, this place scares me," he said in almost a whisper. "It's full of rattlers and panthers and ghosts. Indians, I reckon. We killed plenty of 'em around here."

"You a religious man?" Indy asked.

"What's that got to do with it?" the man snarled.

"Then you read your Bible, don't you?"

"Of course I've read the Bible," he said.

"Then you know about the wilderness," Indy said. "And about how God uses it to test the hearts of men. That's what he's doing with you, right now. This is your test."

"Ain't no test."

"No?" Indy asked. "You're right about one thing. We do have gold. It's over there in that knapsack. Show it to him, Ulla."

Ulla opened the knapsack and took out one of the ingots.

"Shoot," the man said. "I ain't never seen so much gold in all my life. What am I saying? I've hardly seen *any* gold."

"This would make you rich."

"I'll be able to sleep in a bed again," the man said wistfully. "With sheets. And have breakfast in the morning. Steak and eggs. Then go to the store and buy myself a new suit."

"You'll be able to do all those things," Indy agreed. "But there's only one catch."

"What's that?"

"You're really going to have to kill us for it."

"Mr. Jones!" Ulla said. "Speak for yourself."

"She's right," Indy said. "All you have to do is kill me."

"Naw," the man said. "I'll have to kill you both so's there'll be no witnesses."

"Okay," Indy agreed. "In that case, it ought to be pretty easy, seeing as how all I have on right now is a towel. No knife. No gun. I'm not even wearing shoes. It may be a little harder to kill her, because she may run. Or, I'm guessing, she'll choose to fight. You had better be pretty quick in reloading that antique. But make no mistake, mister, this is not the hard part."

"It's not?"

"No," Indy said. "The hard part comes when you're sleeping in that big bed, and eating your steak and eggs, and buying your new clothes. Do you think you can do that when you know you're a murderer?"

The man thought for a moment.

"Yeah," he said. "I reckon I can do that."

He took aim at Indy's chest.

"I was afraid he was going to say that," Ulla said.

"What the—"

The barrel of the gun suddenly pitched upward and the rifle fired into the night sky.

The gun had been knocked from the man's hands by an oak staff, swung by a bare-chested wild man with gray shoulder-length hair and a wooden cross around his neck. His eyes were wild and across his throat was a poorly healed scar from long ago. He threw aside the staff, took a well-honed knife from his belt, and scrambled atop the would-be killer. With one hand he grasped the mop of black hair while he raised the blade high with the other, in preparation for a killing blow.

"John Seven Oaks," Indy said.

The blade paused.

"Don't kill him," Indy pleaded.

The wild man looked questioningly over his shoulder.

It was enough to allow his quarry to squirm out from beneath him. The man stumbled to his feet and ran headlong into the darkness, leaving his rifle behind.

The wild man shook his head. He got up, his knife still clasped firmly in his right hand. He pointed toward the running man and made a jerking motion with his knife.

"Yeah, he probably deserved it," Indy agreed. "But now he can tell stories about you at the Pine Springs Café. That's better, isn't it?"

The wild man smiled.

"Thank you," Ulla said. "I don't know what—"

"It's a little early for that," Indy cautioned her. "Besides, he can't answer you."

"Who is this fellow?"

Indy told her.

John Seven Oaks walked over to the campfire and inspected the gold bar that lay on the ground. Then he nudged the knapsack with a bare toe, and his eyes took note of the other two ingots.

"What's he doing now?" Ulla asked. "Stealing it for himself?"

"He doesn't have any use for gold, except maybe to protect it," Indy said. "I know, because I saw his footprints in the treasure cave." He paused. "No, I'd say that what he's doing now is deciding whether he should take *our* heads."

"This *is* awkward," Ulla observed.

Seven Oaks turned to Indy, made a fist with his free hand, and clutched it against his heart. Then he flung his fist toward the ground.

"What's that mean?" Ulla asked.

"Indian sign language," Indy said. "He says that he is very sad—his heart is upon the ground."

"How do you know that?" she asked.

"I was a Boy Scout."

Seven Oaks pointed to the gold and then held up his

hand, palm out and fingers spread, and waggled it very slowly.

"He's asking me why I took the gold," Indy said.

"This ought to be good," Ulla whispered. "If I didn't believe it, how are you going to make him understand?"

"He's not deaf," Indy said. "Just mute. He can understand what you're saying. So just keep still for a minute, will you?"

"I should have left you in the cave." Ulla shook her head in disgust.

"Look," Indy said to Seven Oaks, "I'm trying to fix something. I'm sorry that I can't explain this so that you'll understand it, but I need the gold to fight an evil that has been unleashed, in the world where our hearts dwell."

Seven Oaks crossed his arms and eyed Indy suspiciously, as if to ask what he knew of the place where hearts dwelled.

"All people," Indy continued, "are on the same journey. It is called by many names, but there is only one path. Many stray from the path, many walk in the wrong direction, and many simply stumble with their eyes clos—"

While Indy was speaking, Ulla had crept up, planted her feet, drawn back her fist, and expertly struck a pressure point behind John Seven Oaks's left ear.

The wild man went down in the dirt, unconscious.

"What did you do that for?" Indy asked.

"I'd rather die than listen to that explanation of yours again," she said as she took the knife from Seven Oaks's outstretched hand.

"Where did you learn to do that?" Indy sputtered.

"All good Viking girls learn to fight," she said. "We just avoid it until it is absolutely necessary." Then she felt for a pulse on the side of the bronzed man's neck.

"He's fine," she said. "But he'll be conscious in a few minutes and angry. Let's get out of here while we can."

* * *

Slewing behind a plume of red dust, the aging cattle truck wheeled from the county road and pulled up to the entrance of the little airfield on the outskirts of El Paso. The truck bounced through a particularly deep pothole, gave a bone-jarring shudder, then came to a tire-skidding stop in front of the hangar.

Indiana Jones jumped from the staked bed of the truck and landed unsteadily on the ground. The knapsack was slung over one shoulder.

"You in one piece?" the cowboy called from the driver's seat.

"More or less," Indy said as he pulled the rest of the bags from the back of the truck. Then he used his hat to knock the straw and dust from his clothes. The manure stains on the back of his pants, however, resisted being dealt with so easily.

"Mister, you said you were in a hurry," the cowboy said. "And like I said, I like to drive fast and not so straight."

"I can only imagine how well you'd do if you had any springs left in this thing," Indy said. He reached in through the driver's window and shook hands with the cowboy.

"My pleasure," the cowboy said, then jerked his thumb at Ulla, who was sitting in the passenger's seat. "It ain't often I have a heifer this pretty ridin' shotgun."

"Thank you," Ulla said with a forced smile. "I think."

"That's quite a compliment," Indy told her. "Judging by the smell in the back, I'd say he's hauled his share of cattle."

Ulla offered the cowboy a five-dollar bill.

"I hope this is enough for your trouble," she said.

"Put your money away, miss." The cowboy tugged at the brim of his ragged straw hat. "It's no good with me."

"Thank you," Ulla said and got out.

"Well, gotta run, amigos. The boss is gonna have my hide when he finds out I've been gone for five hours," the cowboy said. "Adios!"

Indy waved as the truck lurched forward. The driver gave a rebel yell as he wheeled around and tore back down the entrance toward the county road.

"Enthusiastic youngster," Ulla commented. "That will be a ride I won't soon forget."

"Me neither," Indy said. "Every time I swallow, I get a little taste of Texas."

"What kind of place is this?" Ulla squinted against the sun as she took in the hard-packed airfield and the paint-blistered hangar that had obviously been a horse barn in the not-so-distant past. An impressive sign over the office door proclaimed, in red-and-gold letters: WARD BROS AIR CARGO. Beneath was a handwritten addendum: *We don't ask questions.*

"Do they have regular flights out of here?" Ulla asked. "Can I get a plane back to the East Coast?"

"You see that red-and-silver plane out on the field?" Indy asked.

"Yes."

"That's their flight to the East Coast. Or the west. Or Canada or Mexico, for that matter," he said. "It's the only plane they've got. This is a cargo service run by a bunch of guys that grew up in Erbie, Arkansas. It's not a passenger airline."

"You're kidding," Ulla said.

"I never kid, sister," Indy informed her as he paused at the door of the office. "If you want to fly out of here today, you'll be doing it with me."

"Clarence!" Indy called as he stepped into the office. "Donny! Anybody around here?"

There was a Mason jar on the newspaper-strewn desk.

Indy picked it up, swirled around the clear liquid it contained, and sniffed.

"Whew," he said.

"Kerosene?" Ulla asked.

"Just about," Indy said. "Moonshine."

"How quaint," Ulla remarked.

"Prohibition's over, but old habits are apparently hard to break."

Indy stepped through the open door into the hangar. Despite the disarray of the office, the hangar was as orderly as an operating room. Rows of wrenches and other tools hung neatly from pegs. In the center of the room a radial airplane engine was hanging from a hoist, and beside it was a table on which its pistons and connecting rods were laid out in a row.

"It looks deserted," Ulla said.

"Not quite," Indy corrected.

He walked over and kicked a pair of boots that stuck out from beneath the worktable.

"Hey!" came the drowsy reply.

"Get up," Indy ordered. "You've got business."

A big man crawled out from beneath the table. He was about the same age as Indy, and on the breast pocket of his blue coveralls was the name Bob.

"Oh, it's you," the man said, rubbing a hand over his face. "I was just resting my eyes, thinking about putting the pins in those pistons."

"Sure you were, Clarence," Indy said. "I've smelled your jar of inspiration in the office."

"Now, I'm not drunk," the man said, slurring his words just a little too much to be convincing. "I just keep that stuff up front for snakebite. You know how thick the critters can get on the field."

"Right," Indy said.

"Your name's Clarence?" Ulla asked. "But your name tag . . ."

"He's Clarence, regardless of what the label says."

"Now, Indy," Clarence protested. "You know I'd prefer to be called Bob. That's why I put it on my coveralls."

"His middle name is Robert," Indy explained. "For some reason, he doesn't like Clarence. Where's your brother?"

"Donny went down to Juarez," he said. "Won't see him for a couple of days, at least."

Indy shook Clarence's hand. Then he unshouldered the knapsack and lowered it to the concrete floor with a clunk.

"What've you got in there?" Clarence asked. "Bricks?"

"Never mind that right now," Indy said. "I need a favor, old friend."

"Oh no," Clarence said. "When you need a favor it usually means trouble. What is it this time, Jones? You're not talking me into flying something out of the Yucatán again. The last time it took me a week to patch up all the bullet holes."

"This is a no-sweat deal," Indy said. "All you have to do is make a short flight for me."

"For *us*," Ulla corrected. "You're not leaving me here, Mr. Jones. You've already ruined my research expedition to the Guadalupes, at least while Okies and wild men live."

"Who's after you?" Clarence asked.

"Nobody," Indy said. "Well, nobody since I left Kansas. They think I'm dead."

"Great," Clarence said.

"Look, it was just—"

Clarence held his hand up. "The less I know the better. That way, when somebody threatens to break my fingers, I can tell them I don't know a thing about it. Besides, I can't do it."

"You mean you won't do it," Indy said.

"No, I can't," Clarence repeated, and motioned toward the plane on the field. "I've got this job the day after tomorrow running some oil-well equipment to Mexico City, and the crates have already been loaded on *Missy* out there."

"No problem," Indy said. "You'll be back in time."

"I've heard that before," Clarence said as he picked up a combination wrench from the table and wiped it moodily with a shop rag. "Two days has a funny way of turning into two weeks with you."

"This will be a piece of cake," Indy said. "Strictly a milk run. Do you have a phone around here?"

"There's one on the wall," Clarence said, motioning with the wrench.

"Terrific," Indy said. "You just think about it. There's money in it for you."

"I've heard that before."

After several minutes and a half-dozen operators, Indy was connected to Brody's office at the American Museum of Natural History in New York.

"Indy!" Marcus Brody exclaimed. "You're lucky you caught me. I was just on my way out. I have to admit, old man, that I've been worried like the devil about you. Did you find what you were looking for?"

"And then some," Indy said as he looked back at Ulla.

"Outstanding," Brody said. "And the map?"

"Yes, I still have the map."

"Even better."

"Ah, there's just one problem," Indy said. "Due to circumstances beyond my control, the map has been reduced to a wet glob about the size of a tennis ball."

Brody made a sputtering noise deep in his throat.

"Now, Marcus," Indy said. "I'm sure the experts at the museum can put it back together as good as new. I've kept the map wet—that's what you're supposed to do, isn't it?—and your technicians are the best in the world."

"Of course," Brody said. "But they aren't miracle workers. How bad is it?"

"Well, it's pretty bad," Indy admitted.

"Indy," Brody chided. "Oh, Indy."

"I'm sorry, Marcus. If the map can't be restored to its original condition, I'm prepared to pay for it." Which will take approximately until the year 1972 on my salary, Indy thought.

"Well, there's no use jumping to conclusions," Marcus said. "We will see what the boys downstairs can do. More importantly, Indy, are you all right?"

"I'm fine," Indy told him. "Thanks for asking."

"By the way," Brody said, "you have received a cable here. The message is rather cryptic, I'm afraid."

"What's it say?"

"Just a moment." Brody fumbled in his pockets for his glasses and then for the telegram. "Here it is. 'To Indiana Jones, care of Marcus Brody. Interested or not? Time nor tide will wait, and you're wasting both. Will wait on the street until Tuesday, then the party's over.' It is signed, 'Your admiring colleague.' Does any of that make sense to you, Indy?"

"I think so," he said.

Indy closed his eyes. Why did the arrogant so-and-so have to play games? Would an address or a phone number be too much to ask?

"Indy, are you there?"

"I'm here. Marcus, what's today? I've lost track."

"Tuesday, of course."

"Terrific."

"Indy, there's something else," Brody said. "Those chaps from army intelligence have called again. They are rather keen to get in touch with you."

"Did they leave a message?"

"They left a number."

"Give it to me," Indy said.

There was a pencil hanging from a string on the wall, and Indy used it to write the number on his sleeve.

"They said it was rather important they get in touch with you."

"I'll call them the first chance I get," Indy said. "Got to run, Marcus. Thanks for everything."

"Indy," Brody asked. "Indy, won't you at least tell me where you are?"

But Indy had already hung up.

He slapped his hands together and walked back to where Clarence and Ulla were waiting.

"Have you thought it over?"

"It depends," Clarence said. "Where do you want me to take you?"

"New Orleans."

"New Orleans?" Clarence and Ulla asked in unison.

"Aw, I can't fly you that far and get my cargo to Mexico City on time."

"Sure you can," Indy said. "Look, you're practically there—just a short hop across the Gulf."

"Indy, you need to look at a map," Clarence said.

"I don't want to go to New Orleans," Ulla put in. "I thought you were going to take me back to someplace on the East Coast, where I could get a ship for home."

"New Orleans is a port," Indy said. "And it's *almost* on the Atlantic."

"Oh no, Mr. Jones." Ulla shook her finger at him.

"Mr. Jones?" Clarence asked. "Why did you lie to this nice young woman? Didn't you tell her who you were? Did you promise to take her home? What kind of deal are you trying to pull here, Indy?"

"I'm not pulling anything—"

"I'm really ashamed of you," Clarence scolded.

"What do you mean?" Ulla asked. "Who are you, anyway?"

"I kept trying to—"

"Why, this is Indiana Jones," Clarence said. "I'm sorry, Indy, but I'm not going to lie. I won't ask questions, but that's different from asking somebody to lie, isn't it?"

"You mean you really *are* Indianapolis Jones?" Ulla sputtered. "I knew your last name was Jones from your hat, but I thought you were pulling my leg about—"

"Indiana," he said. "My name's Indiana. And yes, that's me."

"That's him," Clarence said. "He's famous in all the forty-eight states, and even in some foreign countries. You know, I've got a wall full of newspaper clippings in the office. There's pictures and everything. My name is even in some of them. But mostly just the arrest reports."

"Don't give her the wrong idea," Indy said. He turned to Ulla. "I've never been arrested."

"Aren't you forgetting that time I got you out of that little jail at El Cedrál on Cozumel?" Clarence asked. "And then there was the time in Costa Rica—"

"Those were different," Indy said. "That El Cedrál thing was in connection with my work, and the charges didn't stick. And Costa Rica was just a misunderstanding."

"Well," Ulla said. Her arms were crossed and she was tapping her right foot furiously. "I'm sorry. I guess I should have believed you."

"Look, there's no time to argue about all of this," Indy said. "I need to get to New Orleans, and I need to get there as quickly as possible."

"It's close to eleven o'clock now." Clarence glanced at his watch. He walked over to a map of North and Central America that hung on the wall. He used the width between his right thumb and little finger to walk off the distance. "New Orleans is a thousand miles away, give or take. *Missy* will cruise at close to two hundred miles an hour. If we're lucky, I can have you on the ground in Louisiana by four o'clock this afternoon."

"Then you'll do it?" Indy asked.

"What's it pay?" Clarence asked.

"Send me a bill," Indy said. "You're already loaded, right?"

"You could say that," Ulla said under her breath, remembering the mason jar in the office.

"Yeah, but I need to make sure the tanks are topped off," Clarence said. "New Orleans is about as far as I can go in a single hop. You all go ahead and climb on board while I lock up."

Indy shouldered the heavy knapsack. "Ulla has some bags out front," he told Clarence.

"I'll grab them. You just go ahead and get on the plane."

Indy and Ulla walked out onto the airfield, where the twin-engine DC-2 waited. The silver skin of the aircraft was nearly blinding in the sun. A coat of flat red paint covered the nose. Beneath the pilot's window, in black script, was the aircraft's name: *Miss Adventure*.

"How do we get in?" Ulla asked.

Indy opened a trapdoorlike hatch in the belly.

"We climb up," he said.

Indy knelt down and let Ulla step on his shoulders, then boosted her up into the interior of the plane, in spite of her protestations that she could handle it herself. Then he climbed in after her.

"It's like an oven in here," she said.

Indy stepped up into the cockpit and slid open the side windows. It helped, but not much. In a few minutes their clothes were soaked with sweat.

Ulla brushed a clump of limp blond hair from her eyes with the back of her hand as she looked over the crates in the cargo bay. Most of them were clearly marked as containing machinery, and were well secured, but a couple of crates were open and loosely packed. These were full of toys—dolls, tops, whatever one could find at the local five-and-dime.

"Who sends toys with this kind of cargo?" she asked.

"Nobody," Indy said. "But Clarence buys the toys himself and distributes them to the kids in the slums in Mexico City. Other times he takes them food, or clothes."

"Remarkable," Ulla said.

When Clarence had finished checking the tanks, he passed the bags and wheel chocks up through the hatch to Indy. Then he swung up inside the plane and secured the hatch behind him.

"You all better strap yourselves in for takeoff," he told them as he eased his big frame into the pilot's seat. "All the rain we've had has turned the field into a regular washboard."

"Doesn't it take two people to fly this thing?" Ulla asked.

"That *would* be nice," Clarence said as switched on the starboard engine. It started with a gust of black smoke and a sputtering, whining sound.

"Is that normal?" Ulla asked nervously.

"More or less," Clarence replied as the engine settled into a reassuring throbbing roar. Then he looked out the cockpit toward the other engine as he brought it to life as well.

Indy buckled himself into the copilot's seat. Ulla chose to remain in the bench behind the cabin bulkhead.

"I'd rather not watch," she grumbled. "I saw sausage being made once, and I've regretted it ever since."

Clarence stuck his head out the window to check the control surfaces as he turned the wheel hard to the left and right.

"Take a gander out your side, buddy," he shouted. "The rudder, flaps, and so forth. They all moving okay?"

"Check." Indy nodded.

Then Clarence wrinkled his nose.

"What's wrong?" Indy asked.

"I'm not sure," Clarence shouted. "There's a peculiar smell coming from someplace. I'd swear it's fresh cow pie, but we ain't had no cattle on the field since Donny flew into one last year."

6

FAT TUESDAY

Even at four-thirty in the afternoon, Bourbon Street was
a sea of revelry and mayhem. Leading Ulla by the hand,
Indiana Jones threaded his way through the crowd
toward the refuge of the old St. Charles Hotel, still some
blocks away.

"Have all of these people gone insane?" Ulla asked
above the cacophony.

"Yes," Indy said, "but only temporarily. It ends
tomorrow—the first day of Lent."

He released her hand so they could pass on either side
of a man standing next to a lamppost, playing a saxophone.
A battered hat with some loose change was at the musician's feet.

"Do you have anything like this in Copenhagen?" Indy
asked, striding ahead, anxious to get to the hotel.

When there was no answer, he turned to confront a sea
of unfamiliar faces.

"Ulla!" he shouted. "Where the devil are you?"

Indy made his way back through the crowd to the saxophone player, who was working hard on a mediocre rendi-
tion of a popular tune.

"Excuse me," Indy said.

The saints kept marching in.

"Have you seen a tall blond woman?"

The saints stopped.

"Man, I've seen plenty," the sax player said as he rolled his eyes. "But the one you're lookin' for was hauled inside that green door behind us. I figured you'd come looking for her."

"Thanks," Indy said.

"Hey!" the sax player shouted.

"Sorry," Indy said. "No change."

Indy pushed his way over to the stout wooden door the musician had indicated. As he grasped the brass knob a large man with a bald head and a beard leaned against it and slammed it shut. Rings glittered from his fingers.

"Where do you think you're going?" he asked Indy.

"I'm looking for a friend."

"Ain't none of your friends in there," the man said.

"Oh, sorry," Indy said.

As he turned away he scooped up a beer bottle from the sidewalk, then spun around and hit the bald man over the head. The bottle shattered, and blood trickled down the bald man's face.

"Now, wha'd you do that for?" the man asked as he slumped to the ground. Indy propped him up beside the building, then dashed inside the green door.

It was dark and smoky inside.

"Ulla?" he called.

There was a muffled cry from the back.

Indy ran toward the sound, but his eyes had not adjusted yet to the darkness. He stumbled over a table and chairs.

"Stay where you are, or we'll kill her," a voice warned.

"Let her go," Indy said.

"Are you kidding?" the voice called back. "You know

what a dame like this will bring on the white slave market?"

"She's more trouble than she's worth," Indy called.

"Then we'll kill her anyway."

Indy reached inside his leather jacket and drew out his whip. Then he walked cautiously into the darkness, making his way around the tables of the closed bar. Just enough light filtered through the shuttered windows to allow him to thread his way across the room.

"Stay back."

Indy heard a gun being cocked. He looked in the direction of the sound and noticed the faint orange glow bobbing in the darkness.

He lashed out with the whip.

It made an ear-splitting crack and the cigarette dropped to the floor in a shower of ashes.

"What the hell was that?" the voice asked.

"You want some more of it?"

"Forget it," another voice said. "He can have her."

The kidnappers fled, leaving the green door open behind them. Indy got only a glimpse of their backs as they ran. Light flooded into the room, and perched on top of the bar Indy could see Ulla. Her hands and feet were bound and a dirty bandanna was stuffed into her mouth.

"I can't turn my back on you for a second," Indy said as he freed her hands and feet. "Are you hurt?"

Ulla jerked the bandanna from her mouth and spat on the floor.

"No," she said. "It happened so fast, I didn't have time—"

"I know." Indy pulled her toward the door as he spoke. "Let's get out of here before they work up their courage for another try."

At the hotel, on St. Charles between Common and

Gravier streets, he led Ulla up the impressive steps to the large double doors.

"We're staying here?" she asked, looking up at the massive facade.

"I have a weakness for history," Indy explained. "This was the most important hotel during the slave trade, built in 1837. It was the favorite of wealthy planters, and slaves were sold in the hotel's exchange. God seemed not to like the arrangement, however, and the original hotel burned in 1851. They rebuilt it, and it burned again. What you see here is the third incarnation, constructed about the turn of the century."

They crossed the massive lobby to the front desk, where a bald man in a suit watched their approach warily. He glanced at the pair's disheveled appearance and chuckled to himself.

"May I help you?" he asked condescendingly.

"We need a room," Indy said.

The man closed the guest book and, for extra measure, leaned his forearms against it.

"Ah, I'm sorry," he said. "But we have no vacancies."

"No rooms?" Indy asked. "You have a wall full of keys behind you."

"The rooms are being cleaned right now." The man sniffed.

"All six hundred of them?"

"I'm sorry, but we have nothing. You'll have to take your—er, business—elsewhere."

Another couple walked up to the desk. They were older, and their costumes looked a little more comical than either probably would have liked. The man was an aging Marc Antony and the woman, complete with a dark wig, was Cleopatra.

The man put down their bags and struck the bell on the counter.

"Service!" he cried.

"You'll have to excuse me," the clerk said to Indy.

The clerk chatted briefly with the couple. Marc Antony signed the guest register, exchanged some cash for a key that the clerk took from the wall behind them. Then they went upstairs, a bellhop trailing behind them with their luggage, while the man's sword clanged on the steps.

"I thought you said you had no rooms," Indy said through clenched teeth.

"Quite right," the clerk confirmed. "We don't."

"Come on," Ulla said. "We will go someplace else."

"I don't want to go anywhere else," Indy said. "I want to stay here."

"Well, you can't," the clerk said. "Off with you, or I will have to call the police."

"Do you have a safe here?" Indy asked.

"What? Of course we have a safe," the clerk said. "This is a first-rate hotel."

"Good." Indy lifted the knapsack onto the counter. He removed the three bars of gold and placed them in front of the clerk. "Look, we've just flown into town on business and I haven't had a chance to take this to the bank and exchange it for cash."

The clerk reached out for the gold, then drew back his hand.

"May I?" he asked meekly.

"I'd be very obliged if you would lock this up for me," Indy said. "And then I'd like for you to call your manager so that I can discuss this matter with him. I always stay at the St. Charles when I'm in New Orleans."

"I am the manager," the man said. "I mean, I'm the acting manager. The manager is out with his krewe."

"Then I would like to talk to the owner," Indy said. "I believe his name is . . . what is it, Dubois?"

"No need for that," the clerk said brightly. "You see, I

thought you just meant a room. I didn't understand that you wanted a suite. And I believe the Pontalba Suite just came available, if that would suit you."

"It will," Indy said, "if it has separate bedrooms. Also, you said this was a full-service hotel, did you not?"

"Of course."

"Then I would like you to have someone run out and get us some proper clothes," Indy said. "We need the full treatment—shirt, trousers, socks, belt, shoes. Boxers and an undershirt. A dress for the lady."

"Please, no," Ulla said. "Not a dress. Men's clothes, if you please."

The clerk searched for a piece of paper then furiously began taking notes.

"Yes, of course," he said. "May I inquire as to sizes?"

They told him.

"From a sensible shop," Indy instructed. "Not the most expensive, but certainly not the cheapest. You may add ten percent for your trouble, but no more."

"Very good," the clerk said. "Thank you, sir."

"Also, we feel somewhat out of place," Indy said. "We need a couple of costumes."

"But, sir," the clerk stammered. "It is Mardi Gras, and—"

"But I'm sure that you have connections," Indy said. "What would you like to be?" he asked Ulla. "No, wait. Allow me to choose. Something Shakespearean for the lady. Not a lady-in-waiting, mind you, but a queen. No, wait, that's it—a Danish queen. Are you familiar with *Hamlet*? Good."

"Please," Ulla said. "I would rather be anyone but Gertrude. Ophelia, perhaps."

"So be it," Indy said.

"And will you be Hamlet, sir?" the clerk asked.

"No," Indy said. The clerk winced. "I've never been that

indecisive. I rather fancy myself as the hero type. Fortinbras, don't you think?"

"Of course," the clerk said.

"I'm not done," Indy said.

The clerk groaned.

"I suppose the banks are closed?"

"They are now, sir."

"Call a banker you trust," Indy said. "At home, if you have to. Tell him I would like to exchange these ingots as quickly and quietly as possible. There's a law now against private ownership of gold, you know. Tell him that I will pay a premium for prompt service."

"Yes, sir. I know a Mr. James who might be willing to help you."

"Good," Indy said. "And one last thing."

"Oh my God." The clerk shuddered.

"Relax," Indy told him. "This is an easy one. I would like reservations for seven o'clock tonight on the balcony of the restaurant upstairs. I want a table that is rather secluded, but which has a good view of the street. And make the reservations for three persons."

"Three?" Ulla asked.

"Trust me," Indy said as he signed the register. Then he looked up at the clerk. "What's your name?"

"Edwards," the clerk said.

"Nicely done, Edwards," Indy said. "By the way, I am holding you personally responsible for the safekeeping of this merchandise until it can be exchanged. If you do it well, I will offer a good word to Mr. Dubois on your behalf. Understood?"

"I'm afraid so," Edwards said nervously.

The wine steward opened a bottle of Bordeaux and poured a little of it along with fragments of the cork into Indy's glass. Indy sniffed the wine, took a little sip, then nodded.

The steward then took the glass, discarded the contents, and poured both Ulla and Indy nearly full glasses.

"May I compliment you both on an excellent choice of costumes," the steward said as he backed away, looking at Ulla's multicolored gown and braided hair. "Especially the lady. Very nice."

Indy smiled, then held up his glass.

"A toast," he told Ulla. "To a long and healthy friendship. May we never again find ourselves lost in the dark."

"Just in the dark," Ulla added.

They both drank.

"Mm," Ulla said, wiping her lips with her napkin. "I had been in the wilderness so long I had almost forgotten what benefits civilization offers."

"They are many." Indy sighed. "He is right about that dress, you know. You look as if you were born for it."

"Really?" Ulla asked. "It makes me feel somewhat naked. But your costume is rather dashing. Perhaps I should have been Hamlet."

"The sword is rather a bother, isn't it?"

"I wouldn't know," Ulla said. "And, it's a rapier."

"Well, I prefer my whip."

"It looks rather authentic, if that is any consolation," Ulla said. "I suppose that's to be expected, considering the number of fencing schools in New Orleans."

"Really?" Indy asked.

"Yes," she said. "It is really the only place in the New World that one can learn the ancient art with any proficiency. Probably because of all those silly antebellum duels they fought."

"I hope nobody challenges me tonight," Indy said.

"Don't worry." Ulla smiled. "I would be your second."

Indy laughed.

"You are quite a different person when you are relaxed," Ulla observed.

"Aren't we all?"

"You know, I really haven't known what to make of you," she continued. "And I still don't. You seemed so unsavory when we first met, with all of these wild stories and schemes, and yet now you seem as reliable as the rising of the sun. Tell me, did you get what you hoped for from the exchange this afternoon?"

"I got what I could have expected," Indy said. "Because of the historical value of the pieces, I received rather more than I would have strictly by weight. But then, I was technically a criminal, keeping so much gold in my possession. Properly, it should have been reported to the government."

"And it hasn't been?"

"No," Indy said. "At least, that's now the problem of the Pelican Bank of New Orleans. Which, to them, is likely not a problem at all."

"Good." Ulla nodded. "The government probably would have just used their share to buy guns and bombs."

"Or to feed people," Indy said. "You know, if it wasn't for the relief and some of the other programs, people would be in far worse shape than they are. That is what gives me hope in humanity, you know—given the choice, I think, most people would prefer to be charitable."

"Ah, but there's the rub," Ulla said. "Many people don't have the choice."

"Are you one of the lucky few that have the choice?" Indy asked.

"Are you asking if I am rich?"

"Well, you don't seem to have what we Americans call any visible means of support," Indy said.

"I appreciate your gift of the clothes today," she said. "But I could have paid for them myself. My family is one of the richest in Denmark. My father is a shipbuilder."

"Longboats?" Indy asked.

"A long time ago our family did make wooden ships," Ulla said. "Although longboats were a rarity. Now we make these wonderfully modern cargo ships of steel, driven by oil-fired engines."

"No more wooden boats?"

"Every so often," Ulla said, "we will make a wooden boat in the old style, for the bear hunters in the Arctic Circle. Wood is very forgiving, and will remain tight when a steel ship would be crushed like a sardine can in the floes."

"Ugh." Indy winced. "Sounds painful."

At that moment the waiter arrived and asked if they would care to order.

"Not yet," Indy said. "We are still waiting for our guest."

"Indy," Ulla whispered. "I'm famished. That sandwich we had earlier in the room did not stay with me, I'm afraid."

"Just a few more minutes," Indy said.

The waiter bowed and went away.

"Who are we waiting for?" Ulla asked. "You're being so mysterious about all of this."

"The reason I came to New Orleans," Indy said, then looked at his watch. "He is making us wait, as usual."

"How does he even know that we are here?"

"He knows," Indy said. "New Orleans is one of his adopted cities, and he has eyes and ears everywhere. Besides, he knows that I always stay at the St. Charles, and our conspicuous table with its unoccupied third seat is an unmistakable invitation for him."

"Well, I will have some more wine in that case." Ulla reached for the bottle. "Would you care for some?"

"No, thanks," Indy said. "I have some left."

On the street below, the carnival was in full swing, with a seemingly endless procession of marching bands and floats streaming by. The krewes—the fraternal organizations that built and paraded the floats—threw trinkets to the crowd, and occasionally some of the cheap jewelry landed on the balcony.

Indy picked up one of the necklaces that landed near the table, and Ulla allowed him to loop the cheap string of beads around her neck.

"Thank you," she said. "I will keep it to remind me of our friendship."

"As something cheap and disposable?" Indy teased.

"No! As something unexpected and remarkable," she said. "Not everything that is precious starts out as gold, Dr. Jones, but is made so by the warmth of our hearts."

"You're a poet as well an adventuress," Indy said.

"All people have poetry in them," she said, "whether they can express it or not. Even you, Dr. Jones, can wax poetic when talking of certain things—like beasts that must be tamed in order to save redheaded sirens from certain death."

A particularly large float, shaped like a pirate ship, glided by on the street below. As decks of cannon spewed fireworks and smoke it suddenly veered toward the side of the street where the St. Charles stood. The crowd parted with some jeers and curses, but the helmsman good-naturedly pantomimed fighting the wheel. The rigging of the float was so tall that Indy found himself looking at the end of a yardarm, from which billowed a sail emblazoned with the skull and crossbones.

Suddenly a pirate swung from the end of a rope onto the balcony, then turned and gave the helmsman a salute. The ship lurched away, inching back toward the center of the street.

The pirate stood for a moment with his hands on his hips, regarding Indy and Ulla. He was a small man, dressed in black, and a mischievous smile tugged at the corners of his mouth. Then he swept off his plumed hat and bowed low. When he came up he tossed the hat on the floor, settled into the empty chair, and began taking off his gloves.

"Easter comes early this year, *n'est pas?*" he asked.

"Really?" Indy asked. "From your entrance I would have thought it was Halloween. Ulla, I would like to introduce you to René Belloq."

"*Au contraire,*" Belloq said. "I am Jean Lafitte, at least for tonight. Lafitte was the black sheep of my family who saved New Orleans for Americans. A terrible mistake."

"It's hard to believe your family could have a black sheep, René," Indy said. "They are all black sheep, aren't they?"

"Lucky for you I have a sense of humor," Belloq said. "So stop your weak attempts at wisecracking and properly introduce me to your charming companion."

Belloq took Ulla's hand and kissed it.

"Miss Ulla Tornaes of Copenhagen, may I introduce you to Monsieur Belloq of Marseilles," Indy said. "Remember, I warned you about him earlier."

"This is the monster you spoke of?" Ulla asked.

"Ah, but a gentle monster when the occasion calls," Belloq said. "Beauty tames the beast."

"I thought beauty *killed* the beast," Indy quipped.

"Only in American movies," Belloq said. Then he picked up the wine bottle and regarded it with disdain.

"I'm disappointed in you, Jones," he said. "I would have expected a little more imagination from you. After all, style is the sauce of life."

"Do you have what I require?" Indy asked impatiently.

"Not so fast, Jones," Belloq warned. "We are civilized people here. We must eat first. That is what you intended, no?"

"Yes," Ulla said. "Let's eat."

Belloq snapped his hands and summoned the waiter, who offered a menu.

"No, no," Belloq said. "I know what we want. Allow me. We will start with scampi and gumbo, and then go on to *cuisses de grenouille*. For the main course, let's try the blackened brisket. And for dessert we will have pecan pie and coffee."

Indy made a face.

"What's wrong, Jones? You do eat pecan pie, don't you?"

"It was the frog legs I was thinking of."

"Ah, but we must taste the local flavor," Belloq said. "Have you ever had gumbo, my dear? It is fabulous. When in New Orleans it would be a mortal sin to waste the cuisine. And waiter—bring me an absinthe, please. And the real thing, from Paris, not what you give to the tourists. Jones, will you join me?"

"No thanks," Indy said. "That stuff will rot your brain."

The waiter left.

"How have you been, my old friend?" Belloq asked.

"I'm not your friend," Indy said.

"Jones simply has a hard time acknowledging our mutual admiration," he said. "We are quite similar, really. We just work in somewhat different ways."

The absinthe arrived and Belloq swirled the potent green liquid around in the short glass. Even from where Indy sat, he could smell the strong licorice aroma.

"I have knowledge of your Miss Dunstin," Belloq said.

"I hope it's not biblical," Indy said with a snarl.

"Oh, no," he said happily. "She's definitely not my type. But this one, at your side tonight—well, I might be inclined to fight you a duel for *her* hand."

"She's yours," Indy said. "Tell me what you know."

"Dr. Jones!" Ulla said.

"I'm sorry. What I meant to say is that Ulla and I are

just good friends, but you had better treat her with respect or I'll give you the horsewhipping of your life. Now tell me about Alecia."

"She's with the Nazis."

"I don't believe it."

"Oh, it's true," Belloq said. "I don't have the details, of course—I assure you that I am not involved—but it seems that she has agreed to help them on some wild quest in the Arctic if only they would spare your life."

"You're lying."

"I don't lie," Belloq said. "At least not when the truth is more profitable."

"Do the Nazis think Alecia can help them find Ultima Thule?"

"Yes, that's the place," Belloq said. "I couldn't quite remember their peculiar name for it. At any rate, Alecia is quite psychic, is she not? The Nazis are working on some crazy thing called distant viewing—an attempt to map unknown terrain through the use of telepathy. Ah, here comes the first course of our meal. *Bon appétit.*"

An hour later, when the dishes had been cleared away, Belloq scooted his chair back and lit a cigarette.

"Well, my dear?" he asked. "What did you think?"

"It was wonderful." Ulla smiled. "The gumbo, however, was visually challenging. All those shells and things."

Belloq laughed, then took a sip of his coffee.

"Now can we get on with it?" Indy asked.

"Of course," Belloq said. "You've been more than patient. Do you have the money?"

Indy handed over a paper sack containing five wrapped bundles, each containing twenty one-hundred-dollar bills. He piled them on the table in front of Belloq.

"You don't have to count it," Indy said. "It's all there."

"Indulge me." Belloq picked up one bundle after another and thumbed through the stacks. "If it were me, I would be tempted to pack the interior with paper cut to size."

When Belloq was satisfied that he indeed held ten thousand dollars in cash, he reached inside the sash of his pirate costume and produced a folded sheet of teletype paper. He handed the paper to Ulla, who gave it to Indy.

Indy took a breath, then unfolded it.

The paper contained three pieces of information: *14.350 58N 32'10" 5W 07'14"*.

"What is this?" Indy asked.

"The information you desire," Belloq said. "Those last set of numbers are coordinates in the North Sea. It's the last known position of that little yellow canister that you seek. But it is the first set of numbers that are the key."

"Fourteen point three fifty?" Indy asked. "It doesn't make any sense to me."

"We live in a marvelous age," Belloq said. "All of these technical marvels at our fingertips. Do you remember when I packed the skull into the canister before handing it over to the Nazis on board the submarine at Marseilles? Well, I included a little something that would help locate the skull if something unfortunate happened to the U-357."

"A radio transmitter," Indy said.

"Yes," Belloq said. "But one that would be activated only in the event the canister came into contact with water. That number is the frequency upon which the radio transmits a pulse, every thirty seconds. But your time, I fear, is running out."

"What do you mean?"

"Batteries last only so long," Belloq said. "The signal has grown weak, it comes and goes. In a few short days there may be no signal at all. And, the Germans have the frequency—they are looking for it as well, I fear."

Indy pounded his fist on the table.

"I was expecting something a little more substantial," Indy said through clenched teeth. "Someplace where I could go and snatch the bloody thing and be done with it. Now I have to search all across the North Sea while keeping the Nazis off my back?"

"No. I expect it is no longer there," Belloq said. "It has probably been swept north by the currents, or perhaps far out into the Atlantic. Who knows?"

Indy stood up.

"You bloody little weasel," he said, half drawing his rapier from its scabbard. "I ought to—"

"Yes, by all means." Belloq drew his cutlass. "Lay on, Jones!"

Ulla stood up.

"Sit down, both of you," she shouted. "You're acting like children."

"Yes," Belloq said. "Sit down, Jones. You are making a fool of yourself. You're dismissing the value of what I have given to you."

"*Sold* me," Indy corrected. "You sold it to me, you wormy little frog coward."

"Indy!" Ulla said.

"You have insulted me, you have insulted my family, and now you have insulted my country," Belloq said quietly. "I am a baron, I'll have you know."

"Baron of what?" Indy spat. "Of intellect? Or of morals?"

"I demand satisfaction, Dr. Jones," Belloq said. "In the grand tradition."

"You're insane."

"Ah, who is the coward now?" Belloq smiled. "As well as the dullard. Without the information I have provided—and the risk I took in placing the equipment in the canister in the first place—you wouldn't have a ghost of a chance. And you repay me with insults?"

Indy grumbled.

"Dawn, at St. Louis Cemetery No. 2. You know the place, of course," Belloq said. "And I must warn you about my skill with the blade."

"This has finally gotten interesting," Ulla said. "But you can't be serious. Can he? Can you?"

"Oh, I'm serious enough for both of us," Indy said. "Dawn, then. But isn't the challenger usually allowed to choose the weapon?"

"If you wish." Belloq shrugged.

"Then I choose pistols."

"Revolvers?" Belloq cried. "How barbaric!"

"Single shot," Indy said. "Muzzle loading. Is that grand enough for you? I'll be happy to load yours if you don't know how."

"No need," Belloq said. "I know how to aim one as well."

"I'll be Indy's second," Ulla said quickly.

"Alas," Belloq said. "I will have to rely upon my old friend Captain Dominique You, for my second. I don't think his ghost will mind, since it will be so close by."

"Who's he talking about?" Ulla asked.

"A veteran of the Battle of New Orleans," Indy said. "He was one of Lafitte's pirates, and he died about a hundred years ago. He's buried in the cemetery."

"What about the weapons?" Indy asked.

"It's up to your second to procure them," Belloq said. "You had better get busy, my dear. My time in New Orleans is almost up, but I think I have just enough left to show one very beautiful Danish visitor some of the more famous sights in the French Quarter, and perhaps even an antique dealer who will accommodate your needs."

"Do I have to jump off the balcony with you?" Ulla asked.

"Of course not." Belloq offered his arm. "This time I

will take the stairs." He paused, then saluted Indy with his sword. "Adieu, Dr. Jones. Until the dawn. Oh, and don't bother waiting up."

"Don't worry," Indy promised as he finished his coffee.

"Oh, and Dr. Jones," Belloq added. "Tonight is the last of the revelry. I do hope you haven't decided to give up something precious for Lent—like your life, perhaps."

Indy unlocked the door to the Pontalba Suite and unbuckled the rapier as he entered the room. He threw the weapon on the couch in the sitting room, then squirmed out of the doublet and folded it beside it.

He sat for a moment on the couch, his head in his hands.

"What have I done?" he mumbled.

Indy was tired. He knew he needed sleep, but he also knew that he didn't have time for sleep. He wearily got up, walked into the bedroom, and searched for the pile of old clothes he had shed earlier in the day. They had been washed, and pressed, and were laid in a neat bundle on top of the newly made bed. His fedora, freshly cleaned and blocked, was next to the bundle.

"Swell," Indy muttered as he unwrapped the twine around the package. He shook out the shirt, found the left sleeve, and held it beneath the light. The number he had penciled there was still visible, but barely.

He reached for the phone, got the hotel operator, and gave her the number. The operator said she would ring when she had made the connection.

Indy eased himself down on the bed and closed his eyes.

A few minutes later the phone woke him.

"Jones?" a crisp voice asked. "This is Colonel William Markham. We've been trying to reach you. What in thunder are you doing in New Orleans?"

"Business," Indy said. "Get to the point."

"I understand you may be able to help us," Markham

said. "You're an expert on this hokum that the Nazis believe in. True?"

"I'm an archaeologist," Indy explained tiredly. "But sometimes my research does take into account ancient beliefs that can seem rather strange to us today."

"Well, the Germans are flying about the Arctic in one of their dirigibles," Markham said. "They seem to be looking for some kind of lost civilization. But the cables we have intercepted seem to suggest they are looking for something of military and not historical importance."

"Go on," Indy said.

"They keep referring to some obscure power source, something called Vril. Are you familiar with it? Is it a kind of mineral or something?"

"I don't know for sure," Indy said.

"Well, their cables to Berlin indicate that this stuff has the ability to manipulate matter, to transform or control it in some way. If they find it, that would fulfill their dream of becoming some type of super race."

"Look," Indy said. "You seem to know as much about all of this as I do. I really can't tell you much more. It seems like fairy tales to me, except—"

"What is it, Dr. Jones?"

"Well, there are some who believe fervently in the legend. It is a matter of national pride, I suppose. I've had a couple of run-ins with them, and even if the story is a myth, they're treating it as gospel. They are prepared to kill for their beliefs, even if Vril has no basis in fact."

"I agree," Markham said.

"Then why are you asking me about it?"

"Because we'd like you to lead an American expedition into the region where the Nazis are searching," Markham said.

"Why me?"

"Because you have some unique talents that other

scholars seem to lack," Markham said. "In the remote event that the Nazis find something up there that would be better off in our hands, we'd like to know about it."

"Spy on them, you mean."

"Spying is a nasty word," Markham said. "Just dog their heels. Consider it research, if you like. After all, much of that territory is unexplored, and it wouldn't be the first time that a scientific expedition had a military component."

"I'm not prepared to lead a land expedition into the Arctic," Indy said. "I don't have the experience. It would be suicide."

"This is the twentieth century, Dr. Jones," Markham said. "Who said anything about dogsleds and frozen toes? What we had in mind was polar aviation. We have the prototype of a new bomber, the Douglas B-18, at your disposal. Twin engines, a crew of six, and a range of more than twelve hundred miles. From your base camp on Greenland, or Spitsbergen Island, you could survey the area in relative comfort."

"Polar aviation scares me," Indy said. "Too many people have never been seen again."

"Like Amundsen?" Markham asked. "Well, that was years ago. Flight, even in the Arctic, has become as safe as driving your Ford to the corner store."

"Why don't I believe you?" Indy asked.

"I may be exaggerating a bit," Markham said, "but the fact remains that this would be the safest expedition to that area, ever. What do you say, Dr. Jones?"

"It sounds insane," Indy said.

"There's something else," Markham said. "It's the real reason I have tried so desperately to reach you. I hate to mention it, because I have always hesitated to introduce any emotional component—"

"I already know that Alecia Dunstin is on board that zeppelin," Indy said. "And yes, that is the reason I will lead your infernal expedition, because I can't stand the thought of her being left for dead on some ice floe after those bastards are through with her."

"Given the choice," Markham said, "I felt you would rather be in a position to help her than not."

"I have a few conditions, Colonel."

"I'm listening," Markham said. "Name them."

"I want complete control over what you have so loosely defined as my research. And I want a friend of mine as the pilot. Or, at least, copilot. I trust him."

"Understood," Markham said.

"I also need the best radioman the army has," Indy said. "He must have the latest direction-finding technology and be able to improvise in a crisis. Fearlessness wouldn't hurt, either. Do you have anyone that meets those requirements?"

"Of course," Markham said. "I will send you my own radio operator from the cryptography office. He is by all accounts a genius with anything electric and I know he is fearless."

"How do you know that?"

"He's seventeen," Markham said. "All teenagers think they'll live forever. And I know he'll gladly volunteer, because he's bored to death by the daily routine around here. What else?"

"You're welcome to whatever we find or can take from the Nazis up there—and I doubt if that will be anything at all—but I want my participation in the expedition kept quiet. After all, I have an academic reputation to protect."

"Some would say it's too late for that," Markham said. "But yes, all right. I agree to every condition. And get some sleep. The aircraft will be on the field at Shushan Airport at zero nine hundred."

An hour after Indy had hung up the phone, the light came on in the room. Ulla had returned from her tour of the French Quarter, and she had a large wooden box and a book beneath her arm.

Indy was lying on the couch, his fedora over his eyes. He was dressed in his khakis and had his leather jacket on.

"Have a good time?" he asked.

"René is quite charming," Ulla said.

"Monsters often are," Indy said.

"Look what I found." She placed the wooden box on the coffee table and opened the lid. "A matched pair, a forty-five-caliber, real museum pieces, circa 1840. René knew the owner of a quaint little antique store on Rampart Street that opened for us."

Indy picked up one of the pistols and examined the barrel, which was covered in a splotchy brown patina of rust and gun oil.

"Sure they won't blow up in our faces?" Indy asked.

"Quite sure," Ulla said. "I insisted that the gentleman test-fire both of them first. With all the commotion and fireworks tonight, nobody gave the shots a second thought. Also, he had a copy of this splendid little book—the *Code Duello*."

"Splendid," Indy said halfheartedly.

"Why are you dressed?" Ulla asked. "You need your sleep. Dawn will be here in just a few hours. I know I am anxious to hit the hay myself, as you Americans are fond of saying."

"I've been busy," Indy said.

"What on earth with?"

"Making travel arrangements for points north," Indy said. "It seems I'm going on an air expedition of the Arctic in search of the Nazi dirigible that Alecia's on."

"So you're going, just like that," Ulla said.

"Well, I'm going to kill Belloq first," Indy said. "What is it that you want me to say?" He replaced the pistol in the case.

"I want you to ask me to go with you."

"What?"

"You need me." Ulla crossed her arms. "You just don't know it yet. The Nazis are going after Thule, and they're not going to find it from the air. They're not going to find it on the surface, either. Sooner or later they are going to lead you underground, and for that you need me."

Indy paused.

"That's what Baldwin's journal said, wasn't it?"

"I don't know," Indy stammered. "It was stolen before I got a chance to—"

"But he was descending into the mouth of a volcanic crater," Ulla said. "You told me that much. Now, how far down do you think he went?"

"The Nazis won't even find the right—"

"They have the journal," Ulla said. "You don't. Your only hope is to find them, and then to follow where they lead. If you would only have put some thought into it, you would have realized that meant far beneath the surface."

Indy ran a hand across the stubble on his jaw.

"All right," he said. "But we have to get one thing straight. I'm the leader of this expedition. I will listen to your advice, but you must not argue with me. It's too dangerous."

Ulla nodded.

"And another thing," Indy said. "To hell with Ultima Thule. My primary objective is to get Alecia back alive. Then, and only then, do we deal with this Nazi fantasy."

"Superb," Ulla said. "This is the chance of a lifetime."

"Yeah," Indy said. "Or the chance to end a lifetime."

"What are you worried about?" Ulla asked. "Belloq may kill you before you get a chance to board the plane."

7

THE SILVER SHIP

The mist seemed to seep from the very graves as Indiana Jones and Ulla made their way past the narrow mausoleum-lined alleys at St. Louis Cemetery No. 2. The sky was overcast and, in the east, was beginning to take on the color of burnished brass. A light rain was falling as they emerged in a small clear space in the center of the cemetery, dominated by a huge oak that wept with Spanish moss.

"This place gives me the woollies," Ulla said as she rested the boxed pistols on a low headstone.

"The slaves used to hold their voodoo rituals here," Indy said. "And the word is willies."

"Woollies, willies," Ulla said, and suddenly her Danish accent became thicker. "It just plain gives me the creeps."

"Bonjour," Belloq said, causing Ulla to jump.

The diminutive Frenchman, dressed in a black frock coat, was sitting atop the unmarked concrete grave of Marie Laveau and drinking a cup of chicory coffee. Scattered around the grave of the voodoo queen were offerings of food and hoodoo money—curious two- and eleven-cent combinations—and a dozen or so candles that had burned away to nothing but pools of colored wax.

Belloq produced a red candle from his coat, struck a match on his heel, and carefully lit the wick before placing it at the base of the grave and making a cross on the concrete with a shard of red brick.

"For luck," he explained.

"You're going to need more than that," Indy said.

"Ah, Dr. Jones, I'm glad to see you haven't lost your spirit." Belloq laughed. "At least, not yet. Would you care for some coffee?"

"No, thanks," Ulla said, and opened the case. "I took the liberty of loading the guns back at the hotel. Each has forty grains of powder, one patched ball, and fresh flints. I hope that was all right with you."

"Of course, my dear," Belloq said.

"I also have a first-aid kit here in case it is needed."

"Doubtful," Belloq said. "I shoot to kill." He jumped down from the gravestone, walked across the muddy ground to where Ulla stood with the pistols, and picked one up.

"Magnificent pieces, really," he said.

"According to the book," Ulla said, thumbing through the pages, "I believe this is the point where the seconds attempt to negotiate a peaceful reconciliation of differences. Because I am the only second, I will begin by playing the devil's advocate for René."

"What a nice choice of words," Indy remarked.

"Also," she said, "it is my duty to remind you both that dueling is against the law in Louisiana."

"A felony, in fact," Belloq said.

"Yes," Ulla continued. "That means that if we're caught, we all could be facing criminal proceedings and possible jail time. The charges would be more serious for you, as participants, of course, but I believe I am clearly guilty of aiding and abetting the crime."

"And how well you do it." Belloq bowed with a flourish.

"If you get tired of—well, doing whatever it is that you actually do, Miss Tornaes—there is always a place for you in my organization in Marseilles."

"On the other hand," she continued, "some may argue that there is a higher law at stake here, that of a person's honor, and that the breaking of the laws of the state of Louisiana is simply an unfortunate, but unavoidable, detail. Since I take it that the illegalities of your intended act are a mere nuisance, I will go on to the gist of the matter."

"Do hurry," Belloq said. "Dawn is nearly upon us, and being caught in the cemetery in full daylight by the local police is an even more unpleasant prospect than sneaking in under cover of darkness."

She nodded. "Dr. Jones. Will you not apologize to René Belloq for casting aspersions on his character, his family, and his country? Will you not give him the benefit of the doubt concerning his motives for selling you the information?"

"For that," Indy said, "and a thousand other slights, no."

"Monsieur Belloq," Ulla called. "Will you not reconsider your challenge? Does your heart not soften when you think of your association with Dr. Jones? Is forgiveness not possible?"

"It is not," Belloq said.

"All right, then," Ulla concluded. "Let's get on with it. I see that you gentlemen have already chosen your weapons. The rules of engagement are as follows: You will stand back-to-back beneath the oak, and on my count you will stride off ten paces. Twenty would be more sporting, but we have room only for ten. At the conclusion of the last pace, you are to turn and take aim. You will fire simultaneously. Understood?"

"Clearly," Indy said.

"Quite." Belloq smiled.

"If satisfaction has not been achieved after the first round of shots, you may mutually agree to reload. Gentlemen, assume the position and ready your pieces."

They marched to the center of the clearing and pressed their backs together, their weapons held in the air. The rain was falling a little harder now. It dribbled from the brim of Indy's hat and plastered Belloq's hair against his skull.

"One," Ulla counted.

The pair strode away from each other, backs straight, eyes forward.

Ulla continued to count through five.

Belloq thumbed back the hammer, a harsh clockwork sound that exposed the priming pan. Indy heard the sound, but pretended he didn't.

"Six," Ulla counted.

Another step forward. Mud clung to Indy's boots and stained the cuffs of his pants.

"Seven."

Forward still. Indy wrapped his thumb around the top of the hammer, ready to cock the weapon a moment before firing. To do so too long before, he was afraid, would give the rain a chance to dampen the primer.

"Eight."

While Indy strode forward Belloq turned quickly, the tails of his frock coat billowing out. In an instant he had turned sideways to Indy, his left hand behind his back and his pistol hand extended, taking aim at the spot between Indy's shoulder blades.

"Foul!" Ulla cried.

Belloq pulled the trigger as Indy turned. As if in slow motion Jones saw the hammer descend and scrape against the frizen, the flint in its jaws sending a shower of sparks into the priming pan.

Indy sucked in his breath for the blast of fire and lead

that was sure to follow a fraction of a second later, but none came. Instead, the powder in the pan fizzled weakly.

Belloq's powder was wet.

Belloq continued to hold the pistol at arm's length, incredulous. Suddenly the embers found a dry pocket, blazed brightly to life, and a moment later the pistol belched fire, smoke, and lead at Indy.

The ball passed through the upper right sleeve of his leather jacket, cutting a furrow in his flesh, and exited the back side of the jacket to go whining off into the trees lining the cemetery. Blood began to trickle down his arm to the wrist, and where it fell upon the cool ground, it steamed.

"Dr. Jones," Ulla announced. "You may now take your shot, at your leisure."

Indy held the pistol high in the air, cocked it, then lowered it until the heavy barrel was wavering over Belloq's heart. Belloq closed his eyes and his lips went thin. Then Indy jerked the pistol to the right and fired, sending the ball thudding into the side of the nearest tomb.

Belloq breathed a sigh of relief.

"Do you desire another round?" Ulla asked.

"No," Indy said. "I have satisfaction. I have proved that Belloq is a liar, a coward, and an unworthy opponent. Nothing would be gained by killing him."

"*Merci,*" Belloq said sheepishly, wiping the sweat from his forehead with the sleeve of the frock coat. "The affair, then, is over."

"It's over," Indy said.

"I lost count. . . ." Belloq insisted as he replaced the still-smoking pistol in the wooden case. "I believed we were to turn at eight instead of ten. It was a simple mistake. My, I hope that you are not seriously hurt."

"Dr. Jones, you're bleeding pretty badly," Ulla said. "We'd better have a look at it."

Indy held up a hand. "Not here. I don't think those shots will go unnoticed, as quiet as it is this morning."

"It did rather sound like cannon fire," Ulla conceded.

"Let's clear out before we end up in the Crescent City Jail," Indy said. "Besides, we have a plane to catch in just a short time."

Belloq scrambled over the mausoleums toward the cemetery wall, then paused and threw a salute Indy's way.

"*Au revoir*, Dr. Jones," he called. "A happy ending to a desperate circumstance. I hope you heal quickly . . . so that we may meet again on the field of honor!"

"The rat," Indy remarked as he and Ulla hurried out of the cemetery. "Who is he to talk about honor? He tried to shoot me in the back."

"True . . ." Ulla inclined her head to one side. "But he did stand fast and allow you to take your shot after his attempt to cheat had failed. He could just as easily have run away."

"He was probably too scared to make his feet move."

"I don't think that's ever been a problem for René Belloq," Ulla said. "No, he has a peculiar sense of honor—a twisted sense perhaps, but there is some kind of secret code he follows. You did the right thing by not killing him."

"It would have just been too complicated," Indy said. "Too much explaining to do, too many cops and lawyers, and as you pointed out, I could have ended up in jail."

"Yes," Ulla said. "And you would have killed the only person that you truly think is a worthy adversary, regardless of what you said back there. You're a very old-fashioned man, Dr. Jones. A gallant man. I think you were born in the wrong century."

Birds were stirring in the trees now, and a shaft of sunlight had broken from beneath the cloud cover as if to illuminate their exit from the cemetery. Two blocks later they hailed a cab, and as they pulled away from the curb a couple of radio cars raced in the opposite direction, toward the cemetery.

"How's your arm?"

Indy slipped off his leather jacket and let her examine it.

"No bones broken," she said as she cut open the shirt. "And the wound really isn't very deep. It went cleanly through, just beneath the surface. You are bleeding like a butchered hog, however."

"Family trait," Indy said.

Ulla cleaned the wound with antiseptic.

"Wow," he said. "That hurts worse than getting shot."

The cabdriver looked suspiciously in the mirror.

"Than getting *a* shot," Indy corrected, and smiled. "This woman's a nurse, and I'm a doctor."

"Sure, buddy," the Creole cabby said. "Whatever you say."

Ulla bandaged the arm, then Indy slipped his jacket back on.

"Thanks," Indy said. "It feels much worse now."

Ulla placed the boxed pistols on Indy's lap.

"What're you going to do with them?" she asked.

"I imagine that I will put them on the wall of my office at Princeton," Indy said. "Crossed, of course. To remind me of an encounter with a guy who, had it not been raining this morning, would have killed me."

It was still raining at the Shushan Airport, which was built on an artificial peninsula twenty minutes away from downtown New Orleans. The cabdriver pulled up under the canopy of the terminal building and looked over his shoulder at his charges.

"Here we are," he said in his singsong accent. "But I think the regular planes they have left for the morning. Do you want me to wait while you check?"

"No need." Indy thrust some bills in the cabby's hand. "There will be at least one more plane, I'm sure of it."

"I hope she is," the cabby said. "It's a wet day, no?"

"A wet day, yes," Indy agreed.

Indy was traveling light, with only his satchel slung over his shoulder, and Ulla had her things in the knapsack that had previously carried Indy's fortune. Indy watched as the taxi driver sped off into the night with a wave.

"Go with God," the cabby called from the open window. "And don't get shot no more."

The pair hurried into the new terminal building, which had been built by the Works Progress Administration in neoclassic style. The building fanned out like a pyramid from the centrally located control tower.

A young man in a crisp army uniform met them just inside the door. He had a clipboard under his arm, and on his shoulders were the silver bars of a first lieutenant.

"Dr. Jones?" he asked. "I am Lieutenant Goodwin. I am to be your liaison for this expedition."

"Excellent," Indy said. "Did you find my copilot?"

"Yes, sir," Goodwin said. "I had to enlist the help of a military police detachment from the army supply base on Dauphine Street, but we finally located Mr. Ward in the French Quarter."

"What bar was he in?" Indy asked.

"An oyster bar, sir," Goodwin said. "And I have to warn you that he reeks of Tabasco, oysters, and beer."

"Thank you," Indy said.

"Excuse me, sir, but your arm. There seems to be a bullet hole in your jacket and fresh blood. Is anything amiss?"

"No, I'm fine."

Goodwin looked questioningly at Ulla.

"Pardon my manners," Indy said. "This is Dr. Ulla Tornaes, of the Danish Speleological Survey. In addition to being a specialist on this expedition, she will also be my personal assistant."

"There's nothing on the manifest about a female civilian," Goodwin said, looking over his clipboard. "Especially a foreign national. I wasn't informed—"

"I'm informing you now, Lieutenant," Indy said.

"Well, sir, I don't know."

"Didn't Markham tell you I was in charge here and that you were to comply with my needs to the best of your ability?"

"Of course, sir."

"Then put her down, soldier," Indy said. "Right there on the manifest. Pencil her in."

"Yes, sir," Goodwin said.

"And you have Mr. Ward on your manifest?"

"Oh, yes, already taken care of."

"What about my radio operator?" Indy asked.

"Sparks?" Goodwin smiled. "He's already on the plane."

"Very good," Indy said, then sat down on one of the airport benches. "Now run down the rest of the crew with me so I know who I'm dealing with."

"All right," Goodwin said. "Let's see. We have I. Jones, commander. B. Blessant, pilot—"

"I want their full names, their rank, where they're from," Indy said. "And, if you know, what they're like."

Goodwin began shaking.

"Calm down, you're doing fine," Indy said. "How long have you had your commission, lieutenant?"

"A month," he said.

"Well, just give me the skinny like you would one of your buddies in the barracks at basic training," Indy suggested.

"All right," Goodwin agreed. "There's you and Miss Torneas, of course, and me—I'm your navigator and meteorologist. Then there's C. R. Ward, a civilian copilot, whom you apparently know. That makes four, so far."

"Go on," Indy coaxed. "Who don't I know?"

"The pilot is Captain Buck Blessant. He's about thirty, has a wife and kid back in New Jersey, and is one of the Army Air Corps' best test pilots. Your radio operator is a kid named Nicholas Swan, but everybody calls him Sparks. He's a regular nut for anything to do with technology. He's a corporal, by the way. And then we have a crew chief who will be flying with us, a Sergeant Dan Bruce. Bruce can fix just about anything with chewing gum and spit."

"Good." Indy looked pleased. "That makes seven. That it?"

"Yes, sir. The B-18 normally has a crew of six."

"Now, tell me about supplies," Indy said. "I assume the aircraft is fully loaded with arctic survival gear?"

"Well, no," Goodwin admitted. "We don't intend on going down. We just have the usual emergency gear. Rubber life rafts, emergency rations, and that sort of thing."

"Tell me about the aircraft."

"It's a cold-weather prototype of the B-18 that's been delivered to the army this year," Goodwin said. "It's powered by twin Wright Cyclone nine-cylinder radial engines, each of which develops one thousand horsepower. They have been modified for cold-weather operation, including an anti-icing mechanism in the carburetors and along the wings. Maximum speed is 226 miles per hour at 10,000 feet, and the ceiling is 27,150 feet. Range is normally 1,200 miles, but we've added some underwing tanks that increase that to 1,800."

"What kind of terrain does this thing need for landing and takeoff?"

"Well . . ." Goodwin shuffled through the sheets on his clipboard. "A runway is desirable, but this prototype is equipped with skids as well, for landing on hard-packed snow."

"What about water landings?"

"No, sir," Goodwin said. "If we ditch, I'm afraid we're going to swim."

"Terrific. How about parachutes?"

"Um, there are six on board."

"Find another one," Indy ordered.

"Right away," Goodwin said.

"Now, how about armament?"

"We have three machine guns, one mounted in the Plexiglas nose, and another two waist guns. We can also carry up to sixty-five hundred pounds of bombs, but since this is a scientific expedition I was told that the bomb bay would be unloaded. Besides, most of the available bomb weight has been taken up by supplies and the extra fuel."

"Who do we have that can shoot those guns?"

"Sergeant Bruce, of course. And Sparks and I, if we have to."

"What about small arms?"

"Practically nothing, sir," Goodwin said. "Sidearms, but that is all."

Indy winced.

"That will have to be corrected," he said.

"I can get Springfields with no problem."

"No bolt actions," Indy said. "We need automatics. Something easy to carry, with short stocks and barrels. Are you familiar with what some of the elite Nazi troops carry?"

"No, sir."

"Well, you have seen gangster movies, right?"

"Of course."

"That's what I want. Tommy guns and so forth."

"Yes, sir," Goodwin said, disturbed. "Pardon me, sir, but

do you think we're going to have a tactical situation on our hands up there?"

"You haven't been well briefed, have you?" Indy asked.

"No, sir," Goodwin admitted. "I suppose not. I'll see what I can do. We'll be making a short stopover at the naval air station on Long Island for refueling. The marines ought to have something that I can scrounge."

"Good man," Indy said. "Now, let's gather up Clarence and take a look at our aircraft."

"He's in here." Goodwin led the way to the men's room. He opened the door a crack and called, "Mr. Ward? There are some people who would like a word with you."

"Send them away," a ragged voice answered.

"Come on, open up," Indy urged.

"Why didn't you say it was you?" Clarence asked. "What on earth is all this about? A couple of military policemen caught me just as I was about to take off for Mexico City. I reckoned I had been busted for something, and I figured it had something to do with you. Indy, if you make me lose that Mexico account, I'll be forced to punch you in the mouth."

"Forget the Mexico City trip," Indy said. "Neither of us is in trouble. I know you were at an oyster bar making time with a Creole girl, so spare me your sad story. The point is that I need you, and you'll be well paid for your services."

"I've heard that before," Clarence said as he ran a hand over his face. "I haven't been paid for this trip yet."

"Is that all you worry about?" Indy asked. "Now, when you sober up you think you can fly a B-18?"

"Heck, they're both made by Douglas. The 18 is just the military version of my old DC-2, except it has teeth and you can drop the cargo out through the belly," Clarence said. "Where we headed?"

"The Arctic," Indy said.

"The North Pole?" Clarence asked.

"Pretty close to it," Indy said.

"I don't like the cold," Clarence complained as he pushed the pilot's cap back on his head. "What're we going to bomb there?"

"We're not going to bomb anything," Indy said.

"I've always wanted to bomb something," Clarence said.

"We're not going to shoot anything, either," Indy told him. "Unless we have to. But it's going to be a tough flight just the same. Do you think you can handle it?"

Clarence smiled sheepishly. "Do you think I would have been jawing it over if I didn't think I could handle it?"

"Good," Indy said.

"I need to send a cable to Donny in Juarez," Clarence said. "He'll be at Ma Crosby's place, as usual, eating steak tampico and drinking that awful Mexican beer he likes. Not to mention that señorita he's sweet on. I'll ask him to come get *Missy* and fly her to Mexico City. The shipment will be a few days late, but things never run on time down there anyway."

Led by Goodwin, Indy and the others walked out of the terminal building onto the wet tarmac. The B-18P (*P* for *Polar*) sat tail down, her nose pointed in the air. Her silver skin reflected the stormy skies above. The engine nacelles were painted a bright red, as was the nose. Unlike the relatively dull body of her civilian sister, the DC-2, the B-18's fuselage bristled with Plexiglas gun ports, bubbles, and antennae. Also, heat ducts that took their warmth from the engine exhausts snaked across each side of the aircraft, and two shields attached to the fuselage just behind the cockpit were meant to catch any potentially lethal ice thrown by the propellers. A big loop antenna placed just aft of the cockpit was connected to the direction-finding equipment.

"My word," Ulla said. "She looks so modern, so lethal. It's like something out of a nightmare."

"You haven't seen anything yet," Goodwin said. "Douglas has delivered forty-five of these regular models to the army, but they'll be obsolete in just a year or two, when the B-17 gets off the drawing board. That bomber has *four* engines and twice as much firepower."

"Gosh," Ulla said. "I'll bet humanity can't wait."

8

THE TOP OF THE WORLD

After resupplying at Long Island, the B-18P—which Clarence promptly and unceremoniously dubbed the *Penguin*, much to the dismay of Captain Blessant—set a course for Iceland.

Indy spent most of the eight-hour flying time on this first leg of the trip zipped into his sheep-lined flight jacket, catching up on his sleep, while Ulla occasionally roused him to check the bandages on his right arm. At Goose Bay in Newfoundland, Indy rose, stretched his legs briefly on the cold runway, and watched while the *Penguin* was refueled. Then it was across the ocean to Godthaab, on the southern tip of Greenland, and then over more of the angry sea.

Indy made his way forward and leaned into the cockpit.

"How's she running?" he asked.

"Like a charm," Blessant replied. "We have one magneto that's acting up, but no big deal. Bruce can take a look at it when we set down. The only problem I have is that my new copilot here never shuts up."

"Just trying to make conversation," Clarence said. "I

thought he'd be interested in what it was like to grow up in Erbie, Arkansas."

"I feel like I did," Blessant said.

"Did I tell you I flew a Jenny in the Big One?"

"About a hundred times."

"You getting the hang of it?" Indy asked Clarence.

"The bird hasn't been made that I couldn't fly," Clarence boasted. "Besides, you just sort of point this thing where you want it to go."

"That easy?" Indy asked.

"No, it's more like steering a boat," Clarence said. "The controls are so dang slushy and we're so loaded that we might as well have a tiller instead of yokes. I can't imagine what it's going to be like when we strap those skis to the wheels."

Clarence turned to Blessant. "You've test-flighted it that way, right?"

Blessant shook his head.

"That inspires confidence," Indy muttered.

"Don't worry," Clarence said. "We're fine. When you have to worry, I'll let you know."

Indy patted Clarence on the shoulder and went aft.

"Sparks," Indy said. "Any word from Markham on the location of the Graf Zeppelin?"

"No, sir." Sparks was sitting at his station behind the cockpit, a set of headphones mashed over his cap, fiddling with the array of dials and knobs on the equipment that lined the bulkhead. He brushed a shock of tousled brown hair out of his eyes before answering, "Not a word. Do you want me to send something?"

"No reason to let the Nazis know we're coming," Indy said. "Any luck with that frequency I gave you?"

"On twenty meters?" Sparks reached up and spun the wheel that turned the loop antenna atop the aircraft. "Not yet. Do you know exactly what it is that I'm supposed to be listening for? A tone, or a Morse signal?"

Indy shook his head.

"I wouldn't worry, sir," Sparks said. "If there's a target out there to be found, we'll find it. At this height, we have an advantage that we wouldn't have on the ground, because our line of sight is so much greater. And we have absolutely the best equipment in the world—I know, because I built it."

"You built all of this?"

"Designed it, too," Sparks informed him. "You see, I use the standard super-heterodyne receiver that Armstrong invented, but I have coupled it like this to the oscillator." The teenager sketched out a block diagram on his clipboard that looked like nothing but a child's version of a locomotive and a string of cars.

"I'll take your word for it," Indy said.

"Sir, I can get you a rough bearing by turning the loop antenna and comparing it with the signal from the fixed radial on the tail, but to be able to get you a position, we need triangulation—like you triangulate compass bearings from two known points to fix an unknown third on a map."

"I know the principle," Indy said.

"When we find the signal, we'll need to get a reference from another source. A ship, maybe, or a fixed station on a mountaintop. One option is to find the highest ground we can for a base camp and then set up an auxiliary station there."

"Good thinking."

"The only problem, somebody would have to stay behind and operate the radio."

"I don't know if we can spare a crew member for that," Indy said.

"Well, the alternative is to find a bearing where the signal is strongest, and plot a line from there. Problem is, we won't know how far we have to go before acquiring the target. It could be beyond our fuel range."

"I see the problem," Indy said. "We'll do the best we can. Keep monitoring that frequency, and let me know if you pick up anything."

"Sir?" Sparks asked.

"What is it?"

"We haven't had much of a chance to talk, and I just wanted—" The freckles on his cheeks were engulfed in a blush of red. "Well, I just wanted to thank you for allowing me to be a part of this. My father's dead, and my mother back in Iowa had to sign the papers to allow me to join the army, since I'm not eighteen yet."

"What town in Iowa?" Indy pulled up a crate and sat down.

"You probably never heard of it," Sparks said. "It's a little place called Payne Junction."

"I know the place," Indy said. "It's on the Missouri River. There's some Indian mounds nearby that I visited once."

"Right!" Sparks exclaimed. "My dad ran a little filling station there until a truck tire he was fixing exploded. The rim got him right in the forehead. I guess that's why he never let me fix flats."

"I'm sorry," Indy said. "It's tough to lose a parent. My mother died of scarlet fever when I was twelve. I still miss her."

"That's horrible," Sparks said. Then he added: "I still miss my dad, too. He was a great guy. He kept telling me that anything was possible if you just worked hard enough—and had enough imagination."

"He sounds like a great guy," Indy said.

"He was kind of a science buff, and when I was little I started reading all these magazines he had around the shop—you know, stuff like *Amazing Stories*. They're published by a guy named Hugo Gernsback, and I guess he wanted everyone to get excited about technology and what the future could be like. That's what got me hooked on electronics. I still read 'em, too."

"Your dad gave you quite a lot," Indy said.

"Yeah." Sparks smiled. "My mother still doesn't understand, though. She hates those magazines, mostly because of the robots with the naked girls on the covers. I joined the army because I was tired of building crystal sets and knew I couldn't get my hands on equipment like this anywhere else. Also, to help my mother out. We had to sell the station after Dad died, and it's been pretty rough on her."

"The Depression's been pretty rough on everybody."

"She told me that if you're a soldier, you have to expect to get shot at. But isn't that what we fought the Great War for?" Sparks asked. "I mean, so nobody would have to be shot anymore?"

Indy swallowed and looked away.

"That's the idea, Sparks," he said. "But sometimes things don't work out the way we hope. There's still a lot of evil in the world, and I'm afraid we might see some of it on this trip. We might even get shot at."

"I know," Sparks said. "I'm not afraid. I just wish everybody could see the future like my dad did."

"Everybody gets afraid," Indy told him. "It's nothing to be ashamed of. But if things do get dicey around here, I want you to stick as close as you can to me. Now, I've got to go check on the rest of the crew. Keep listening, okay?"

"Roger," Sparks said.

Indy climbed into the cockpit.

"Clarence." Indy tapped the pilot on the shoulder. Clarence took off his headphones and they put their heads together so they could talk privately beneath the engine noise.

"You need to promise me something," Indy said. "If

anything happens to me, I'd like for you to personally look after our radio operator. Sparks is a bright kid, and I couldn't stand it if anything happened to him."

"Sure," Clarence joked. "But if anything happens to you, who's gonna look after me?"

Indy laughed and slapped him on the leg as he climbed through the cockpit and down into the nose, where Goodwin was at the navigator's desk in the bombardier's Plexiglas compartment. He was filling a cup from a thermos of coffee and updating their position on the map with a grease pencil.

"Wow," Indy said as he looked at the clouds and the ocean whispering past beneath them. "Doesn't this view ever bother you?"

"No," Goodwin said. "I'm not particularly afraid of heights."

"I didn't think I was, but this view may change my mind," Indy said. "Everything on schedule?"

"Like clockwork so far." Goodwin glanced at his wristwatch. "We'll set down at Reykjavik in about twenty minutes and refuel again. Do you have any idea yet where we're going to set up base camp?"

"No," Indy said. "I don't have enough information yet. I need some kind of indication where the Graf Zeppelin is. Without that, we could be locating camp a thousand miles in the wrong direction."

"Quite so." Goodwin held a finger up and pressed the headphones against his right ear. "Captain says Sparks has a message," he said. "Maybe it's about the big tin balloon we're looking for."

"Thanks." Indy made his way back up the cabin. "What is it, Sparks?"

"I've received a coded message from Markham," the boy said as he worked out the letters on his clipboard against a mimeographed code key. "I've about got it. There. What's LZ-127?"

"That's the Graf Zeppelin," Indy said.

"LZ-127 sighted off South Cape of Spitsbergen Island by Norwegian fishermen at zero-nine-thirty hours," Sparks read. "Heading NNE. Altitude five hundred feet. Speed unknown. Acknowledge."

"Where the heck—"

"It's here," Goodwin said as he unrolled a map. He had come up from the nose to hear Sparks decipher the message. "At the edge of the arctic ice pack. A group of islands owned by Norway and known officially as the Svalbards, but commonly called by the name of the biggest island, Spitsbergen."

"Where's the Graf headed?" Indy asked.

"Nor-northeast will take them around the edge of the islands, possibly into the ice pack itself," Goodwin said.

"What are they doing so low?" Ulla asked.

"They're either meeting with a refueling ship," Indy explained, "or they are searching for something in the water. My money is on the latter. How far away are we now?"

Goodwin used a protractor to measure the distance.

"About fifteen hundred miles," he said.

"Right," Indy said. "And the top speed of the Graf Zeppelin is about eighty miles an hour."

"But from the sighting, she appears to be going considerably slower than that," Goodwin said.

"Let's say she finds what she's looking for and heads flat out. Theoretically, we could catch up with her how soon? Somebody, help me out."

Sparks made some furious computations.

"It will take us six and one half hours to reach Spitsbergen, where we refuel," he said. "That will give the Zep a head start of about five hundred and thirty miles, which we can close in another two hours and twenty minutes. But by then, the Zep will have put another sixty miles or so between us. What that boils down to is a rendezvous point that is twenty-one hundred miles away—less than ten hours, with just the one refueling stop. After Reykjavik, of course."

"Let's say they make a dead run for it, in any direction," Goodwin said. He took a compass from his flight suit and drew a circle representing a six-hundred-mile radius around Spitsbergen Island.

The penciled circle passed over the northeastern coast of Greenland, across a thousand miles of sea to thinly slice the coast of Norway, and through the Barents Sea to within a hundred miles or so of the North Pole.

"No matter which direction they turn," Goodwin said, "we can catch them within ten hours. Not only that, but we'll still have enough fuel left to make it back to Spitsbergen, no sweat."

"How will we know if they change their heading?" Indy asked. "There won't be any Norwegian fishermen where they're headed."

"The closer we get," Sparks said, "the better the odds we have of picking up their radio traffic to Berlin."

"That's right," Goodwin said.

"Unless they're maintaining radio silence," Indy said.

"Even so, it's the only chance we've got," Goodwin said.

"Five minutes to landing at Reykjavik, Commander," Blessant called over the intercom. "I suggest everyone don their cold-weather gear now, if you haven't already done so."

" 'Commander'!" Ulla punched Indy in the ribs, a little harder than playfulness would allow. "I like that better than Doctor."

"We have to make a decision now," Goodwin said. "Or else we'll just waste time on the ground."

"Hold it," Indy said. "Let's take a minute and consider

the disadvantages of the plan. First, we've already been in the air for nearly twenty hours. Sergeant Bruce, how is the *Penguin* holding up?"

"That magneto has gone out," Bruce said, struggling into his fur-lined suit, "and it will take at least an hour to change. If we go on, we'll have to count on the redundants. No real risk there, I suppose. Otherwise, the *Pen*—I mean, the *B-18P*—seems to be holding up quite well. All systems nominal."

"All right," Indy said. "What about the weather?"

"It's clear and holding. Barometer is steady."

"Good. Now, what about a base camp?"

"No time to set one up," Goodwin said.

"Maybe not." Indy paused. "Sergeant, how long will it take to refuel at Spitsbergen?"

"Twenty minutes, tops," Bruce said.

"Okay," Indy said. "That's enough time to unload our camp gear and leave one person behind to set it up and operate the radio."

"But which one of us?" Goodwin asked.

Indy looked apologetic. "You, I'm afraid."

"Not me," he said. "I'm the navigator. Anyway, I have to stay with the stupid plane, because Markham put me in charge of all the paperwork."

"Well, I need Sergeant Bruce in case something goes wrong," Indy said. "Blessant is necessary, for the obvious reasons, and Sparks is indispensable. That leaves Ulla and Clarence."

"The civilian woman would be the clear choice," Goodwin suggested.

"Not really," Indy said. "And don't ask me to explain. It will be clear when the time comes. Goodwin, can you fly this aircraft?"

"Fly it?" he asked. "No, sir."

"There you have it." Indy shrugged. "Clarence stays as

well. You're getting off at Spitsbergen and setting up the radio and base camp there. You can hand your paperwork over to Sparks."

"But Colonel Markham—"

"Colonel Markham put me in charge of this expedition, down to every rivet in this aircraft," Indy said. "I don't have time to justify my position to you. Besides, you're the only one of us besides Sparks who is capable of triangulating radio positions on a map, correct?"

"I suppose. . . ." Goodwin didn't look happy.

"Then climb into your cold-weather gear," Indy said. "Ulla and I will help you get the supplies unloaded as quickly as we can while the others ready the plane. Don't look so glum, Lieutenant, you've just pulled the safest detail on this expedition."

"Yes, Commander," Goodwin said stiffly.

"Oh, and remember," Indy told Goodwin. "If you get a bearing on anything of interest on that radio equipment, you act as if you are a remote observing station radioing back to our grounded plane on Reykjavik, right?"

"Right."

"Sir," Sparks interjected. "Colonel Markham is waiting for an answer. What should I send him?"

"Tell him this: 'Message received. Unable to intercept because of mechanical difficulty. Landing Reykjavik for repairs. Will advise. Out.' "

"But, sir!" Sparks cried. "That's against regulations."

"What do you think the odds are that the Nazis are listening to us and can break our codes as easily as we break theirs?"

"The odds are excellent," Sparks said.

"So why tell the buggers we're coming after them?" Indy asked. "Let them—and Markham—think we've broken down. They've known every move I've made so far. Let's throw 'em a curveball on this one."

Sparks nodded appreciatively.

"But, Dr. Jones," he said. "If we are deceiving our own people about our location as well as the Germans, and won't be giving our coordinates back to Goodwin at base camp on Spitsbergen, then who will know where to find us if we're forced down on the ice?"

Indy had no answer to this question.

As soon as the wheels had stopped rolling, the crew of the *Penguin* went to work. While Clarence fueled the aircraft Blessant and Sergeant Bruce worked to attach the strange-looking skis to the landing gears. The wheels themselves fit through the middle of the skis; in flight, the gears would be unable to retract completely, but would be tucked up under the aircraft like some kind of awkward bird.

"I hope this field is level," Blessant shouted to Bruce as he quickly ratcheted the bolts on the skis down. "There's not six inches difference between the skis and the bottom of the wheels."

In twenty-three minutes, the hatches were closed on the *Penguin* and the engines started.

"What's the barometric pressure?" Blessant asked Sparks over the intercom.

"Twenty-eight five," he answered. "Elevation above sea level here is eight hundred twenty."

Blessant adjusted the altimeter.

"I'd hate to run into that famous volcano they have here," Blessant joked. Then he checked manifold pressure and oil temperature on both engines.

"Everybody strapped in?" he asked over the intercom.

"We're ready to roll back here," Sparks answered. Bruce was beside him, still sweating from the exertion.

"We're go down here as well," Indy reported. Ulla was in the navigator's seat and Indy was strapped into the forward gun position, with the runway just beneath his legs.

"Throttle up," Blessant said. "Clarence, you're going to have to help me hold her steady on the runway. There's a wicked crosswind. Keep a light touch on the rudder, but keep her straight."

"Check," Clarence said.

As the engines revved to a screaming pitch and Blessant took his heels from the brake, the *Penguin* lurched forward and began to pick up speed. The starboard wheel hit a hole and bottomed out the skid, which threatened to send the aircraft slewing off the runway.

"Keep her straight," Blessant shouted.

"I will, if you can avoid the potholes," Clarence grumbled.

At fifty miles per hour the runway was a blur of gray beneath Indy's feet, but the plane seemed reluctant to leave the ground. He could see the end of the runway approaching, and beyond it a pile of the black volcanic rocks.

Indy closed his eyes.

"Remind me not to sit up here again," he called back to Ulla.

Blessant pushed the throttles forward again, and at sixty-five miles per hour, the wheels lifted off the ground. Then the tail came up, and the plane floated on ground effect for a moment but hesitated to go any higher.

"Flaps!" Blessant yelled, and Clarence adjusted the wheellike device between the cockpit seats.

The aircraft now took flight in earnest, and Blessant pushed the throttles nearly to their stops. The engines screamed and the *Penguin* gained altitude as it made a sweeping turn to the northeast.

"Need to make a note that the flaps should be set steeper on takeoff when using the skids," Blessant said calmly.

"Yeah," Clarence said. "And I need to make a note

about carrying a change of undershorts. Boy, I'll bet landing will be a hoot."

The landing at Spitsbergen was not quite the "hoot" that Clarence had predicted. The *Penguin* settled gently down and skidded to a rest on a vast snow-covered plateau that served as the airfield adjacent to a Norwegian weather station. Indy helped Goodwin unpack the base camp while the others—after a bit of haggling and pleading with the weather crew about the necessity for more fuel—rolled out fifty-gallon drums of aviation fuel.

As the *Penguin* taxied around the ice and then roared back down the snow-packed runway, Goodwin stood with his new Norwegian companions and waved gamely. The sun had dipped below the horizon behind them, turning the western sky into a fiery orange smudge.

"I've got a signal," Sparks said an hour later.

"Are you sure?" Indy asked.

Sparks closed his eyes and cupped his hands over the earphones, in an effort to mute the noise from the engines. Then he reached out his right hand and tweaked the frequency dial just a bit.

"Yes, I'm sure," he said. "It's weak, and warbling a bit, but it's at fourteen dot three-five-zed. It's a tone, every thirty seconds."

"Let me listen to it," Indy said.

Sparks offered him the earphones.

Indy heard nothing but static for a few seconds, and then there was a peculiar *dwit!* sound. He returned the phones to Sparks, who clamped them back over his cap.

"Can you get a bearing?"

"I'll try," he said, then punched his intercom. "Sir, could you hold it steady as possible for a few moments? I think I have a target. What's your heading now? Good, keep it there and I'll let you know."

Sparks closed his eyes and spun the antenna wheel

around this way, and then that, and then adjusted some switches. He swung the wheel again, then settled on one spot where the signal seemed to be the loudest. He looked up at the face of the antenna compass and jotted down the bearing on his clipboard.

"Captain Blessant?" he asked. "I think I've got it. Your heading, whatever it is now, let's call that zero. Now come port thirty-seven degrees."

The plane banked slowly and in a few moments leveled out again.

"Now, let me check." Sparks spun the antenna to the left, then stopped. "Back a degree or two." The change in direction was nearly imperceptible this time. "Good, that's it. The signal is straight off our nose."

Sparks made a note of the bearing and the time on his clipboard.

Indy went to the cabin window, which was badly frosted. He tried wiping the ice away with his sleeve, but it was on the outside.

"It's still dark," Sparks said. "You won't be able to see anything. The sun won't be up again for another couple of hours or so."

"That soon?"

"Land of the midnight sun," Sparks said. "We're well within the Arctic Circle now. The nights will get successively shorter until, on June twenty-first, the sun won't set at all."

"Where is this heading taking us?" he asked.

"Well, we're heading almost due east now," Sparks said, looking at the map. "There's nothing out there but sea and icebergs."

"Do you think the signal will last?"

"Hard to tell," Sparks said. "It appears to be wavering in strength, and I'm sure it isn't strong enough for Goodwin to pick it up in Iceland. We're ten thousand feet in the air and two hundred miles closer."

"So we can't triangulate it," Indy said.

"No, sir. All we can do is follow it and hope it lasts."

Sparks took off his cap and headphones and ran a hand through his tangle of hair. His ears ached from the strain of constant listening.

"This is a different target than the tin balloon, isn't it?" Sparks asked. A cloud of vapor from his breath hung between them. "If you don't mind my asking, sir, what *is* that thing?"

"It's a canister," Indy said. "Probably bobbing around on the waves. Swept into the Arctic Circle by the North Atlantic current."

"What's in it?"

"It's classified." Indy was too tired to explain; besides, he didn't think Sparks would believe him.

"What about the zep, sir?" Sparks asked. "Do you want me to keep trying to locate them?"

"Not if it means losing this signal," Indy said.

"I think I can do both." Sparks replaced the cap and the headphones. "But what if the zep goes one direction and your target goes another?"

"They won't," Indy said.

Sparks pushed the intercom button. "Hey, Captain. It's cold back here. Are those heat ducts working? . . . Yeah, that's what I thought you'd say."

"What did he say?" Indy asked.

"He told me to drink more coffee," Sparks informed him. "I don't drink coffee, but it may be time to start."

Thirty minutes later the signal had grown weaker.

"Dr. Jones, I'm afraid we're going to lose it," Sparks said. "I've done everything I can, but it's just fading away."

"You said that higher is better, right?"

"Well, yes," Sparks said. "But we're already high

enough. Any higher would just put more distance between us and the target." He paused to adjust the receiver. "There, the signal is gone. I can't find it."

"But the sea is pretty rough down there," Indy said. "Suppose the tops of the waves are chopping off the beacon, or some icebergs or something are in the way. Wouldn't going higher help that?"

"Yeah," Sparks agreed, "but then we have another problem."

"What's that?"

"The loop antenna is on top of the aircraft," he said. "The higher we go, the more we are increasing the angle from the ground, and eventually the body of the plane is going to be blocking the signal. Ordinarily that wouldn't mean much, but with a target this weak it could be the difference between finding it or not."

"Why didn't you put the antenna on the bottom?" Indy asked.

"Honestly, sir, I didn't think of it," Sparks said. "The antenna is really designed to locate powerful targets that are above the deck, not something bobbing around in the sea giving off maybe a watt or two of power."

"What if we flew high and upside down?"

Spark's eyes got wide.

"We can't turn this tub over," he said. "I mean, sir. This isn't a fighter. The wings would snap right off."

"Well, it was just a thought," Indy said.

"But you may be onto something," Sparks said. "If we went up to our ceiling, and then dived back down to cruising altitude, that would pitch the nose down and give the antenna a more or less right-angle approach at the target. That, we can do."

"Terrific," Indy said.

Sparks called Blessant and told him the plan, and the

pilot announced it over the intercom. Then Sparks reached beside his seat and produced an oxygen bottle and mask.

"What're you doing?" Ulla asked.

"You can't breathe at twenty-seven thousand feet," Sparks said. "You'll black out."

As the *Penguin* climbed, Ulla and Indy strapped on their masks and cracked open the valves of the oxygen bottles. A few minutes later the aircraft was high enough to catch the rays of the sun, just about to reappear over the horizon. Then the aircraft nosed over and began a dive that got progressively steeper. The sound of the air whistling over the wings became louder than the sound of the engines, and the plane began to vibrate.

Sparks, breathing through his mask, listened through his headphones and cranked knobs frantically. A few seconds later he looked back at Indy and nodded.

"All right," he told Blessant. "I've got it again. Soften this curve."

"Good advice, son," Blessant shot back. "I've been trying, but the aircraft doesn't want to cooperate."

The wind grew to a shriek and the plane began vibrating so badly that Indy was afraid the rivets would pop out. Ulla reached out and clasped his arm—the one that had been shot—and squeezed. Indy winced, but did not remove her hand.

"Stop fighting the wheel," Clarence told Blessant.

"What do you want me to do?" the pilot snapped.

"Let me have it," Clarence said.

"It's yours."

Clarence eased the yoke forward a notch. The vibrating stopped, but the plane was pitched even more steeply down. Suddenly Indy felt himself rising above his seat as gravity lost its hold on the interior of the plane. Every loose object began to float: coffee cups, pencils, the papers on the radio console.

"This is unusual," Ulla said.

"Clarence," Indy shouted as he tore off his oxygen mask. "What're you doing?"

"He's going to kill us all," Blessant said over the intercom.

"Naw," Clarence said, letting his mask dangle from his face. "You have to smooth everything out first by pitching forward into the dive, then you bring it out."

"This isn't a Jenny!" Blessant screamed. "What do you think, this is some air show? You'll never be able to pull out of this."

"I do it all the time in my big ol' plane back home," Clarence said as he watched the sea rushing up to meet them. "The trick is to ease back on the yoke and do a slow roll to one side—"

Gravity reasserted itself with a vengeance as the nose came up. A coffee cup broke on the floor between Indy's feet as he was slammed back down into the seat. By the time the *Penguin* was level again, they were skimming the wave tops.

Sparks took off his oxygen mask.

"Whew," he said. "Remind me to put the damn directional loop on the bottom next time. I mean darned loop, sir."

"No problem," Indy said. "Did you get a bearing?"

"Yeah," Sparks said excitedly. "Ninety-two degrees, a fairly strong signal this time. I think your target must be drifting with the current."

"Ninety-two?" Blessant asked. "Are you sure?"

"No, I mean *twenty-nine* degrees," Sparks said. "I'm sorry. I tend to transpose numbers or otherwise get things backward when I'm under pressure."

Clarence returned the controls to Blessant, who adjusted the heading and trimmed the aircraft.

"Did you feel something at about ten thousand feet?" Clarence asked.

"Yeah, the end of the world," Blessant said. "My seat was shaking so much I couldn't tell what was happening. My butt feels like it's been strapped to a Missouri mule."

Three and a half hours after leaving Iceland, over the vastness of the Barents Sea, Sparks called Indy and offered him the headphones.

"What is it?" Indy asked.

"Listen for a couple of minutes."

The signal was clear, with no warble, but each *dwit!* seemed lower in pitch. The signal was also a little softer each time, as if somebody were steadily turning down the volume on a table radio.

"What does that mean?" Indy asked.

"We just passed over it," Sparks said. "About six minutes ago, I think. I charted it on the log."

"Then we go back," Indy instructed, and moved up to the cockpit.

"How can you guys see out of these windows?" he asked. Although the heating ducts were working, the visibility had been reduced on each side to a hole about the size of a basketball.

"It ain't easy," Clarence said.

"Listen, Sparks just said he thinks we passed over the target, about twenty miles back. We need to make a U-turn and go back."

"No problem." Blessant began to bring the plane around. "But we've picked up a lot of weather down there. We're going to have to be right on the deck to see anything."

"Then do your best," Indy said.

"Dr. Jones?" Sparks called. "I've lost the signal. Completely. Not a trace of it left."

Four minutes later the *Penguin* had descended through the clouds and fog to five hundred feet. The air was warmer at the lower altitude, and most of the ice had broken away from the windscreens.

"This is no good," Clarence said. "I still can't see a thing."

"Then we go lower," Blessant said.

At a hundred feet, they were still in thick fog.

"This is no good," Clarence repeated. "We're flying nearly blind. I can't even see the water, can you?"

"Nope," the pilot answered.

"I'm going down into the nose," Indy said. "Maybe I can see a little better down there."

Ulla followed him down and sat at the navigator's desk while Indy took the gunner's chair. Enough ice had melted off the Plexiglas that Indy had a good view of nothing but cloud vapor. The sun was well above the horizon now, and the fog seemed to glow.

"This should be the spot," Indy said. "For all the good it does us. I can't see a thing down there. To be so close and—"

"What happened to the sun?" Ulla asked.

The fog in front of the aircraft had gone dark. Then, suddenly, the cloud vapor cleared and Indy had a razor-sharp view of the sea—and of the nose of the Graf Zeppelin hovering above them, blocking out the sun and clearing the fog from an area the size of a football field with the wash from her engines.

From his vantage point in the nose of the *Penguin,* Indy was close enough that he could see the astonished expressions on the faces of the passengers and crew in the glass-windowed control cabin, which was slung underneath the nose of the airship like a giant double chin.

"My God!" Indy shouted into his microphone. "Pull up, pull up! No, wait, don't pull up!"

The *Penguin* dipped and throttled back but still passed close enough to the underside of the control cabin that

Indy could see the cleats for the lines and the instructions printed in English and Portuguese for the benefit of foreign mooring crews. Then they were past the cabin and sailing slowly beneath the belly of the leviathan, and Indy noticed that there was a kind of fighter plane he'd never seen before secured to a trapezelike mechanism amidships.

"I think we found the zep," Blessant said calmly over the intercom as he pushed the *Penguin* down to within a few yards of the water. Indy gaped upward. The aft cargo hold was open in the Graf's belly, and from it a yellow canister swung from a slender cable. The canister was a few yards above an inflatable raft with a couple of men on board, and obviously had just been recovered. In as much time as it took Indy to recognize the scene in front of him, the *Penguin* had overtaken the raft.

"This is going to be interesting," Ulla said as she drew her knees up and braced for impact.

Confronted by the twin-engine bomber barreling at them, the men in the raft jumped overboard into the sea. Blessant pulled up and tried to veer away, but the starboard wingtip snagged the cable and the yellow canister vaulted into the sky.

The *Penguin* lurched to starboard from the drag of the cable while at the same time the canister was shot toward the wingtip as the slack in the cable was taken up. The canister wedged itself between the wing and the underslung fuel pod with a sickening crunch. Then the cable snapped, and the aircraft seemed to wallow through the air. Fuel began to spew into the sea from the ruptured tank.

The yoke was slammed backward into Blessant's hands.

"Throttle up!" he shouted to Clarence as he struggled to push the yoke forward. "We've got to get some airspeed or we're going to stall."

Clarence slammed both throttles forward. The port engine screamed, but on the starboard wing the engine backfired and began to sputter. The nose rose in the air as the *Penguin* chewed at the air and began a sickening spiral.

"Lean it out," Blessant ordered.

"I'm trying," Clarence said, adjusting the fuel mixture.

The starboard engine coughed, as if clearing its throat, and then began to smooth out. Within a few seconds it was at full power again.

Blessant slammed the yoke forward and the aircraft skimmed the sea with its starboard wingtip before pulling back into the air. But they were still beneath the tail of the zeppelin. Indy saw the leading edge of one of the dirigible's stabilizing fins knifing toward them. On the side of the fin was a huge black swastika in a red circle.

"Are you blind?" Indy screamed. "There's a swastika the size of my house coming right at us!"

The *Penguin* rolled hard to the left, narrowly missing the massive fin, then whipped back to level.

A moment later, when he discovered *Penguin* was still flying, Blessant shook his head and asked: "Do we still have flight control?"

"I think so," Clarence said. "We've got one wingtip that's pretty boogered up, but the flaps and gizmos seem to be okay."

"Gizmos?" Blessant asked.

"You know," Clarence said. "Ailerons."

"We're dropping fuel like crazy from the starboard pod," Blessant said. "Shut it off so it doesn't drain the rest of the wing."

"Check," Clarence said.

By the time Indy popped his head up from the nose compartment, the Graf Zeppelin was a shadow far behind them.

"I'm not sitting down there in the nose again," Indy

ranted. "What are you guys trying to do to me? Clarence, you did that last thing on purpose. Just wait until we get on the ground, I'm going to—"

"Settle down, buddy," Clarence said. "Nobody did anything on purpose. That was the purest example of luck I've ever seen. In the middle of nowhere we dang near crashed smack-dab into the most famous airship in the world, which would have killed us and thirty or forty people on board it. Probably would have started some kind of war, too. As it is, we're pretty lucky—maybe all we did was kill ourselves."

"What do you mean?"

"Look out this here window," Clarence urged. "You see that thing wedged under our wingtip and that stuff spilling out from the tank? That's our reserve fuel."

"The canister," Indy said. "It won't fall off, will it?"

"You've got some strange priorities, Jones," Clarence told him. "Now you get back down there in the nose and plant your butt in the gunner's seat."

"I'm not going back down there."

"You'd better," Blessant said. "The Graf Zeppelin just dropped a pursuit plane on our tail. Sparks and Sergeant Bruce will have to take the waist guns."

"I'll take one of the waist guns," Ulla offered as she climbed through the cockpit and went aft. In her excitement, her English began to deteriorate. "Leave Sparks at the radio. Besides, I shoot good, no?"

"I've got a really weird feeling," Indy said as he reluctantly dropped back down into the nose. His companions, however, could not have guessed what that feeling was—it was the feeling he had had when he walked into the library of the British Museum and stared into the hypnotic eyes of Alecia Dunstin for the first time: a curious combination of fear and fascination.

• • •

On board the Graf Zeppelin, Alecia Dunstin pressed her hands against the cold panes of the observation window on the starboard side of the dining room and watched as the damaged American bomber passed out to sea.

"Indy," she whispered.

Reingold pulled her roughly back from the window, causing her red hair to spill over her eyes. She was wearing the black tunic of an officer, but devoid of any insignia except the lightning bolts at the collar and the red-and-gray piping of a specialist. On the black velvet band of her cap was a grinning skull and crossbones, the *Totenkopf* of the SS.

The dark uniform made her eyes and skin look even paler.

"Don't get your hopes up," he said.

"Why shouldn't I?" she asked, brushing her hair back.

"Because you're on the other side now," Reingold said. "For whatever reason, it was the right choice. It is the side that God Himself is on."

Alecia crossed her arms.

"Wait till Indy gets his hands on you," she said.

"Ah, your talents are amazing," Reingold said. "I was unsure myself whether Jones was on that aircraft, but your reaction leaves little doubt, doesn't it?"

"It was just a guess," she said. "Not a divination."

"I know you better than that," Reingold said. "You never guess. Your powers should prove quite useful in the coming struggle."

"The deal is off," she said.

"Once you make a deal with us," Reingold said, "you can't back out. It's like a marriage—until death do us part."

He reached out and rubbed a strand of her hair between his finger and thumb. She slapped his hand away.

"We are near our goal," Reingold said. "Too bad Dr. Jones won't be around to share your triumph. But I will."

"You promised you wouldn't hurt him."

"Ah, we promised we would leave him alone," Reingold said. "But now that he has come looking for us—well, that's another matter. Besides, we thought he was dead."

"You thought—" Alecia stammered. "You mean you agreed to leave him alone because you thought he was *already dead*?"

Reingold took a cigarette from his silver case, tapped it on the crystal of his watch, and put it in his mouth—but did not light it. Then he motioned toward the observation window, where the dirigible's fighter plane was thundering over the waves in pursuit of the bomber.

"We cannot allow this American gangster to jeopardize our well-laid plans," he said, "or to get away with the canister, for that matter. I think it was a stroke of brilliance when our captain decided to hang an escort plane beneath our belly for this expedition, no?"

9

LOST!

The fighter was an experimental Messerschmitt specially designed to be light enough to be dropped from a dirigible but fast enough—thanks to a growling, twelve-cylinder engine—to counter any potential threat to its mother ship. It had a top speed of 342 mph, a 34,450-foot ceiling, two machine guns, and two 20mm cannon. In short, it could fly rings around the *Penguin.* But because Germany was still forbidden to rearm by the Treaty of Versailles, only the Nazi leadership and the fledgling Luftwaffe knew of the existence of the prototype Messerschmitt Bf.107a. About to join the circle of initiates, in a rather spectacular fashion, was the crew of the *Penguin.*

Within a few minutes the Messerschmitt had overtaken the *Penguin,* and as it streaked overhead Clarence muttered, "What in the world was that? It must be doing three hundred miles an hour."

Blessant keyed the intercom.

"Let's stay cool for a moment," he told the crew. "Don't get trigger-happy. Let's see what their intentions are first."

The Messerschmitt slowed to let the *Penguin* catch up with it. Then it veered over and placed itself off the bomber's starboard wingtip, and Indy could see the pilot assessing the damage to the *Penguin* and radioing the information back to the Graf. Indy imagined that at least part of the conversation included the condition of the yellow canister wedged beneath the wingtip. As the fog and clouds grew thicker the Messerschmitt nudged even closer to the bomber.

"I can blow him right out of the sky where he sits," Sergeant Bruce commented as he lined up the sights of the fifty-caliber on the cockpit.

"Hold your fire," Blessant said.

"Sparks, can you get his frequency?"

"Sure," Sparks replied, dialing down the ten-meter band. "But what good is it going to do us? I don't speak German."

"I do," Ulla called from the port gun.

"Coming right up," Sparks said. "Got him."

Sparks piped the transmission over the cabin monitor.

"He's advising that we are leaking fuel and that one of our landing skids is damaged," Ulla translated.

"News to me," Blessant said.

"Must have been the pop you heard during the dive," Clarence suggested.

"He's asking if he should bring us down," Ulla said. "Now comes the answer, no, not over the water. They're afraid they would lose the canister. They want him to herd us over the ice, and then shoot us down."

"Can I blow him up now?" Sergeant Bruce asked.

"No, not yet," Blessant said. "Commander, this is your call."

Indy swallowed and pressed the intercom button.

"What are our options?" he asked.

"Not many," Blessant replied. "No fuel to make it to a suitable landing spot. In fact, the valve on the starboard pod is screwed up and it's draining the rest of our fuel from that wing. We could take this Teutonic weasel out where he sits, but that wouldn't help our situation."

"If we're going down," Bruce said, "we should at least take this clown with us."

"Wars have been started over less."

"What do we care?" Bruce asked. "We'll be dead anyway."

"Put a sock in it, Sergeant," Indy said. "Nobody's dead yet. Nobody's going to die, not as long as we keep thinking. Sergeant, do we burn the same type of fuel that Richthofen here does?"

"Sure do."

"If we can make a safe landing on the ice, can you repair that leaking valve?"

"I'd put money on it."

Indy swallowed.

"Okay, we need to get this clown to land on the ice with us somehow," Indy said. "Ulla, I want you to talk to him."

"Me?" she asked.

"Yeah," Indy said. "Sparks, I want you to talk first. Act like you're searching for the right channel, so that we don't know what his real orders are. Then, when you've got him, act really relieved and hand the mike over to Ulla."

"What do you want me to say?" she asked.

"Tell 'em we're sorry about the near collision, we were lost, and that we're real glad to see him. Really ham it up. Ask if he'll be good enough to follow us to the ice, where we intend to land and make repairs."

Ulla nodded.

"Mayday, this is the twin-engine Douglas off your port wing," Sparks said, then adjusted the frequency. "Mayday, I repeat, this is the American—"

"Was?" came the bewildered reply.

"Boy are we glad to see you!"

"Wie bitte? Ich spreche kein Englisch."

"You don't speak American, is that it?" Sparks asked. "Hold on, partner."

He traded places with Ulla.

"*Hallo!*" Ulla said. "*Guten Tag.*"

There was no reply.

"Nice to see you," she continued in German. "We're awfully sorry about the confusion back there, and it is awfully good of the Graf to have sent you out to check on us."

"*Ja?*"

"As you can see, we have suffered some serious damage and are losing fuel at an alarming rate. We need to make repairs as quickly as possible. Would you be kind enough to follow us to the ice? We're planning to set down there and try to stem the flow of gasoline."

Ulla waited.

"He's switched to another channel to talk to the Graf," she said to Sparks. "He knows they've heard the discussion, and he's not about to make a decision on his own."

The Messerschmitt pilot was back in a moment. He said he would be more than happy to follow them to the ice pack, which was only a hundred or so meters to the north. By the way, he asked, would the American bomber mind identifying itself?

"This is the 23 *Skidoo*," Ulla said as she shrugged her shoulders. "We're an American scientific expedition sent to study weather patterns in the Far North. We've been releasing radio balloons and were attempting to retrieve one of them when we crossed paths."

How many are on board? he asked.

"Six," Ulla said.

There was a pause.

Would the American scientist Indiana Jones be among them?

"No!" Indy shouted from the nose.

"Nein," Ulla said.

Then who was in command?

"Why, I am," Ulla said, then paused. "It's actually a joint Danish-American expedition. I'm Dr. Ulla Tornaes. What's your name?"

The pilot's name was Dieter.

Ulla signed off.

Twenty minutes later, with the Messerschmitt still off their starboard wing, and with the skies beginning to clear, Blessant spotted the ice below them.

"Okay, Professor," he began. "Here's where it gets interesting. Is he going to let us land and then strafe the hell out of us, or is he going to take us in the air?"

"I don't know," Indy said, biting his knuckles. "We need to get his plane on the ground with us in one piece, though. Ulla, get on the horn again and play to his fear of destroying the canister."

"All right." Ulla took up the microphone again.

"Dieter," she began in German, "this yellow thing that is lodged under our wingtip—it is something the Graf would like to have back, no?"

"Ja."

"Then why don't you land with us and we can exchange it?"

Dieter said ice landings were hazardous and that he was afraid to attempt it.

"Liar," Bruce said. "He's planning to walk over our bodies in about ten minutes. Look at those oversized tires on that thing. It could land anywhere."

The Messerschmitt began to drop back.

"He's getting ready to make his move," Blessant guessed. "As soon as we're on the deck, he's going to nail us from behind. That way, they'll be sure not to lose the canister—even if we blow up, it's pretty safe on the wingtip."

"He'll be right behind us?" Indy asked. "Not higher?"

"Not much," Blessant said. "His guns point the way his plane does."

"What's our altitude?" Indy asked.

"Hard to say," Blessant answered. "The altimeter just went screwy all of a sudden. It says we're below sea level, but that can't be."

"Unless we're in a depression or something," Sparks suggested.

"What kind of depression do you find on ice floating in the ocean?" Blessant asked.

"Start looking for a nice clear spot to land," Indy said.

"Are you nuts?" Clarence asked. "It'll be a duck shoot for him. We can't get a clear shot. Besides, what about the landing gear?"

"We need his plane in one piece," Indy said. "Can you open the bomb bay?"

"Sure, but why?" Blessant asked.

"I don't have time to explain," Indy said. "There's a good patch of ice up ahead. Nice and smooth. Head for it, and start dropping altitude. Open the doors when I tell you to."

"All right," Blessant said.

"I need the parachutes." Indy was growing impatient.

"All of them?" Bruce asked.

"Just find them, will you?"

"I think I know what you're getting at," Bruce said as he helped Indy gather up the parachutes.

"Okay," Indy said. "When the doors open, you rip open your three and dump them and I'll dump mine. Try to get as big a pattern as you can."

"We're getting close to the deck," Blessant announced. "Our boy has taken his position and is closing the gap. Here he comes."

There was the stutter of machine-gun fire in short

bursts, followed by a pinging sound as the bullets found the top of the tail.

"He's got our range now," Blessant said. "The next ones are going to be through the hull."

"Open the doors," Indy ordered.

A blast of cold air and snow filled the cabin of the bomber as crates of supplies and miscellaneous equipment fell from where they had been stacked around the bay. The ice streaked past below them. The engines throttled down to a near idle.

The Messerschmitt opened up again, and this time slugs began to spew around the *Penguin* like spray from a garden hose. Through the open bomb bay, Indy could see tracer bullets falling toward the ice.

"Now!" he shouted, and pulled the cord on the first parachute. "Full throttle, Captain!" The parachute was followed by a second, and a third, and then all of Bruce's chutes, while bullets began chewing at the tail of the bomber.

The parachutes billowed open in the prop wash from the bomber, and it seemed to the Messerschmitt pilot that he was suddenly confronted by a forest of giant silk mushrooms. He pulled up, missing the first two parachutes, but the third snagged on his landing gear. The next hung on the cockpit of the Messerschmitt, then washed off, while the next two missed entirely.

Indy grabbed the seventh and last parachute, pulled the cord, and tossed it down with a vengeance. It billowed open and blanketed the nose of the Messerschmitt, and as the propeller blades tried in vain to eat through the silk, the cords wound around the hub.

The Messerschmitt lost power and slammed into the ice, crushing the landing gear. It spun in a headlong circle on its belly while the machine guns continued to chatter, kicking up tufts of snow in a hundred-yard radius. Its propellor broke itself to pieces on the ice, and shards of the blade were thrown like shrapnel into the air.

Over the radio, they could hear Dieter's last transmission—a long scream punctuated by the sound of grinding metal and breaking glass. Then the transmission ended abruptly as the last and largest piece of the three-bladed prop smashed into the front of the canopy.

Then, after cutting its long groove in the ice, the Messerschmitt creaked to a stop and the guns were silent.

"Bingo!" Sparks cried.

"Close the doors," Indy ordered. "Then circle around and land—away from the guns."

"What about our damaged landing gear?" Clarence asked.

"Fly this thing, son," Indy said, brushing snow from his shoulders. "That's what I brought you along for."

"Next time," Clarence said, "you can just leave me at home."

The *Penguin* made an awkward but upright landing on the ice as the port landing gear sagged and groaned but held in a half-locked position. Before the engines had died, Indy drew his Webley and raced across the ice toward the rear of the downed Messerschmitt. When he clambered up on the wing and peeked inside the ruined canopy, he holstered his revolver. Dieter was dead, having been decapitated. The edge of the propellor blade was buried deep into the seat back. Dieter's dead hands were frozen on the stick, his right index finger still squeezing the firing button.

"How is he?" Ulla asked when Indy strode back to the bomber.

"*Kaputt,*" Indy said.

Sergeant Bruce dropped down out of the hatch and onto the ice, followed by Sparks.

"Make sure your parkas are secure," Indy told them.

"The cold is our most immediate enemy now." Already, ice had begun to form around his mouth.

Bruce motioned for the bomber to taxi closer to the downed fighter, to make the transfer of fuel easier.

Indy blinked hard at the white landscape around him, then realized his eyes were hurting. He brought a pair of dark goggles from the pocket of his parka and put them on.

When the shadow of the starboard wing of the *Penguin* covered what was left of the Messerschmitt, Blessant cut the engines. Then he and Clarence dropped down from the hatch to help Bruce with the hoses and hand pumps.

"We'd better hurry if want to get back into the air before the Graf gets here," Indy said. "Sparks, do you have any idea where we are?"

"No, sir," Sparks said. "Compass readings are pretty much useless this far north. I could try to shoot an angle off the sun."

"Do it while we still can see it," Indy said. "It looks like the clouds are going to swallow us up in short order."

Indy climbed on the wing of the Messerschmitt, where Clarence had knocked open the fuel door and was inserting a hose attached to one of the hand pumps.

"Did you have to use *all* of the chutes?" Clarence asked.

"You'd look like poor Dieter there if I hadn't," Indy said.

"Your aim could have been a little better," Clarence mumbled. "Why couldn't you have gotten him with the first chute instead of the last?"

"You'd complain if you won a million dollars," Indy said. "Hand me that crowbar and shut up."

From the wing of the Messerschmitt, Indy was just high enough to reach over his head and jam the crowbar behind the yellow canister. He tugged a couple of times, and then put all his weight into it and hung from the crowbar.

The canister came loose, glanced off Indy's wounded arm, bounced off the wing of the Messerschmitt, and landed in the snow. Holding his arm, Indy jumped down. The canister was badly dented and covered with rust, except for the shiny areas where it had been wedged up against the aircraft. The skull-and-crossbones warning, however, was still legible.

"Hey," Clarence said. "That looks like a poison-gas canister from the Great War."

"That's what it looks like," Indy agreed as he drew back the crowbar and struck the end of the drum as hard as he could. Clarence ducked as the lid sprang off and the canister rolled, emptying its contents out on the snow.

Amid the wires and vacuum tubes of the ruined transmitter was the Crystal Skull, which had spilled from its interior packing and was sitting upright on a patch of black cloth. A mesmerizing rainbow of arctic sunlight shimmered around it.

Indy sighed and took off his goggles.

"Happy now?" Ulla asked him.

Just then a dull rumble shook the ice, followed by a grinding sound. Then came a tremor that made them all struggle to keep their footing.

"What was that?" Clarence asked.

"It's the ice," Ulla said. "I think it's breaking up."

"Where's Sparks?" Blessant asked.

"Nicholas is over there." Ulla pointed toward a ridge of ice about two hundred yards away, where Sparks stood with a sextant in his hand. "He's trying to get a position on the sun."

Indy fell to his knees in the snow and quickly wrapped the skull in the black cloth. Then he tossed it up to Clarence.

"What do you want me to do with this?" Clarence asked.

"Stow it someplace safe," Indy said. "Inside the plane."

"Where're you going?"

"To get Sparks," Indy called as he ran across the ice,

Ulla behind him. By the time they reached the teenager, they were both breathing hard.

"Come on," Ulla said, grabbing Sparks by the arm. "We have to get back to the ship."

"Why?" he asked. "I've almost finished taking my readings, and you won't believe—"

"There's no time," Indy said. "The ice pack is breaking up."

There was another rumble, followed by the shriek of ice buckling and a popping sound like cannon shots. A plume of white spouted at the far end of the field, marking the place where the ice was separating, and the tear spread its jagged fingers toward them.

"Hurry," Indy shouted. *"Run!"*

The break crossed their paths twenty yards ahead of them and moved quickly down the field, cutting them off from the *Penguin* and the rest of her crew. The ice was lifted up so violently that the trio were thrown to the ground, and when they managed to get back to their feet they saw they were separated from their companions by a twenty-foot chasm with seawater at the bottom.

"This is bad," Indy observed.

"What do we do?"

"Hey!" Indy shouted. "Throw us a line, something!"

Clarence scrambled over to his side of the ravine with a coil of rope, but the ever-widening tear was now forty feet across. The rope was only thirty feet long.

"Great," Indy said. "Our side of the ice is drifting out to sea."

"Throw us some supplies, then," Ulla shouted. "Food. Whatever you can find."

Clarence and the others gathered what they could from the scattered supplies on the ice, and heaved them over the chasm, but only a fraction of the missiles landed on the other side. Most splashed into the frigid water between them.

"Okay," Indy shouted. "We're just wasting equipment."

"What'll we do, boss?" Clarence asked.

"Get the *Penguin* in the air," Indy said. "Then hightail it to the closest base and send a rescue party back after us. We can survive for a few hours."

"All right," Clarence said. "Good luck!"

As the massive ice floe drifted away they could see the silhouettes of Clarence and Blessant and Bruce waving to them, unwilling to turn their backs on their companions as they drifted away.

"All right," Ulla began. "The first thing we need to do is to get organized. We each have the proper clothing, no? Keep your gloves and hoods and boots on at all times. Expose as little of your flesh to the weather as possible."

"I'll bet you could catch a killer cold up here," Sparks said.

"There are no colds here," Ulla said. "It is too cold for the germs which spread the common cold to live. That should give you some idea of how really harsh the conditions are.

"Now, we need to make an inventory of our supplies. First, let's put them in piles—food, medicine, weapons, camp gear. Okay? Sparks, you collect the food and medicine, Indy will take care of the weapons, and I will assess the camp gear."

A few minutes later Indy said, "We have no weapons, except these two hunting knives. And my revolver and my whip."

"Where are the automatic rifles and such?" Ulla asked.

"I think we dropped them out of the bottom of the plane while we were fighting Dieter off."

"What a waste." Ulla shook her head. "How much ammunition do you have?"

"Five shots," Indy answered.

Ulla nodded as she strapped on one of the hunting knives and gave the other to Sparks. "Well, we'll have to save those for an emergency situation. What about food and medicine?"

"We have five cans of beans," Sparks said, "and they are frozen solid. A couple of them have busted open. We also have a tub of lard, a tin of sardines, and two Hershey bars. We have one standard camp medical kit, nothing fancy."

"Not bad, considering," Ulla said. "Now, for my report. We have two sleeping bags, a blanket, one white-gas stove with a small canister of fuel, a box of matches, and one small American flag."

"No tent?" Sparks asked.

"No tent," Ulla said. "But we can build igloos instead. I will show you how. It's tough work, but it will be worth it in order to have some protection from the elements."

"It could be worse," Indy said. "Ulla, do you have any idea how large this piece of ice might be?"

"It's hard to tell," Ulla said. "But I would say it is at least a quarter of a mile. When we get our camp established, one of us should carefully walk the perimeter to see."

"Sparks, did you manage to fix our position?"

"That's what I was trying to tell you when the ice started to break," he said. "The fix I got from the sun doesn't make any sense at all. And look at the sun—look how red and strange it is. It's far above the horizon still, but it's like looking at a sunset, through layers of atmosphere."

"The position," Indy said.

"According to the fix I got, and my charts, we ought to be far below the Arctic Circle—like somewhere on the Norway coast. Obviously, we aren't."

"Can you explain that?"

"No," Sparks said. "But it's like we're on the lip of a huge—something—that's folding back into the earth. I know that's impossible."

"Take another reading in a few more hours," Indy instructed. "Maybe you just made a mistake with the charts in the excitement after the landing."

"I beg your pardon, Dr. Jones," Sparks said, "but I don't make mistakes with calculations. As a matter of fact, I find them strangely comforting."

"Try it again, anyway," Indy told him.

"With no radio," Sparks said, "and on a moving block of ice, how are they ever going to find us again?"

"Everybody up!" Ulla called. "Prepare your knives, or whatever else you can find to dig with. We are going to erect some proper shelter."

Six hours later Indy lay exhausted inside the dome-shaped igloo of snow and ice while Sparks warmed a can of beans over the little stove. He reached for the tin of sardines and was about to open them when Ulla snatched them away.

"I was going to share." Indy looked a little wounded.

"These will serve us better as bait," Ulla said. "I can fashion a hook and we have some cord here to use as line. Maybe we can catch a fish that will feed us all day instead of just for an hour."

"You've done this before, haven't you?" Sparks asked.

"Not exactly under these conditions," Ulla said. "But yes, at various places around the world, my survival has often depended upon making the right choices at the right times."

"Where's that American flag?" Indy asked, still smarting a little from Ulla's reprimand.

"Why?"

"I'm going to plant it on top of the igloo, to help whoever is searching for us," he said. "I can think, too, you know."

When Indy had crawled outside with the flag, Ulla leaned over to Sparks. "Men!" she scoffed. "You must be careful not to bruise their egos too much. I was going to put the flag up myself, but we'll let Indy do it. It may make him feel better."

"Gee," Sparks said, and bit his lower lip so he wouldn't cry. "You have anything to make me feel better?"

Ulla put her arms around him and hugged him.

"Don't worry, Nicholas," she soothed. "If you want to cry a little bit, if that will help, then go ahead. But we're going to get out of this all right. We just have to keep thinking, keep working, and above all not give up hope."

In three days the food was almost gone, and Ulla had caught only one fish with the sardines from the tin. Indy had scouted for a quarter of a mile in either direction from their camp, but could see no end to the huge block of ice.

"It's time we moved," he said when he returned.

"I think we would be better to stay here," Sparks said.

"There's nothing left here," Indy said. "We're out of food. We need to go on a foraging expedition. I have my revolver, and you can put your knife on the end of the flagstaff to make a spear."

"But shouldn't we stay here so they can find us?"

"Nicholas . . ." Ulla sighed. "It's been seventy-two hours and we have heard no noise, no airplanes overhead. If the *Penguin* did get off the ice and send a rescue plane back, they obviously don't know where to look. Now is the time to move."

Sparks nodded and began packing his things.

They set out toward the south, and for the next twelve discouraging hours they saw nothing but snow and ice. The monotony of the empty plateaus was occasionally broken by dangerous crevasses of glittering blue, sometimes with green seawater at the bottom.

"Have you noticed something odd?" Indy asked. "The sun hasn't set. I know the day up here is something like twenty hours long, but in the three or four days we've been here it hasn't gotten dark."

"Isn't this the land of the midnight sun?" Sparks asked.

"Yes," Ulla answered, "but it doesn't stay light all day until the summer solstice, June twenty-first. We haven't been up here that long."

They continued marching, growing ever more tired. After three more hours of the grueling trek, Sparks sat down dejectedly in the snow.

"We're lost," he moaned, his chin in his gloved hands.

"We may be lost, but we're still alive," Indy reminded him. "Come on, let's go. You can't just sit here, you'll freeze to death. We have to keep moving. Just a little while longer, all right?"

"Oh, all right," Sparks snapped. "You sound like my father."

Indy and Ulla paused.

"I'll take that as a compliment," Indy said.

The three trudged on. Two hours later they spotted a clump of dark bundles on the ice, and their hope gave them strength. As they approached, however, their spirits again plummeted.

It was a campsite. A half-dozen corpses lay strewn about, and the carcasses of many more dogs, some still hitched to their sledges. Most of the bodies were covered in snow and a sheet of ice, but a couple of the men were still inside their rotting tents. Their heads, feet, and hands were bundled in rags. They looked as if they had simply lain down to go to sleep—until you noticed their noses, which had turned black and fallen away.

"Why aren't they skeletons?" Sparks asked.

"Putrefaction is caused by microbes inside the body," Indy explained, kneeling down to inspect one of them. "The cold keeps them dormant. Well, we have a knife here, and a rifle—but I'm afraid it's useless. The cold, it seems, hasn't stopped the rusting process."

"You can't be thinking of robbing their bodies?" Sparks gasped in horror.

"I'm sure if they could speak, they would say we were welcome to whatever could be of use," Ulla rationalized as she began to pick through one of the sledges.

"Who are they?" Sparks asked.

Indy knelt down and inspected one of the victims. The revolver in his belt was of the percussion variety, and beneath his heavy coat, his clothes were decidedly Victorian. On one of the sledges was tacked a large flag, and although it was heavy with ice, Indy could discern the pattern of the Union Jack beneath.

"British, probably mid-nineteenth century," Indy said. "I'd say they were attempting to find the Northwest Passage. Probably the Lord Dwyden expedition."

"You mean these guys are nearly a hundred years old?" Sparks asked.

"The gentleman over there with the muttonchops is Lord Dwyden himself, more than likely," Indy said. "Sparks, why don't you make a quick survey of the site, and attempt to mark its location by dead reckoning from where we left the *Penguin*. This is of historical significance."

"All right," Sparks said, a little awed. He took out his notebook and paused. "How do you want—"

"Make a note of the location of each of the bodies, and of the sledges, and of the dogs. If you're up to it, you may poke around the bodies and see if you can get a name from each one. The least we can do is to notify their families back in Britain."

"You mean their descendants," Sparks said. "They look

like they all died at about the same time. Isn't that kind of strange? Do you think it was disease, or what?"

"Or what," Indy said. "I'd say they died from vitamin A poisoning."

"How can you tell that?" Ulla asked.

"It's a logical guess," Indy explained. "In the early days of arctic exploration, people were in the habit—when their sledges grew lighter and they no longer needed as many dogs—of eating the surplus."

"Ech!" Sparks was horrified.

"They used Huskies to pull these sledges, but what they didn't know was that the husky stores an incredible amount of vitamin A in its liver," Indy said. "The liver was considered a particularly tasty and nutritious part of the dog. After a few dozen meals of husky, you ended up with vitamin A poisoning and died."

"How do you know that?" Ulla asked.

"I like dogs," Indy said. "I read about them. I'm *named* after a dog, after all."

"Now you're pulling our collective legs," Ulla said.

"Nope." Indy shook his head. "I adopted my own nick-name. It drove my father nuts."

"What's your real name?" Sparks asked.

"When we get out of this," Indy said, "I promise to tell you."

"I won't count on finding out, then," Sparks said. His discouragement had returned. "I'm afraid we're going to end up like these guys, and somebody will come along in a hundred years and say, 'What a shame—they didn't know that the combination of Hershey bars and sardines is fatal at arctic temperatures.'"

"Then it's a good thing I used them for bait," Ulla said.

"Sparks is clever even when he's whining," Indy said.

"Have you found anything useful?" Ulla asked.

"Maybe," Indy said. "Lots of bear skins. Most of them

are pretty ratty, but some we can use. Candles. Half a jug of whiskey."

Indy uncorked the whiskey and took a sniff.

"Ugh," he said. "I don't know what this has turned to, but it's not drinkable."

"Well, take the candles. We can eat the tallow if we have to. And I think this sledge is in pretty good shape," Ulla said. "The runners are good, the harness is in one piece, and the wood seems strong enough. Two of us could pull it while the third one rides. We could take turns."

"Good idea." Indy brought the bear skins over and piled them on the sledge. "Sparks, I said you'd be able to rest soon. Sir, I give you your throne, at least until the next shift."

"Swell," Sparks said, plopped down on the sledge, and covered himself with the skins.

"Is there anything else we can use?" Ulla asked.

Indy thought for a moment. "I don't think so. Most of this stuff is pretty far gone. But I took the poles from the tents, thinking we could use them for spears or to pitch our own tents with the bear skins."

Ulla took up half of the harness and threw the other half to Indy.

"Let's go," she announced.

"Wait," Sparks said. "Don't you think we ought to say something? Like a prayer or something?"

Indy paused.

"Sparks is right," he said.

"May I?" Ulla asked.

"Be my guest."

Ulla took the knife from her belt and held the blade aloft.

"We give thanks to the Old Ones who have given us a thirst for life and have allowed us to drink deeply of one more day! We give thanks to the Dead Ones who have graciously shared their possessions to ease our journey! We give thanks to this vast and inhospitable world for the opportunity to test ourselves and know ourselves better than the timid ones who cower at home by their fires! And finally we give thanks to our enemies, for without them our swords would not gleam so bright nor our hearts beat so strong!"

"Wow," Sparks said. "I was thinking of the Lord's Prayer, but that was swell, just the same. I'll have to try to remember that one to tell my pastor back in Iowa."

"Ready?" Indy asked.

"Mush!" Sparks said.

"You're not getting my whip," Indy said.

They made better time with the sledge, but it was strenuous going for the two "dogs." It wasn't long before Indy's back and calves began to ache, but since Ulla didn't complain, he wasn't about to mention it. Six hours later, when he couldn't stand the pain anymore, he sat down in the snow beside the sledge and rested his back against it.

"I thought you would never stop," Ulla panted.

"Come on, buddy," he said as he shook Sparks awake. His lips were so blistered it was hard for him to speak. "It's your turn to be the dog. Let Ulla rest for a spell."

"I'm fine," Ulla said painfully. Her cheeks were sun- and wind-burned, and her lips were even more blistered than Indy's.

"I know you're as tired as I am," Indy said. "One of us has to rest first. It might as well be you."

"Oh, all right," Ulla grumbled as she gave up the harness and took Sparks's place in the sledge.

"Do you smell the sea?" the teenager asked.

"I've been thinking that myself for the last half hour," Indy said. "But there's so much frost up my nose I wasn't sure."

"It's definitely the sea," Sparks said as he struggled into the harness. "And the terrain has gotten a bit hillier, too. Sort of like sand dunes, only made out of snow."

"Yeah," Indy agreed. "It makes it a little harder to pull the sledge up one side, but we kind of slide down the other."

After twenty minutes of pulling, Indy's legs felt like rubber and Sparks was sweating profusely.

"Let's take a break," Indy suggested. "Be careful to wipe the sweat off your eyelashes, or your eyes will freeze shut. It's happened to me a couple of times already. And I think my nose is getting frostbitten."

Sparks nodded as he leaned against the sledge.

Ulla sat up.

"What?" Indy asked.

"Did you hear that sound?"

"What sound?"

"Shush." She placed a finger to her lips. "Don't move, don't speak."

Barely audible, the sound of something moving across the ice behind them, behind the last dune, reached their ears. It would take a few steps, snort, and then take a few more steps. It sounded like a moose or some other big animal. Then it growled, a low, frightening sound, and there was no doubt.

"Polar bear," Ulla whispered. "Indy, you had better get your revolver out."

"You're kidding," he said.

"No, I'm not," Ulla said. "I thought it had been tracking us for the last half mile or so, but I wasn't sure. They have a keen sense of smell, and when they're hungry they will eat just about anything."

Indy drew the Webley.

"Perhaps it's a small one," Ulla said. "Then we'll have something fresh to eat."

"And if it's a big one?" Sparks asked.

"The handgun won't stop it," Ulla said. "And we can't run away from it. It can run at about thirty-five miles per hour forever."

The top of the bear's white head loomed above the dune, sniffing the air. Its coarse fur was matted and its muzzle was flecked with the dried blood of its last meal.

"It's been hunting seal," Ulla said. "But it still looks hungry. It's going to charge us in just a few seconds. Indy, you put as many shots as you can into it."

"Where do I aim?" he asked.

"The skull is too thick for your little gun," she said.

"My little gun?" Indy asked, holding up the Webley.

"A thirty-eight will do little more than make it angry," Ulla said. "But it's all we've got, I suppose. If we're lucky the bear will stand up—they usually do when they're about to attack—so they can use their front paws to tear you apart. Then shoot as if you're shooting to kill a man— the heart, the lungs. But lower, beneath the shoulders."

The bear climbed up on top of the dune, stretching its long neck toward them. It bared its teeth, shook its head, and growled again. Then it paused, apparently unsure of its next move.

"My god, it must weigh a thousand pounds."

"More," Ulla said. "Some say that the polar bear can be bigger even than the Kodiak."

"Maybe it'll go away," Indy said.

"It won't." Ulla had her knife in her hand. "Sparks, be ready to use your spear if it charges you. If it charges Indy or me, you just run as fast as you can."

The bear came loping down the dune toward them, snarling, with its head down. Its fat stomach rolled from side to side as it walked. Its fangs were bared and the claws on its front paws gleamed like black razors.

Indy took aim, holding the Webley in both hands.

"Not yet," Ulla whispered. "Wait."

The bear roared, then stood up on its hind feet. It was nearly twice the height of a man. It was thirty yards away, and Indy took aim at an imaginary target the size of a pie plate in the center of its rib cage. He fired twice, in quick succession. The bear rolled over to one side on the snow, bellowing in anger.

"You got him," Sparks said.

Then the bear got up and charged directly at them. Indy got off one more shot, which struck the bear in the center of the skull, but it had no effect. Indy had two rounds left, and he was planning on saving them until the bear had him in its paws, when he would jam the Webley into its mouth and pull the trigger.

At that moment a report that sounded like a cannon blast echoed across the snow and the bear was knocked sideways, ten yards away from the sledge. Another shot came as the bear tried again to rise, and this time particles of its skull and brains were scattered across the snow. The bear gave one last defiant look at its intended prey, then collapsed.

"Where did that come from?" Indy asked.

Ulla pointed at the ridge of a dune two hundred yards behind them. A hunter was standing on top, a heavy rifle in his hands.

"What's he carrying, a howitzer?" Indy asked.

"Bear gun," Ulla said. "Fifty-caliber or better."

"Like I said, that's a cannon."

The hunter shouldered his weapon and walked down the dune. He was a big, barrel-chested man dressed in bear skins—even his hat was made of bear skin—and he had wild hair and a full, graying beard.

"One of your Viking ancestors?" Indy asked.

The man smiled and gestured toward the fallen bear while he chatted with Ulla.

"He wants me to have the honor of the kill," Ulla said. She took her knife and cut off one of the bear's ears.

"An aficionado," Indy remarked.

Sparks blinked, and then fell to the snow, vomiting. Nothing much but water came out.

Indy pulled him up.

"Gentlemen," Ulla said. "I would like to present our rescuer, Captain Gunnar Erickson. He says he has been tracking this bear for most of the day, and that he was happy because he had almost decided to give up and go back to his boat—in which case he would not have gotten his trophy, and we would have lost our lives."

"His boat?" Sparks asked excitedly. "He has a boat?"

Ulla spoke with the man briefly in Danish, then smiled.

"Yes, it is only a mile or so away," she said. "The boat is one of the wooden bear-hunting vessels manufactured by my father's company. Gunnar says we are welcome to the hospitality of the *Berserker*, although it is small and quarters will be cramped. He will understand if we prefer to go our own way."

"Is he kidding?" Sparks asked.

"He's trying to be polite," Ulla explained. "He knows we cannot afford to turn down his offer, but he doesn't want to treat us like beggars, either."

"Doesn't berserk mean crazy?" Sparks asked.

"No," Ulla said. "It means one who wears the bear shirt, one who takes the fighting spirit of the bear in battle. The word has been misunderstood for centuries."

"Tell Gunnar that we will be delighted to accompany him," Indy said. "And please commend him on his marksmanship."

Ulla did as she was asked; then Gunnar replied, and she frowned.

"The captain says he is sorry that he doesn't speak English so that he may talk man to man instead of having to communicate by way of an excitable and possibly inaccurate female."

Indy suppressed a laugh.

"I'm glad you find it amusing," Ulla said. "Oh, by the way—there is only one problem."

"What's that?"

"Gunnar's lost," Ulla said. "He's been sailing farther and farther north tracking bears, and has been following a rocky, barren shoreline where the currents don't make sense."

"That sounds familiar," Indy said.

"Does he have a radio?" Sparks asked.

Ulla repeated the question in Danish.

"No," she translated. "He doesn't trust any disembodied voice. He says he hears enough voices when he is alone anyway."

Gunnar field-dressed his kill and loaded it on the sledge, and all of them pulled for a quarter of a mile to a spot where a dinghy was beached upside down on the ice. Indy and Sparks helped Gunnar slide the boat off the ice into the water, and when it was fully loaded, they abandoned the sledge and Gunnar began rowing through the billowing fog.

"I hope he knows where he's going," Sparks said.

"Of course he does," Ulla told him. "Look."

She pointed to where a green light glowed in the mist.

The *Berserker* was a twin-masted schooner with a bleached bear's skull nailed to its prow. The hull was made of South American evergreen sheathing three-inch oak planks, and the entire ship was rounded, with a flat bottom, so that it would rise upon the ice instead of being crushed by it. The decks and sides were insulated with cork and reindeer hair so the interior remained warm and dry, and for the times when the wind was not generous, in the aft hold was a six-cylinder gasoline engine to provide power.

"She was designed after the *Fram*," Ulla explained as Indy helped her over the side and onto the ice-covered deck. "In the 1890s, Nansen tried to reach the Pole by letting a specially designed ship, the *Fram*, drift with the ice. He came very close, but did not make it. He and his ship, however, returned unscathed. This ship is about half the size of Nansen's, of course, but the principle is the same."

"She's marvelous," Indy said. "What is she, a sixty-footer?"

"A little less," Ulla said. "And twenty feet at the beam."

They went below, and Gunnar began to boil water for coffee. Sparks removed his gloves and parka, then tried to take off his boots. They were a frozen mass of ice, and he had to hold them near the stove until they had thawed enough for him to undo the laces. Finally he got them off, peeled away his wet socks, and then a feeling like pins and needles in his feet quickly escalated to something that felt more like fire.

"Aw," Sparks said, "what's happening?"

"It's your circulation." Ulla sat down next to him and inspected one foot while Indy took the other. Sparks's feet were an angry red, and there were white spots on the ends of most of his toes, and on his soles.

"I'm afraid you've gotten frostbitten," Indy said.

"Am I going to lose my toes?"

"No," Indy said. "Not unless gangrene sets in. But you don't look all that bad. I've seen worse. A little skin and flesh may slough off, though."

"Will it grow back?"

"Hopefully," Indy said. "Ulla, can you get us a pan of warm water? Not hot, just warm."

"A small price to pay for being alive," Sparks said.

"You're getting tougher," Ulla said as she drew the water.

"I have to be to run with your crowd," Sparks said.

She brought the pan and Sparks placed his feet in it.

"I'll see if Gunnar has anything for the pain," Ulla said. "Then Indy and I had better look at our own feet. I'm sure they don't look any better."

Gunnar went to the cabinet and offered whiskey or aspirin. Ulla took the aspirin and Gunnar took a shot of the whiskey before replacing it.

"Gunnar says we can try some bear steak for dinner," Ulla told them. "He says that it is unwise for us to eat too much at once, however—one must become acclimated to the peculiar, oily flesh of the polar bear. And, he adds, bear steak is all that he's got."

"Then bear steak it is." Indy gave the aspirin and a cup of coffee to Sparks.

"Ugh," Sparks said. "More coffee."

"Drink it," Indy urged. "It's warm."

Sparks took a sip.

"It needs about a ton of sugar," he said.

Indy turned to Ulla.

"Ask Gunnar about the shoreline."

Ulla did as he requested.

"Gunnar says you will see much of it," she said. "As it turns out, at the moment he is out of gasoline for the motor, the sails are frozen to the spars, and the *Berserker* is drifting at the mercy of the current . . ."

10

THE MAELSTROM

Indiana Jones leaned over the ice-covered railing and stared at the dark shore shrouded in mist. The fingers of his right hand slipped inside his parka and felt the stone that was on the thong around his neck, and he thought of Baldwin.

"It's getting warmer," Ulla observed.

"I was thinking that myself," Indy said. "A few more degrees, and maybe we can peel the sails away from the spars."

"And then what?" Ulla asked. "We seem to be in a dead calm. Gunnar isn't even at the wheel anymore; he's just letting the boat drift along with the current. Besides, how would we know which direction to go until we can get a glimpse at the stars?"

Indy shrugged.

"How's Sparks?" he asked.

"Still sleeping," Ulla replied.

"Good. He needs it."

At that moment Gunnar approached, his boots pounding on the deck. He came over and leaned on the rail between Indy and Ulla. He had a knife in one hand

and a piece of nearly raw meat in the other, which he offered to the couple.

"No thanks," Indy said.

Ulla took a chunk of the meat and began chewing. It was as tough as a leather boot.

Gunnar began to talk quietly with Ulla.

"What's he saying?"

"Gunnar is telling me I have too much spirit to be a woman, that the gods must have made a mistake." She smiled. "He says that when the Valkyries come for the chosen ones, those who will help the Old Ones fight the last battle against chaos, I will be among them."

"*Ragnarok*," Gunnar said.

"The Doom of the Gods," Indy said. "When the bifrost bridge appears and the stars fall from the sky."

"So you know the story?" Ulla asked.

"I've read the Icelandic Eddas," Indy said. "And the Volsungs. When the trumpet blows announcing dooms-day, the rainbow bridge that leads to Asgard, the home of the gods, will appear. The last battle with evil will take place, and then the stars will fall, and the earth will sink beneath the sea."

"It is an interesting thought." Ulla smiled again. "Perhaps I will be there—a single woman in a legion of men, the bravest sons of the earth. I don't know which of the traditional weapons I would prefer. No sword nor ax for me. Poetry, I think, would be my weapon."

"Poetry?" Indy looked surprised.

"I would count each man that falls and compose a verse for him," she explained. Then she began to sing: "Wealth dies, kinsmen die, a man himself must likewise die. But one thing I know that never dies—the verdict on each man dead."

"And each woman?" Indy asked.

She nodded. "In my version."

"Does it bother you being constantly compared to men?" Indy asked. "I mean, even in your religion there are only places for men. Women are either harpies who pick over the battlefields or are the barmaids of the gods."

"But some of the most powerful gods are women," Ulla said. "It is a complex belief system. What bothers me most is the way people treat me in this life, as some kind of freak."

"I've never thought of you in that way."

Ulla shrugged.

"Life is hard. The power of the gods is not eternal, Dr. Jones. It will end, as all things end. Ragnarok truly is the herald of doom."

"Do you believe that?"

"What do you believe?" Ulla said.

"I think there is truth in all of the old stories," Indy said. "Most civilizations have creation myths which are amazingly similar, and there were saviors who died and were resurrected long before Christianity adopted the notion. Your god Odin wounded himself with his spear and hung for nine days on the Tree of Woe and was renewed. In the process he became the master of the runes, of reading and writing."

"Yes," Ulla said, "but the afterlives are different. In Christianity the savior redeems the world, while in my belief system the world is unredeemable. Evil is destined to win the final battle. What matters isn't faith, but courage in the face of certain defeat. That is the only reward. After that—oblivion."

"It is a depressing prospect."

"Not really." Ulla looked at him, her eyes alight. "It wonderfully concentrates the mind on the moment, and gives value to our actions as momentary events, instead of bargaining chips for the next life. That is why I prefer to think of myself as an adventurer, a person of action instead of contemplation."

Indy smiled.

Ulla folded down her hood and gazed at him.

"You're a handsome man," she said. "That is saying something, because I am not usually attracted by men. And I know by the way that you sometimes look at me that you think I am not unattractive, either."

"How could I not?" Indy said. "Not only are you smart and strong, but you are beautiful as well. A very rare combination in any individual."

"Then perhaps we shouldn't allow this moment to pass," Ulla suggested as she gripped his arm. "Sparks is asleep, and Gunnar doesn't care what we do as long as we don't sink his boat."

She kissed him, cautiously, because their lips were still blistered.

"Ulla." Indy touched her face. "I care for you, but in the way I care for my other friends. Your suggestion is tempting, but it would change our friendship in a way that neither of us is prepared to handle."

"I was just suggesting an hour's pleasure," she murmured sullenly, and pushed him away. "I mean, if we're about to be sucked into this thing that your old friend said was waiting for us, why not? I wouldn't mind it. But I wasn't asking to have your babies. The very idea is revolting."

"Well, you know I'm—"

"I know, *in love* with the redheaded sybil on the Graf," Ulla said, and made a face. "You're very straitlaced, Jones. Sex must scare you a lot."

"About as much as snakes," he snapped.

"Scared of snakes, too? Hah! No sexual overtones there, huh? A psychoanalyst would have a field day with your head. I'll bet you can't bring yourself to eat an apple, either."

"I like apples just fine," Indy said. "Ripe, red, juicy ones. Sometimes I have two or three a day."

Down the rail, Gunnar was laughing.

"I thought he didn't speak any English." Indy was clearly annoyed.

"He doesn't," Ulla said. "He's just enjoying our fight. But maybe we ought to let him in on the discussion so he can appreciate its true richness."

Indy looked up.

"Shush," he said.

"What?"

"Engine noise."

"Don't try to distract me."

"I'm not," Indy insisted. "I hear something, and if you would shut up for two seconds and listen, you'd hear it as well."

Ulla scanned the clouded sky.

"Is it the *Penguin*?" she asked hopefully.

"No," Indy said. "It's over there, off the port bow. A big shadow in the clouds."

"The *Graf*," Ulla said.

"They're searching."

"Maybe they'll pick us up."

"They can't even see us," Indy said. "The weather's too thick. And even if they did pick us up, they'd probably torture us before shooting us and pitching us over the side."

"Well, it'd be better than sitting here on this little boat with you," Ulla concluded, and went to the cabin. Gunnar laughed again and patted Indy on the shoulder as he followed her down.

The current quickened now and the *Berserker* was drawn inexorably into the rugged bay, where her hull bumped and ground against a dozen rocks. Gunnar and his passengers managed to push her clear each time with poles and oars, but even though they managed to save the ship, they couldn't stop her headlong rush toward the mouth of the river on the dark shore. The river was dark and wide and flowing inward, and as they drifted, the weather grew increasingly warmer and the rest of the ice fell from the decks and masts. At one point Gunnar unfurled the sails and attempted to check their progress, but there was no wind and the attempt simply made the little boat swirl dangerously in the middle of the water.

The weather was worsening as well. The clouds became even darker, and blotted out the sun. For the first time in days they were in darkness. Up ahead they could make out the dim outlines of a smoldering red peak, but never could they get a clear view of their destination.

"I wish I had some proper equipment," Sparks said. "A radio transmitter, or a compass that worked, or even a theodolite. I keep checking the barometer in the cabin, but it just keeps rising with the storm."

"There's no way to fix our position?" Indy asked.

"Not without the sun or the stars," Sparks said. "If there's no landmass under the arctic ice, then where are we? You don't have rivers running over the ice, and from what I can see of the terrain, it's solid rock. Maybe we're lost in some fjord in Norway."

"I don't think so, Sparks." Indy patted the boy's shoulder.

As they neared the smoky peak the river began to run faster and the clouds closed down upon them. Rain lashed over the deck and lightning streaked around them, sometimes hitting the shore and reducing a boulder to so much smoking rubble. Around the tops of the masts the eerie blue light of Saint Elmo's fire danced and bobbed.

"This is too weird for me," Sparks commented as he

hung desperately to the rail. "My mother was right. I should never have joined the service. This isn't worth twenty-three dollars a month."

Gunnar looked at him and nodded, understanding the sentiment intuitively but not the specific words of the boy. The captain tamped his pipe, lit it, and murmured something in Danish.

"What'd he say?" Indy asked.

"You don't want to know," Ulla said.

"Come on, tell us."

"Well, our captain believes that we're all dead," she explained. "He thinks it happened when he picked us up after killing the polar bear—he doesn't know how, exactly, but he presumes that the boat sank and we all drowned since we're still together—and that we have sunk to the netherworld."

"In other words," Indy said, "he thinks we're in hell."

"You got it."

As they spoke Gunnar began distributing pieces of rope to each of them.

"What's this for?" Indy asked.

"He's telling us to lash ourselves to the masts," Ulla said. "The river is running too fast, and he says we are bound to be smashed to bits on the rocks at the base of the mountain, or blasted to bits by the lightning. He says the three of us can decide to jump off, if that's what we want, but he doesn't have a choice. He's the captain, and he's determined to go down with his ship."

"Jumping off would be suicide," Sparks observed.

"I guess it depends on your perspective," Ulla said. "It doesn't make much difference, unless you think we're still alive."

"My vote's for alive," Indy said. "And I'm still the leader of this expedition, so that's your vote, too."

"You've done a helluva job so far, Commander," Ulla said. "Which mast do you want?"

Indy and Ulla tied themselves to the forward mast while Sparks secured himself to the aft one. Gunnar lashed himself to the wheel pedestal, in some vain attempt to retain control over his ship.

The river had turned into a ribbon of whitecaps. The boat continued to pick up speed until the wind whipping through the lines made a whistling sound. The glowing mountain peak was above them now, and at any second they expected the *Berserker* to be dashed against the rocks.

Indy closed his eyes against the spray coming over the bow, and Ulla squirmed uncomfortably against the ropes. Sparks began to recite the Lord's Prayer, while Gunnar gritted his teeth and chewed on the stem of his long-cold pipe.

The ship pitched forward, as if to slam against the side of the mountain, but instead was swept into a tunnel that could not be seen through the storm outside. The tops of the masts were snapped off like pencils by the roof of the chasm, and lines and spars came crashing down onto the deck.

They seemed to hang in the air for a moment, as if on the lip of a waterfall, and then the *Berserker* hurtled downward in the darkness, trailing its wreckage behind it. There was no light in the shaft, and all had the sensation they were swirling down a gigantic drain.

Sparks screamed.

At the bottom of the shaft the little ship struck an underground lake with such force that she dove deep beneath the surface. The water surged over the decks with an explosive fury that nearly knocked Indy out. Tied by his hands around the mast, he could feel his body twisting helplessly in the water. But thanks to her watertight hull, the *Berserker* shot back to the surface like a cork.

Indy gasped.

It was perfectly still in this new pool of water. He took his pocketknife and cut himself clear of the mast, then freed Ulla.

"Are you all right?" he asked.

She gagged and threw up some water.

"I'll take that for a yes," he said.

Then Indy crawled aft, where he found Sparks unconscious but alive. He and Gunnar untied him and laid him on the deck, which was listing badly to port.

"How are you, Captain?" Indy asked.

Gunnar smiled and showed him a wrist that had obviously been broken while he was attempting to control the wheel. The bones were protruding through the skin.

"Ulla," Indy called. "Gunnar's injured. We have to take care of it right away."

Ulla staggered back to the wheel.

"Is this thing going to stay afloat?" she asked.

"I don't know," Indy said. "It looks pretty badly beaten up."

"Wait until I see my father and tell him about the shoddy workmanship on his bear-hunting boats," Ulla said. "Would an even deck be too much to ask for?"

With that, she went off to retrieve the whiskey from the cabin, then poured it over Gunnar's wound. Then, while Indy held a rope attached to Gunnar's right hand and pulled, she delicately pushed the bones of the forearm back beneath the skin.

Gunnar groaned and bit the stem of his pipe in two.

"We're not done yet." Ulla smiled. "I have to feel around a little more and make sure the ends match. Indy, I need a little pressure this time, just enough to—there, that's it."

Gunnar's eyelids fluttered.

"Indy, get me some sheets from below so we can bandage his arm up. It wouldn't be much of a splint, but it's the best we can do right now."

Then Ulla took the whiskey and turned to Sparks. She held his head while she poured a little of the beverage into his mouth.

He coughed and sputtered.

"How are you?" Ulla asked.

"I know I'm not dead," the boy said. "I hurt too much. My head feels like it's been hit with a baseball bat."

"You've got a pretty good-sized lump on your forehead," Ulla confirmed. "I think one of the spars might have caught you a glancing blow when they gave way."

When Indy came back on deck from the cabin, Sparks told him to look up. There, framed in the volcanic throat of the mountain, which glowed with flecks of lava, was a sky full of stars. And floating peacefully among the stars was the dark cigar-shaped outline of the Graf Zeppelin.

"I'm not getting it." Sparks grimaced. "If the sun never sets up here, then how can we see the stars? Maybe it's like being at the bottom of a well. They say you can see the stars at noon."

"I don't think so," Indy said. "That well thing is a myth. Maybe we're just in that two hours of darkness each day. That one star up there has to be the North Star. See it, just about dead center above us?"

"That makes calculations easy," Sparks said. "Latitude ninety degrees. As fantastic as it sounds, we have to be at the North Pole—or awfully close to it."

"No, we're not *at* the pole," Indy said. "We're *under* it."

Sparks whistled.

"Swell," he said. "How do you think the zep got through the storm?"

"They didn't go through it," Indy said. "They sailed *over* it. We took the hard way."

"And this is what they've been looking for all along?"

Indy nodded. "It's the entrance to something," he said. "I'm not exactly sure what, but something."

Suddenly the hair on the back of his neck and arms bristled. "Hey, do you feel that?" he asked.

"Yeah," Sparks said. "It feels like some kind of electrical discharge."

A nebulous rainbow of colors began to form in the night sky above them. Then the rainbow started to rotate, then it shot down and illuminated the interior of the volcano in a celestial light. The four voyagers were bathed in a mixture of blue and green and rose. The rainbow continued downward, seeming to disappear somewhere beyond the edge of their subterranean lake.

"The northern lights," Indy said.

"At least we can see now," Ulla commented.

The *Berserker* drifted over to the shore of the lake, where they tied it fast to a pillar of rock. Indy jumped down onto the gravel, then stood with his hands on his hips while he turned around and inspected the interior. About halfway up on one wall lay the wreckage of an aircraft.

"What do you think?" Ulla asked.

"I don't know," Indy said. "It must be a half mile away, at least. Do you think we can make it up there?"

Ulla studied the rock formations.

"I think so, without much problem," she said. "There seems to be a natural kind of stairway winding around the inside of the cone."

"Then we have to go take a look," Indy said. "It might be the *Penguin*. Gunnar, you stay here and take care of your arm. Sparks, do you feel like a little hike?"

"My head hurts, but I think I can make it," the boy said.

"I'd hate to think of Clarence and the guys lying up there hurt."

"That's my feeling," Indy told him. "Let's get going."

It took the trio more than two hours to climb to the wreckage, and when they reached the plateau on which it lay it became obvious that it wasn't the *Penguin*, or any other type of twin-engine craft. It was a smaller plane, and although it had obviously tumbled some distance, the red-and-white fuselage was largely intact. It was a hydroplane, and one of its pontoons was missing. On the nose of the plane was a name, clearly legible: THE LATHAM. In white chalk, on the nose, was the following message: CREW DEAD. ATTEMPTING TO USE PONTOON AS CANOE. AMUNDSEN. 26 JUNE 1928.

"Well, now we know what became of Amundsen," Sparks concluded.

"No, we know what became of his *plane*," Indy corrected. "He obviously walked away from the crash. Smart, using the pontoon as a boat. But there's no chance he could fight that current and get to the outside."

"Maybe he didn't go to the outside," Ulla suggested.

Sparks stepped into the crumpled fuselage.

"Where are the bodies of the crew?" he asked.

"Amundsen buried them," Indy said. "In those rock cairns, along the wall here. Look, there's a name chalked on the largest rock atop each of them."

"Good," Sparks said. "I hate corpses."

Indy went deeper into the wreckage. He came out a few minutes later, plainly disappointed.

"The radio is all busted up," he reported. "The batteries are dead, anyway, after six years. And it looks like Amundsen took everything with him that wasn't bolted down, including the log."

"Well, the old man was nothing if not thorough," Ulla said.

Sparks stepped out of the plane.

"It was a long climb up here for nothing," he said.

"Not quite," a voice above them said. "It saved us from climbing all the way down to the bottom to kill you, no?"

"Reingold," Indy snarled.

On the ledge above the wreckage Reingold appeared, followed by his men. They were ten feet above Indy and the others, and the troopers began to scramble down.

"At your service," the SS captain said behind his drawn Walther. "I believe you have already met some of the other members of my squad, especially Sergeants Dortmuller and Liebel."

The officers in question jumped down onto one of the rock cairns, their submachine guns pointed at the trio. They were followed by a half-dozen troopers similarly armed.

"Oh, and of course we can't forget the newest member of the Thule Society, can we?" Reingold added with a triumphant smirk. "Dr. Jones, meet SS Specialist Alecia Dunstin. I believe you two once meant something to one another, but that affair, you could say, was doomed from the start."

He pulled Alecia forward so that Indy could see her.

"She looks rather smart in her uniform, doesn't she?" Reingold taunted. "And I must say, she has earned it. The journal gave us much information, but it was Alecia's clairvoyance that helped us to pinpoint the exact spot. Many people don't believe in that sort of thing, I'm afraid—until they have a well to dig, or a lost civilization to find."

"Don't," Alecia said.

"Dortmuller! Liebel!" Reingold shouted. "Help us down from here. You others, don't take your guns off them!"

Reingold straightened his jacket when he reached the ground. Alecia kept her eyes lowered.

"Specialist Dunstin, observe!" Reingold commanded.

"It looks like Dr. Jones's flame did not last very long for you. It appears that he lost no time in finding a blonde to replace you."

"Don't believe him," Ulla told Alecia. "Indy's not my type."

"Silence the degenerate," Reingold said.

Dortmuller brought the gun up and aimed.

"Not that way, you idiot," Reingold said.

Dortmuller walked over and slammed the butt of his gun into Ulla's stomach. It knocked the breath out of her, but she remained on her feet.

"You give us Nordic types a bad name," Ulla managed to wheeze.

"Leave her alone," Indy said. "She has nothing to do with this. It's me you ought to be slugging in the stomach."

"All in good time," Reingold assured him. "Why don't we begin by asking about that precious yellow canister which you stole from us? Reichsführer Himmler was particularly distressed to learn of its theft. His astrologer assured him it was vitally important to the future."

"Tell Himmler to go—"

"Careful, Dr. Jones," Reingold said. "You shouldn't say that."

"No, but I can think it," Indy spat. "Look, I'll tell you everything if you just let Ulla and the boy go."

"I have all of you," Reingold said. "Why would I let anybody go?"

"Because I'll kill you if you don't?" Indy ventured.

"Reach for that revolver under your jacket," Reingold said, "and my men will cut you to pieces. You're in no position to threaten anybody. Or to bargain, for that matter."

"Captain," Alecia said.

"No, my dear. In German."

"*Hauptsturmführer.*"

"Passable, but you need to work on your accent," Rein-gold said. "You sound like a London guttersnipe."

"May I have a word with Dr. Jones?" she asked, wiping away her tears. "I think I may be able to persuade him."

Alecia walked over, and now it was Indy's turn to stare at the ground.

"Nice boots," he said.

"Will you look at me?"

"No," he said. "You'll do that thing with your eyes and make me agree to anything." Indy paused, his body rigid. "Can you tell me why you betrayed me? Betrayed yourself?"

"I didn't betray you," Alecia said defiantly. "If anything, I was attempting to save your life. You know what these chaps are capable of."

"Too bad I didn't know what *you* were capable of."

"Don't thank me now," Alecia said, and crossed her arms. "Or later."

"Indy, things went so horribly wrong between us," she said, and touched his sleeve gently. "And I kept having these recurring nightmares—prophecies, really—of people dying, even more than during the Great War. Death on the ground, in the sea, in the sky. Death raining down from the sky on civilian populations all across Europe and Asia. Cities reduced to ashes—with nothing but a single bomb."

"Science fiction." Ulla sneered.

"You don't know what it did to me," Alecia pleaded. "My spirit went into shock, my mind into a kind of fugue state. I couldn't eat, I couldn't sleep. And the thing that got to me the most is that I saw you dying. I've seen what's going to happen to you, Indy—thrown into some horrible tomb in the desert with thousands of snakes."

Indy swallowed hard. "Snakes?"

"And then the tomb is sealed shut and that's it."

"*Thousands* of snakes?" He swallowed again.

"Millions of people are going to die, Indy, and you are one of them."

Tears rolled down her cheeks and dribbled onto the SS rune on her collar.

"A city destroyed by one bomb?" Ulla said. "You're obviously some kind of delusional charlatan who needs to justify her own importance."

"I believe her," Sparks said.

"Nobody is really going to win like this," Alecia continued. "I thought I had to do something to keep so many people from dying. Isn't it better that one side wins quickly rather than millions dying in a kind of hell on earth?"

"Not if the winning side is their side," Indy said. "That's the funny thing about life—there are some things worth dying for and some that aren't, and when you lose your ability to make that distinction, you're something less than human."

Alecia removed her officer's cap and looked at it with a wry smile, her thumb tracing the aluminum skull insignia on the black velvet band. Then she threw the hat over the side and began to unbutton her tunic.

"What're you doing?" Reingold demanded.

"I quit," she said.

She wriggled her shoulders and let the black jacket fall to the ground. Her hair spilled over the shoulders of her white blouse.

"Nobody leaves the SS," Reingold warned.

"Watch me," she said as she stepped forward. She took Indy's face in her hands and kissed him passionately. Indy returned the kiss and put his arms protectively around her.

"Get back," Reingold ordered. He advanced with the Walther held tightly in his left hand. "Of course I knew it would come to this eventually. Do you really think we would allow a *woman* into the SS? Quite a nice charade, though, while it lasted, wasn't it?"

"I love you," Alecia said, and kissed Indy again.

Indy saw Reingold's finger tighten on the trigger. He and Alecia were standing side by side, and he was unsure for a moment at which one of them the Nazi captain was aiming. When he finally attempted to push Alecia behind him, it was too late—and in the wrong direction.

When Reingold fired, the bullet flew within an inch of Indy's twisted chest and shoulders. It struck Alecia in the ribs, beneath her right arm, which was still around Indy's neck. Her lips were still pressed against his.

Alecia stiffened in Indy's arms as the coppery taste of blood entered his mouth from hers. The bullet had lodged in her right lung. As Indy slumped to the floor with her and cradled her head, Alecia looked into his eyes and smiled.

"There *are* some things worth dying for," she whispered.

"My God, no!" Indy screamed.

Reingold fired again, this time placing a bullet in Alecia's heart.

Her face tightened with pain, then her features relaxed and her blue eyes became cloudy.

Not a word was spoken. Nobody moved.

Then Indy drew his Webley and took aim at Reingold's chest. Sweat beaded on his forehead and upper lip, and his mouth was twisted in hate.

He pulled the trigger.

The hammer fell, but nothing happened. The cartridge was so waterlogged it would not fire.

Ulla reached out for the nearest soldier and grabbed the back of his collar while she swept his legs out from beneath him. By the time he hit the floor, her boot had already connected solidly with his jaw, snapping his head around at an unnatural angle. She took the short MP-40 submachine gun from his lifeless hands and turned it on the other soldiers.

The first soldier that raised his weapon was hit by a burst that Ulla fired from her hip. He fell over the edge and tumbled down into the throat of the volcanic crater, bouncing off rocks and finally landing in a scalding pool of lava.

The other soldiers lowered their weapons.

"Kill him!" Reingold snarled. "Kill Jones!"

"Be my guest." Dortmuller gestured politely with one hand, then pushed his glasses up on the bridge of his nose with the other.

Reingold took aim at Indy's head.

"I wouldn't do that if I were you," Ulla said over the barrel of the MP-40.

Reingold shrugged, then tossed the Walther over the side.

"Let's get out of here," Ulla said. She reached down and relieved the dead soldier of three ammunition pouches.

"I'm for that," Sparks said. He grasped the barrel of a submachine gun from the nearest soldier and wrenched it away.

"I can't leave her," Indy said.

"I'm sorry." Ulla glanced at him sadly. "But she's dead. We can't bring her back, but we can save ourselves."

Indy didn't look up to meet her gaze. "What's the use?" he said.

With the barrel of her gun still pointed at the soldiers, Ulla walked over to Indy and pulled him with one arm. Free of his grasp, Alecia's head lolled to one side, but her eyes were still gazing at him.

Ulla knelt down and closed Alecia's eyes.

"Are you going to let her die for nothing?" Ulla shouted at him. "She died proving that she loved you—that nothing on this earth was as important, and that she was sorry for her mistakes. It was a perfectly beautiful and courageous act, and I am not going to let you waste it."

Indy gritted his teeth and fixed Reingold with a stare that made the SS captain's blood run cold.

"You reptiles did this to her." He bit out the words. "You took someone who was kind and gentle, and destroyed her, played on her fears of hurting others so that she would do your bidding. And then, when she became herself again, you killed her."

Indy holstered the Webley and held out his hands toward Sparks, coaxing with his fingers for some firepower.

Sparks threw him the machine gun.

"But what you didn't count on is that love is eternal," Indy said as he backed away with the gun, pulling her body after him. "You don't know the power of love because all you have is hate, and that hate has turned your hearts to stone. Well, I'm not going to let you desecrate her body—or her memory."

He knelt down, hoisted Alecia's body over one shoulder, and then stood up. He was still holding the machine gun in his other hand.

"What are you doing?" Ulla asked.

"The only thing I can do," Indy answered. "Bury her."

He thumbed the fire-control button of the MP-40 to full automatic, and as the sharp *click!* echoed from the stones, Reingold and the soldiers dived for cover.

"I'm sorry," Indy whispered, and then heaved Alecia's body over the side. She seemed to sail through the air, her arms and legs splayed and her red hair flaming out behind her. Then her body struck the surface of the lava pool and burst into flames.

The twisting pillar of the northern lights flared to brilliance. For a moment everyone stopped, mesmerized, because Alecia's face was staring back at them from within the supernatural glow.

Impulsively, Indy retrieved Alecia's hat from the ground and stuffed it inside his jacket.

"What are you waiting for?" Reingold screamed. *"Get them!"*

Indy took cover behind the nearest rock as his gun spewed flame and lead, allowing enough cover for Ulla and Sparks to join him. The Nazis returned fire, but the trio was already far down the rocky steps, protected by the undercut ledge. Mixed with the acrid smell of gun smoke was the odor of burning flesh.

11

ULTIMA THULE

Indy and Ulla jumped onto the deck of the *Berserker*, then together they pulled Sparks aboard as he tottered uncertainly on the rail. Ulla crouched behind the gunwale, and at the first sight of a Nazi uniform on the path above, she fired a burst.

"Get below," Indy told Sparks.

"The water is up to my ankles in the cabin," he protested.

"Well, there's going to be hot lead up to your neck if you stay up here," Indy said as he grabbed a broken piece of spar and tried to push the boat away from the shore.

Gunnar asked if the devil himself was after them.

"You could say that," Ulla replied in Danish.

Gunnar's right hand was in a sling, but he picked up an oar with his left and, leaning against the handle with his thick chest, helped Indy push the boat out into the lake.

The *Berserker* bobbed low in the water.

"Keep poling!" Ulla shouted as she let loose with another burst to keep their pursuers at bay. Dortmuller held his weapon above a rock and sprayed the area, but succeeded only in wasting ammunition and stitching the surface of the water.

Soon the lake was too deep for Indy to reach the bottom with the spar, but the current began to draw the boat away. Ulla emptied the rest of her magazine at the shore, then popped in a fresh clip, released the bolt, and waited.

"Keep low," she whispered.

The boat edged slowly toward the sound of rushing water.

"We're not going through another drain, are we?" Indy asked.

"If we are, it beats facing what's back there," she said.

The current began to pick up speed and soon the boat was pulled toward the shallow falls that emptied from the lake. Her bottom grounded on the rim of the falls but, after some nudging from Indy with the spar, slipped over the rocks and entered the mouth of a dark river. Soon they were out of sight from the shore, but they could hear Reingold's curses as he exhorted his men to follow.

"Where are we headed?" Sparks asked, poking his head out of the cabin door.

"Down," Indy said.

A luminescent mist tinted with the colors of the aurora floated over the river as it serpentined into the depths of the earth, allowing just enough light for the passengers of the wallowing boat to glimpse their surroundings. During some portions of the descent, the rocks would take on a majestic quality, as if they were floating through a stygian cathedral complete with bits of stained glass in the form of quartz and amethyst. At other times the passage seemed to be flanked by velvet drapery, or glittering tapestries made of diamond, or the tourmaline tubes of a gigantic pipe organ. Occasionally they caught glimpses of what must have been veins of silver, and at other times of gold. Gunnar's eyes gleamed with greed at the sight.

A narrow path paralleled the course of the river during most of these passages, but occasionally the path would veer off as the river passed between high cliffs or beneath a rocky overhang. Always, however, the path would reappear, as reliably as a railway track running alongside a desert highway.

Ulla estimated that their speed was just sufficient to keep ahead of the pursuing Nazis, but not by much. Her calculation was proved during the infrequent straight stretches when an occasional geyser would rise in the water close to them, followed a moment later by the report of a rifle.

For hour after hour the *Berserker* drifted deeper into this forbidden realm. Ulla remained at the stern of the boat, ever watchful for the flash of a gun barrel behind them, but Indy found himself staring off into the darkness ahead of the boat, holding Alecia's unlikely black hat in his hands—and dreaming about things that now could never be.

As Ulla watched and Indy brooded, the *Berserker* sank lower and lower, until the water left no room at all in the cabin. Gunnar had salvaged some food and a coffeepot before abandoning the lower deck altogether, and he lit a small fire from the bits of the ruined boat, intending to make a modest meal to lift their spirits. It seemed to take a long time for the water to boil, and when it finally did and the coffee was made, it was so unbearably hot that the porcelain cups began to crack.

Gunnar questioned Ulla about it.

"Air pressure," Sparks said, and Ulla repeated the answer in Danish. "The air is becoming denser, and the boiling point of water has risen, like in an automobile radiator."

"You're sure?" Ulla asked.

"Normal air pressure is fourteen point seven pounds per square inch at sea level," Sparks said, as if he were reciting a passage from a textbook. "It must be at least double that now."

"Do you remember everything you read?" Indy asked.

"If it's a number," he said. "Sometimes I can't get to sleep at night because I have all of these figures running through my head—equations, telephone numbers, even sports scores."

"That must be horrible," Ulla said.

"No, it's rather pleasant, actually," Sparks told her.

"How deep do you think we are?" Ulla asked.

Sparks shrugged.

"We're at the bottom of a column of air molecules that extends, in its thinnest form, up to a thousand miles in space," he said. "Air does not compress like water does, which doubles its density every thirty-three feet. But the coffee took three or four times longer than usual to boil, right? My guess is that we're at least three hundred miles down by now, and the pressure is double, maybe triple. Of course, I can't know the precise depth without knowing the precise temperature of the water."

"What about the ship's barometer?" Ulla asked. "Wouldn't it give us some idea?"

"It burst," Sparks said. "So did the thermometer. Anything with air sealed inside is likely to implode."

Ulla translated for Gunnar.

"But we have air inside of us, right?" Ulla asked. "Why don't we burst?"

"Because our bodies are mostly water, not gas," Sparks said. "It doesn't compress. And the air spaces we do have in our bodies are not trapped—our lungs, for example, are breathing air that is the same pressure as the outside, so there is an equalizing effect. The only pressure you might feel is in your sinuses, if you have a head cold. Otherwise, you're fine."

"Is there a risk of the bends?" she asked.

"Deep-sea divers are under much more intense pressure," Sparks said. "If we were experiencing this pressure in the ocean, we'd probably be only between sixty and ninety feet. And the bends are caused by rapid ascent, not descent."

"A hundred miles?" Ulla asked reverently. "That's deeper than a human being has ever gone into the earth, deeper by at least ninety-five miles."

"We may not be the first," Indy said. "Baldwin, remember."

Ulla frowned.

"Well, we're the first on record," she said. "Like Columbus. And explorers get to name their discoveries, right?"

"So what do you want to call this place?" Indy asked.

"The Edda Shaft." She translated for Gunnar, and he nodded.

"What's it mean?" Sparks asked.

"Loosely translated," Indy said, "the Shaft of Poetic Saga."

"I'm impressed," Ulla commented. "You *have* read the Icelandic tales, haven't you?"

Water was beginning to wash over the deck now.

"It looks like we're breaking up," Ulla noted. "And this ship is supposed to be unsinkable."

"It's the cork," Sparks said. "The cork is failing because the pressure is collapsing the microscopic air pockets in it. It has lost its buoyancy."

"Well, for whatever reason, it's about time to abandon ship," Indy said. "Everyone here can swim, right?"

"Why are you looking at me?" Sparks asked. "I know how to, theoretically."

Within minutes, the *Berserker* simply sank away beneath their feet, leaving them to swim for it. Ulla slung the submachine gun around her neck and starting kicking for the bank. For a moment Indy thought Gunnar had gone down with his ship, until he saw him bob to the surface and try to tread water with one hand. Indy grabbed him by the collar and towed him behind. But Sparks was the first to reach the bank, even though he gulped mouthfuls of water and was doing a combination dog paddle and frog kick.

"Gee," Sparks said coughing as he crawled dripping onto the rocks. "You'd think with all this air available, we'd float a little better. Sometimes, science just doesn't make sense."

"Wait a minute," Indy said after he was sure Gunnar was all right. "What is this dense atmosphere going to do to a bullet?"

"You mean the trajectory?" Sparks asked. "It'll retard it, but not enough to make much of a difference."

"No," Indy said. "I mean, with the gunpowder."

"Hmm." Sparks stopped to ponder. "That's an interesting thought. We're so deep now, I wouldn't try to shoot those guns of yours."

"Why?"

"Two reasons. One, the increased pressure will make powder burn at higher, more explosive temperatures."

"Like the coffee," Indy said.

"Right."

"And second?"

"This is the interesting part," Sparks said. "Because of the extra power, and the denser and therefore springier gases inside the barrel of a firearm."

"So, what's that mean?" Ulla asked.

"The gun may blow up in your face," Sparks finished. "Chambers and barrels weren't designed for pressures of two or three times normal, and in the brief instant of a gunshot there's no equalization in the barrel."

"Is there any way to make the guns useful?" she asked.

"Yeah," Sparks said. "Take the bullets apart and reduce the amount of powder by at least half—or two thirds, to be on the safe side."

The sound of boots echoed down the passage behind them.

"You're sure?" Indy asked.

"Don't put me on the spot."

"Well, we're about to test your theory," he said. "You three, go on down the passage. I'm going to stay here for a moment, be a target for them."

"Indy!" Ulla said.

"No, go on," he shouted. "And don't try to use that thing you're holding until we find out for sure."

The other three hurried off farther down the path away from the Germans, while Indy hid behind a boulder and waited. When the sound of the boots were nearly upon him, he jumped out.

"Now's your chance!" Indy shouted.

Dortmuller was in the lead, and his submachine gun was up in an instant. He was about thirty yards from Indy. *"Feuer eroffnen!"* Reingold shouted from behind. "Open fire!"

Indy turned on his heels and ran.

Dortmuller aimed at Indy's back and pulled the trigger. The gun exploded with a flash of light and a deafening *whooomp!* in his hands, and the explosion simultaneously set off the remaining twenty rounds in the gun's magazine. As Dortmuller's torso turned into a red haze, pieces of the gun ricocheted off the stone walls and slashed like shrapnel through two of the troopers standing beside him.

A scalding piece of the barrel nicked Indy in the right calf, sending him stumbling to the ground. Then he got to his feet and continued running, but now with a limp.

"Three for the price of one," he panted as he caught up to his companions and sat down on the ground. "That leaves eight of them, I think."

He pulled up his trouser leg and inspected his calf, which was surprisingly free of blood. "But here's an important tip that Sparks failed to mention—the guns explode like bombs, and pieces go in every direction."

Ulla inspected the ugly red welt.

"It didn't hit anything vital," she said. "And the metal was so hot that it cauterized the wound. But you'll have a lovely scar."

"A lovely scar?" Indy asked. "It hurts. Something that feels like this can't be called lovely."

"Consider yourself lucky." Ulla folded her arms, her lips tight. "It could have hit you in the back of the head."

Indy got up, still limping.

"Let's keep going," he said. "Find a place we can rest for a bit and rig the bullets like Sparks said."

"They're going to figure it out, too," Ulla warned.

"Yeah," Indy said proudly, "but we did it first."

Two hours later the path left the river, apparently for good. When it opened into a wide chamber, Indy called for a rest stop, and while they sat they used their teeth to remove the lead bullets from the cartridges and pour out most of the powder.

"Won't this slow the velocity?" Ulla asked.

"Nope," Sparks said. "Guns work from the compression of gases. Things should work out about equal."

"Should," Indy said. "That's a scary word."

"Where do you think this passage is leading us?" Sparks asked nervously. "Do you think it will ever go back up?"

"I don't know," Indy said. "But I intend to find out."

Indy took his two ruined cartridges from the Webley,

pulled the slugs with his teeth, and then used a little of the gunpowder that Ulla had emptied from her ammo.

"Back in business," he said as he holstered the Webley. "Let's go."

"I'm getting awfully tired," Ulla said. "Gunnar and Sparks don't look any better. Can't we rest a little bit longer?"

"Do you think they're resting?"

"No," she said sadly as she replaced the magazine in the MP-40. "How long do you think this can go on?"

"Until it ends," Indy said.

Ulla stood up.

The Nazis suddenly stumbled into the chamber, unaware that Indy and the others had paused there. The troopers fumbled for their guns, and before Ulla could bring her own weapon around, two of them had already begun firing. The air was suddenly filled with ricocheting lead.

"Cover!" Indy shouted.

Ulla took a step toward Indy and the others, then was jerked backward like a puppet as one of the flattened slugs struck her in the chest. Her face was full of surprise as she landed on her rump and elbows on the ground, the machine gun dangling uselessly from the strap around her neck.

She glanced down at the growing crimson stain, then over at Indy with apology in her eyes.

"Sorry," she said.

Indy ran to her.

He grabbed the MP-40 and fired blindly into the Nazis while dragging Ulla away. Gunnar and Sparks were unhurt, and already running. Two of the Nazis fell dead from Indy's barrage and a third clutched his arm before the gun jammed, refusing to eject a shell that had been loaded with too little powder. Indy dropped the gun and hurried with Ulla down the passage.

The Nazis, who were as tired and dazed as their prey by now, hung back for a moment while they counted their losses.

"Sparks!" Indy cried. "Help me."

Sparks got beneath Ulla's shoulder and together they ran with her down the twisting passage, her feet dragging on the floor, splatters of blood marking their trail. Two hundred yards later the passage narrowed and then opened again—this time revealing a cathedral-like chamber with a blank wall opposite them.

"Oh, no," Sparks said.

They placed Ulla on the floor, and Indy unbuttoned her shirt and took a look. Blood was gushing out of a bullet hole on the left side of her sternum.

Ulla looked up at him from beneath half-closed eyes.

"So you were lying when you said you weren't attracted to me," she quipped.

"Shhh," Indy said. "Don't try to talk."

Gunnar took off his sling and ripped it into strips, which he jammed beneath Ulla's blouse in a desperate attempt to stanch the flow of blood. Then he took off his bearskin shirt, rolled it in a ball, and placed it beneath her head.

"What kind of a chamber are we in?" Ulla asked. "It's brighter in here. And there are people on the walls."

Indy glanced around. The aurora glow was brighter in this chamber, and there were shadows on the walls that looked indistinctly like gargoyles.

"Indy," Sparks said.

"Not now," Indy snapped.

"There's a circle of stones in the floor here."

Gunnar took Ulla's hand, and then he nodded toward where Sparks was kneeling.

"I'll be right back," Indy said. "Don't go away."

There were five crystals in a circle of about a foot in diameter, but there were slots for six stones. The five stones in the slots were yellow, violet, blue, red, and green. The stone at the top of the circle was missing.

"What does it mean?" Sparks asked.

Indy reached for the piece of Icelandic spar on the leather strap beneath his shirt. He gave a jerk and snapped the thong, then held the stone up. It had turned from its original smoky color to a milky white.

Indy placed the stone in the vacant spot.

Nothing happened.

"What's it supposed to do?" Sparks asked.

"I don't know," Indy said impatiently. "But it must do something. Open a door, reveal another passage, *something*."

Sparks bit his lip.

"Maybe it has to do with the order of the stones," he said, and sat down cross-legged in front of the stones.

"The message on the Thule Stone," Indy remembered. "It said, 'I am all colors and I am none. Circle me backward and you are undone.' Does that suggest anything to you?"

"Should," Sparks said.

"Don't say that," Indy told him. "Think!"

"You're making me nervous."

"You're making us dead," Indy said.

Sparks reached for the stones.

"Maybe if we just randomly—"

"No." Indy caught his hand. "You have to be sure. Get it backward, and it will be bad."

"What do you mean?"

"I mean *bad*," Indy said. "You don't mess around with these types of warnings. Now, the white crystal obviously is in the right place, because that spot was vacant. What do we do with the other five?"

Gunnar called out.

Indy could hear the sound of boots approaching.

"You've got about thirty seconds," Indy told Sparks. "I'm going to leave you alone. Do it."

Indy returned to Ulla and cradled her in his arms.

"I know what it is," Sparks cried. "It's the spectrum! Arrange the stones according to their visible light frequencies. Clear goes at the top, because all color is contained in white light."

"Good!" Indy shouted. "Do it!"

Sparks began moving the stones.

Gunnar was on his feet, slapping himself in the face, preparing to fight. He ignored the pain in his broken arm. Blood gleamed at the corners of his mouth.

Indy could hear Reingold scream for the troops to move quickly. They were almost to the last bend in the passage. Indy pointed the Webley down the passage, waiting, but his hand was shaking badly.

"Don't die," he whispered to Ulla. "Please. Hang on."

Her blond hair, where the ends brushed against her blouse, was stained a strawberry color, and to Indy the color seemed eerily like Alecia's. Her skin had turned ashen and her lips were tinged with blue. Her breath was ragged and accompanied by a sickening gurgle.

"Jones," she whispered.

"Don't try to talk," Indy said, and wiped his eyes with the back of his gun hand. "Save your strength."

"Be a man," she rasped.

Indy blinked hard.

"What color is between red and green in the spectrum?" Sparks asked calmly.

"Yellow!" Indy shouted. "Hurry up! They're almost here."

"I told you," Sparks said. "Don't make me nervous."

"You're doing great," Indy said encouragingly. He could

hear Sparks beginning to rearrange the stones, each
making a sharp clicking sound as they fell into place.

"Let's see. White at the top. Then—clockwise, right?—
red, yellow, green, blue, and violet."

The room suddenly became hot, unbearably so, and
the air felt like molasses in Indy's lungs. Then the hair on
the back of his neck stood up.

"Do you feel that?" Sparks asked. "Static electricity. The
air has become supercharged. I don't know why."

The Nazis were nearly upon them.

Ulla opened her eyes and looked over Indy's shoulder at
the blank wall beyond. Her eyes widened and she wetted
her blood-flecked lips.

At that moment the Nazis burst into the chamber and
spread out, their guns trained on Indy. Gunnar sprang at
the nearest soldier and wrestled him to the ground, hands
around his throat. Two others grasped Gunnar's arms and
pulled him back, but he threw them off like rag dolls.

Reingold walked over and placed the barrel of his
Walther at the base of Sparks's neck.

"Stop this nonsense," he ordered.

Gunnar stopped fighting, but Indy kept his gun trained
on Reingold.

"Lower your gun," Reingold said.

"Go to hell," Indy spat over the wavering gun barrel.

"It seems we are already there," Reingold said, tugging
at his collar.

The chamber had become suffused with a crimson glow,
and the heat was stifling. A deep rumble shook the floor,
and behind them they could hear stones crashing down to
the floor of the narrow passage. The shadows on the wall,
Indy could now see, were more than shadows—they were
bas-reliefs of gargoyles and skeleton men, all looking as if
they were about to step down from the walls.

"It's becoming a little crowded in here," Sparks said anxiously.

The skeleton men were stepping down from the walls, moving slowly but determinedly, wielding swords and axes. One of the skeletal warriors wore a helmet from ancient Greece, while another had a Roman breastplate and sword. A creature in a doughboy helmet and wielding a wicked-looking stone bayonet hopped down, apparently more eager than the others for combat, and his jawbone clacked rhythmically as he repeated the words: "Hun! Hun! Hun!"

Another hobbled across the floor using his cavalry saber as a cane. His left foot was missing. Atop his skull, at a rakish angle, was a Civil War kepi. Behind him was a Viking skeleton swinging a double-bladed stone ax.

Other warriors were from periods that Indy had never seen before, much less identify, including a skeleton twirling some sort of hand weapon in the shape of a five-pointed star.

After all of the warriors had descended, the gargoyles and chimeras came to life, flapping their gray wings and gnashing their stone teeth.

"Don't be alarmed!" Reingold announced to his men. "These creatures cannot be real. It is some kind of trick. Hold your ground!"

Sergeant Liebel screamed when a bony hand seized him by the shoulder. He emptied the magazine of the machine gun into the rib cage of the apparition, but to no effect. The skeletal warrior dragged him across the floor, stepped back into the wall, taking the hapless Liebel with him. As the others watched in horror the soldier's skin and uniform turned to stone in front of their eyes. He, too, had become part of the bas-relief, complete with steel helmet and machine gun.

"Sparks, this is what I meant by *bad*," Indy shouted.

The Viking warrior had Sparks by the feet and was starting to drag him away from the stones. "Indy, I got it backward," the boy cried while trying to keep his hold on the crystals. "I should have gone the other way."

Meanwhile the four remaining Nazi soldiers dropped their weapons and ran for the passage, but found it blocked by a giant stone. The gargoyles and skeleton warriors advanced, and each Nazi was seized and dragged toward the walls.

Reingold backed away from a particularly hideous-looking creature, a skeleton that carried a samurai sword in one hand and its head in the other. He fired blindly with the Walther as the creature used the point of the sword to back him toward the nearest wall.

Then Indy felt the clawlike fingers of a gargoyle grip his own shoulder. He smashed the monster with the butt of his gun, but to no effect.

"It's like hitting a piece of rock," he yelled.

Gunnar broke away from the gargoyle holding him and then grappled with the skeleton at Sparks's feet while the teenager desperately tried to rearrange the stones so that the sequence of colors around the circle was reversed. He was almost finished when the skeleton got a grip on both of them and began dragging Gunnar and the boy toward the wall.

The four Nazi soldiers were already a part of the hideous tableau, and Reingold had disappeared in the wall up to his waist.

"Indy!" Sparks shouted. He still had the red stone in his hand. "Do something!"

"Throw me the stone!"

Indy was on the floor, with the stone gargoyle on top of him, and the thing was so heavy he couldn't breathe. Then he managed to bring his knees up and push the nightmare back. Sparks tossed Indy the stone.

The gargoyle snarled and bared its fangs, then rushed. Indy instinctively swung the double-terminated crystal like a knife and caught the creature in the face, knocking some of the granite teeth from its mouth.

Indy scrambled over to the circle and placed the red stone in the open spot.

The glow in the chamber changed from red to blue. At the sound of a trumpet, the monsters all stopped. The skeleton men slowly released their prey and returned to assume their original positions in the walls, while the gargoyles snapped and snarled a bit longer before retreating. Even back in the wall, the doughboy's mouth kept repeating, "Hun! Hun! Hun!" But it slowed and eventually stopped, frozen agape.

"Help me," Reingold pleaded. The skeleton with the samurai sword, who was now back on the wall, had left him buried up to his chest.

Indy and Gunnar each grabbed an arm and tried to pull the SS captain out of the wall, but they could not budge him. Reingold began to scream, his face turning purple with pain.

"It's agony," he said. "Don't leave me this way."

"There's nothing we can do," Indy said.

"Kill me," Reingold pleaded as he squirmed.

Gunnar grasped Reingold's head beneath his left arm and gave a sharp twist, snapping his neck. Sparks looked away. Reingold's body shook convulsively. Then his eyes rolled back, his arms went limp, and his head fell forward.

Reingold's silver cigarette case fell from his tunic.

Indy picked it up and looked at the inscription, which was the SS motto: *Meine Ehre heisst Treue.*

"My honor is pure," Indy translated.

Gunnar looked at Indy and shrugged.

Indy shrugged back.

Then he returned to Ulla and knelt beside her.

Her eyes fluttered open.

"I must be dead," she gasped. "The Valkyries are here.
My God, but they are beautiful."

Indy glanced over his shoulder.

Behind the circle of stones, a doorway had opened in
the once-blank wall. A pleasant breeze wafted from the
opening. A trio of shimmering beings of pure light wafted
into the room. They floated and wove around one another
in the air like butterflies, and as they hovered over Ulla
they became almost too bright to look at.

Ulla held out her hand toward them.

At that moment a tall, athletic-looking man in his mid-
fifties appeared in the doorway. He had a long, thin nose,
his hair was cropped close to his head, and his beard was
neatly trimmed. He wore a turtleneck sweater and had an
air of command about him.

Flanking the tall man were a pair of what appeared to
be Tibetan monks in flowing yellow robes.

"Bring her in," the man commanded in English.

The monks took Ulla in their arms and carried her
through the doorway into the brightness beyond.

The tall man waited in the doorway with his arms
crossed.

"Well, are you coming or aren't you?" he asked.

"Yes, sir," Sparks said, and hurried for the doorway.
Gunnar followed, and as Indy passed the circle of stones
he picked up the piece of Icelandic spar.

"The *lapis exilis*," the tall man commanded. "I'll have
that."

"Roald Amundsen, I assume?" Indy asked as he handed
over the stone.

"The same," the tall man answered.

The doorway closed behind them as the monks, leading
the way, took Ulla to a black casket-shaped trough. They
laid her gently inside of it.

They were on a vast columned balcony overlooking a mist-shrouded sea, and peering over the railing Indy could see that the balcony was only part of a huge complex of buildings whose architecture seemed faintly Egyptian. High in the sky was a ball of light that swirled with the colors of the aurora. Across the sea there was an island, and Indy could see a forest of jeweled spires reaching up through the mist.

"Welcome to Ultima Thule," Amundsen said.

"Or Agartha?" Indy asked.

"Whatever one wishes to call it," Amundsen said. "There was once an outpost on the rip of the volcanic peak you came down, but I'm afraid the world has gotten too small for that now."

The monks worked feverishly now, pouring jugs of a glowing liquid substance into the black trough. Indy walked over and peered into Ulla's face, but she seemed quite dead.

He started to put his hand in the liquid, then stopped.

"May I?" he asked.

Amundsen nodded.

The glowing green liquid felt like nothing Indy had ever experienced before. When he scooped some of it into his hand and held it up to examine, the liquid passed right through his palm and dribbled back into the trough.

Indy wiggled his fingers. His hand felt energized.

In the trough, the color was coming back into Ulla's face.

"Vril?" Indy asked.

Amundsen nodded.

"Curious stuff, isn't it?" the tall man asked. "You can do just about anything with it—build cities, or destroy them. Technically, it is the fourth state of matter—plasma. It was forged in the interiors of stars eons ago, and is a type of ionized gas. It floats through space until attracted by earth's magnetic field, then is brought down here with the aurora, where the Aesir collect it."

"Those shimmering things we saw?"

"Yes," Amundsen said. "What they call themselves can't be translated into human speech, so that's the name I employ. It's the collective name of the old Norse gods. They could not live on the surface, you know—the air is much too thin. They wouldn't survive."

"Are there more humans here?" Indy asked.

"Of course," Amundsen said. "But not many. Mostly they are ones that the Aesir trust, like the monks, or people like me, who stumble down here by accident. I must say, they didn't think much of you. They were afraid that you were as bad as all the rest, going around shooting things up and delighting in the deaths of your enemies. They were touched by your obvious affection for the dead woman and the boy, but they would have been just as happy to let you become part of the wall out there."

"Is this a dream?" Indy asked.

"Oh, this is quite real, Dr. Jones," Amundsen said. Then he held up his hand. "Yes, I know all of your names. And I know the sorry state of the world above, so you needn't fill me in on the last seven years. The world is as it has always been, preparing for war."

"Do you have any technical material on any of this?" Sparks asked. "Especially Vril, and how the earth's magnetic field collects it?"

"Technical material?" Amundsen repeated, and laughed. "I'm afraid not. But don't worry. You won't remember any of this when you get back to the surface, I'm afraid."

"Why not?" Sparks asked.

"Well, you have a choice," Amundsen said. "You may stay here in peace and harmony and glimpse the secrets of the cosmos, or you may return to the world above. But if you return, you won't remember any of what you have witnessed. It will be like a dream you had long ago. What will it be?"

"We don't get to think this over?" Sparks asked.

"No," Amundsen said. "The more memories you accumulate here, the harder it is to send you back. Stay more than an hour, and we have no choice but to keep you."

Ulla sat up in the trough. She brushed back her hair, which glowed with the luminous stuff, then felt for the bullet wound beneath her shirt. It was gone.

"Is this Valhalla?" she asked.

"No, my dear." Amundsen smiled benevolently. "You are still among mortals, I'm afraid, though you came very close to passing to the other side."

"Once a person's dead, then, it's not possible to bring her back?" Indy asked.

"No," Amundsen said. "I'm sorry."

Indy nodded sadly.

"It's so beautiful down here," he said as he looked over the railing at the city beyond the sea. "Who would have dared to dream?"

"Our imaginations are really quite limited and centered on what we already know," Amundsen said. "You teach your students that human civilization on this planet goes back, what, five thousand years? Ha. At least a hundred major human civilizations have come and gone in the last twenty thousand years, and that's not counting the communities of nonhuman intelligences. One day it will all be clear—but not today. Your time here is so short that it would only confuse you."

The monks motioned for Gunnar to bring his broken arm over to the trough. Ulla reassured him in Danish, and he reluctantly approached and dipped it into the plasma.

"Does life continue after death?" Indy said.

"How should I know?" Amundsen asked. "I'm not dead yet. But I know what the Aesir tell me—that everything in the universe is connected, that it's all happening at once, and that the passage of time is just an illusion of human consciousness."

"So love is eternal?"

Indy was thinking of Alecia.

"Love, friendship, compassion, joy—what is death compared to these things?" Amundsen asked. "Now, I must have an answer from each of you. Do you stay or do you go?"

Gunnar looked up. He had been inspecting his healed arm, but he knew the tone of a question. Ulla translated for him.

He jerked a thumb upward.

"I agree with Gunnar," Ulla said. "There are still things to accomplish above."

"Dr. Jones?"

"Back," Indy said emphatically.

"Nicholas?" Ulla asked.

Sparks thought for a moment.

"Wow," he said. "What a choice. But I don't think I can leave my mother alone up there. But thanks for everything—you've been swell."

"Yes," Indy said. "Particularly for bringing Ulla back to us."

"She was deserving," Amundsen said. "Or so they tell me."

"Thank you." Ulla leaned over and kissed Amundsen on the cheek. "You have been a hero of mine since I was a little girl. You are like a Viking god in my hometown, and I am sorry that I cannot bring them news of your good health."

"I miss all of Scandinavia," Amundsen said. "And the wild places on the surface. But I needed new worlds to explore. I am beginning to find out that, like the Bible says, the world is without end."

"Say," Indy interjected. "Are you sure that we won't remember any of this?"

"You'll remember up to the part where you came through the door," Amundsen said. "But nothing of what has transpired after."

"Hey, Sparks," Indy said. "Remember when I promised to tell you what my real name was if we got through this? Well, now's the time. It's Henry, but my dad always called me *Junior*."

"Dr. Jones," Sparks said. "You're a rat."

"Now," Amundsen said, "it is time for you to leave. Please follow the monks. And, farewell."

"Good-bye," Indy said, and shook Amundsen's hand.

They followed the monks along the balcony to an altar placed between two great columns. The star-shaped construction was made from a translucent blue material, and a set of steps led up to it. The rays of the aurora cascaded down onto the altar from a channel high above them, and then trickled like water down a series of broad marble steps to the multicolored sea below.

"Too bad we won't remember any of this." Sparks frowned.

"In dreams, Nicholas," Ulla said. "Only in dreams."

The monks motioned for them to step up onto the altar.

Ulla went first, ascending confidently and then spreading her arms. Her hair flowed about her as if she were floating in a pool of water, and then her body began to glitter. Suddenly she was gone.

Gunnar went next, hesitantly.

Then Indy motioned for Sparks.

"Please," Sparks said. "I'd like to go last, if you don't mind."

"But you will come?" Indy asked.

"I promise."

Indy stepped up onto the altar. He felt nothing at first,

and then a dreamlike feeling rushed over him, and then there was a sensation of floating. He felt his glittering body leave the altar. He was flying up, passing effortlessly and without fear through miles and miles of rock, toward the warmth of the sun.

EPILOGUE

Indiana Jones woke on his back in the snow. A husky was standing over him, licking his face.

"What the—"

He sat up. Then he shook Gunnar and Sparks, who were sleeping next to him. Ulla was already awake. She was sitting in the snow, petting the dog and laughing. There were no footprints around them, not even their own.

They were on a slope overlooking a town that consisted of a dozen buildings, a glittering blue bay spreading out beyond it. At the near edge of the town was an airfield. They could see the *Penguin* shining in the sun.

"Where are we?" Indy asked.

"Ny Alesund on Spitsbergen Island," Ulla answered. "The northernmost town in the world."

"How do you know?"

"That sign on the roof of that hangar says so," Ulla said.

They pulled Gunnar and Sparks to their feet, then all four of them raced down the slope, the dog trotting happily beside them. The sun was shining brightly, and despite the cold, Indy felt incredibly rested and alive.

As they neared the airfield the dog ran ahead, barking.

The commotion brought Clarence to the door of the hangar. He was eating a ham sandwich, and he opened the door to pet the husky and give him a bite. Then he looked up and saw Indy and the others crossing the snow-packed field.

Clarence shot out of the door, crossed the field like a track star, and grasped Indy in a bear hug.

"Buddy, I thought I'd never see you again," he gushed. "I felt so guilty after we got back in the air and couldn't find you. We looked, I swear we did."

"It's okay," Indy said. "Put me down."

Clarence stepped back and shook his head in wonder.

"How did you get here?" he asked.

Indy looked at the others, and they returned his blank stare.

"Buddy," he said, "we're not sure."

"What d'ya mean?"

"I mean we don't know," Indy said. "We can't remember."

"Well, you didn't get far in those clothes," Clarence said. "Somebody had to pick you up or something. But if you don't want to tell me, I understand. This big guy probably found you, whoever he is."

"This is Gunnar," Indy said. "He rescued us on the ice."

"Well, there you are."

"No, a lot more happened after that," Indy said. "I remember parts of the last few days, but not all of it. Reingold and his squad are dead, I know that."

"I don't remember much, either," Sparks said.

"What about your girlfriend on the Graf?" Clarence asked.

Indy looked at Clarence and blinked.

"Alecia is dead," Indy said. "Reingold shot her."

"I'm sorry."

"So am I," Indy said.

"Well, come on in and get warm," Clarence said. "Captain Blessant and Sergeant Bruce are at the trading post, but will they be glad to see you when they get back. And Marcus Brody has been driving us nuts trying to find out what's happened to you."

"You still have the skull?"

"Yeah," Clarence said. "And that thing gives me the creeps. I finally stuffed it in a cardboard box because that cloth you had it wrapped in kept coming off somehow."

"Show it to me," Indy said.

They entered the hangar, and Clarence brought him the box.

Indy peered inside to make sure the Crystal Skull was there, but he did not take it out of the box.

"What are you going to do with it?" Clarence asked.

"Put it back where I found it," Indy said. "Before it has a chance to ruin somebody else's life."

Indy put the box down.

"What're we going to tell Major Markham?" Indy wondered aloud. "What am I going to tell Brody? I'm not sure which parts of what I remember are a dream and what's not."

"The Edda Shaft was no dream," Ulla said.

"Well," Indy asked, "do you think you can find it again?"

"No," Ulla answered.

"Me neither."

"In that case," Ulla said sadly, "it's just another story."

"But you know," Sparks said, "I have the impression that we did something important, like avoiding that final battle that Ulla and Gunnar were talking about."

"Ragnarok?" Ulla smiled. She looked in turn at each of the now familiar faces around her, and then settled her gaze on Indy. He felt her ice-blue eyes looking through him to something beyond.

"It can never be avoided," she said. "Only postponed."

AFTERWORD

The Conquest of Inner Space

As fantastic as hollow-earth theories may seem to us now, they were once a subject of serious scientific debate. The reason so much speculation turned out to be dead wrong may be that the interior of the planet has proved so inaccessible—and, more significantly, unobservable.

Unlike the night sky, which offers clues across the gulf of time and space in the clockworklike movements of stars and planets, the ground resists attempts to probe its secrets by the use of human senses. It was not until the invention of the seismograph in 1897, and the subsequent study of the speed and direction of earthquake shock waves as recorded by a network of seismograph stations around the world, that scientists concluded that the earth was solid.

Such inaccessibility has made the inner earth as much, if not more, of a challenge to exploration than the nearer reaches of outer space. In 1969, human beings crossed a quarter of a million miles of inhospitable space to walk on the surface of the moon; now, nearly three decades later, we have penetrated only seven and one half miles into the crust of the earth, via a borehole in the Kola Peninsula of Russia.

Thanks to intense intellectual exploration, scientists now believe they have a pretty good idea of the composition of the inner earth: its crust ranges from two to seventy-five miles thick, followed by 1,800 miles of rocky mantle, all encompassing a core of molten metal, at which the pressure is 3.6 million times that of the earth's surface. Still cooling from the fires of creation, the inner earth releases heat in the form of convection currents that create volcanoes and earthquakes and push the continents slowly apart.

Worlds Within Worlds

Hollow-earth theories have had a curious link with the history of polar exploration. From the discovery of the continent of Antarctica to the controversy surrounding Admiral Byrd's cryptic remarks following an overflight of the North Pole, such theories refuse to die.

Perhaps it is because both regions remained inaccessible for so long, and our imaginations naturally precede us to those places we can't reach; or, it may be an unwillingness to surrender the power and magic of belief to the often dream-shattering rationality of science. After all, it is more fun to dream of lost worlds beneath our feet than crust, mantle, and core.

And the dreams have been with us longer.

Just as some of our ancestors looked skyward and imagined explanations for the panoply of lights, others pondered the earth and tried to explain what was below. Although the Western tradition has been to ascribe rather unpleasant qualities to the nether regions—the Greeks

imagined Hades as a dismal place populated by the joyless
dead, and Christian hell, traditionally located underground, is a place of eternal suffering for the damned—to
Eastern minds, the depths might harbor utopia. Buddhists
in Central Asia, for example, tell of the ancient Kingdom of
Agartha (or Agharta), a refuge for the survivors of lost continents. The capital city of this underworld paradise is
Shamballah, where the benevolent King of the World
keeps watch over the affairs of humanity through his
magic mirror. A network of labyrinthine tunnels connected to Tibetan monasteries are traversed by monks
who carry his secret messages to the above world.

In 1692, astronomer Edmond Halley (of comet fame)
told the Royal Society of London that there were no less
than three inner earths, each inhabited, and corresponding
in size to Mercury, Venus, and Mars. The Aurora Borealis,
he said, was the luminous atmosphere from these inner
earths seeping from the thin crust over the North Pole.

A St. Louis trading post operator, John Cleves Symmes,
declared in 1818 that not only were there *five* concentric
spheres inside the earth, but huge openings at the poles as
well. In a "letter to all the world," Symmes claimed the
portals would lead to a land that was warm and rich, and
he asked for one hundred adventurers to accompany him
on an expedition northward from Siberia.

Despite widespread ridicule, Symmes won a few con-
verts to his theory, including newspaper and magazine
writer Jeremiah N. Reynolds. In 1828, Congress autho-
rized a polar expedition to search for the opening to
Symmes's interior world, but the expedition met a
decade's worth of political delays. Symmes died in 1829
and Reynolds, tired of waiting for the official expedition,
joined a seal-hunting expedition for the South Seas. He
returned and told stories of a lucrative whaling trade in the
direction of the south antipode, and it was this appeal to

commerce that finally prompted Congress in 1836 to fund the long-awaited search.

The Wilkes Expedition, 1838–42, named for commander Charles Wilkes, was the first to team civilian scientists with a naval crew. Although the expedition found no portal, it made a number of important scientific discoveries and surveyed enough coastline to prove that Antarctica was indeed the seventh continent.

Cyrus Read Teed, a Civil War veteran and herb doctor, contributed a unique twist to both cult religion and pseudoscience in a book he wrote under the pseudonym of Koresh—Hebrew for Cyrus—which claimed that we lived on the *inner* surface of a hollow sphere. A sun at the center, dividing equally into dark and light areas, gave the illusion of rising and setting. Outside the sphere, Teed said, there was only a great void.

Teed believed this reductionistic vision of the universe amounted to nothing less than a religious revelation and based a new religion on it, called *Koreshanity*, and proclaimed himself messiah. He established a church, a college, and in 1894 founded a community near Fort Myers, Florida. When Teed died in 1908, his followers waited in vain for his (self)-prophesied resurrection. His tomb was washed away by a hurricane in 1921, and in the 1960s, the community was turned into the Koreshan State Historic Site.

Other grist for the hollow-earth mill included a long-dead but well-preserved woolly mammoth, colored snow, and—of course—more fantastic tales. In 1846 a woolly mammoth—an extinct species—was found frozen in the ice in Siberia. The animal was in such a retarded state of decomposition that, in its stomach, its last meal could be identified. For decades the discovery stirred controversy, and some claimed that the animal had not been dead for thousands of years at all, but had simply died in the interior of the earth—where mammoths are plentiful—and drifted to the outside on an ice floe. Some arctic travelers reported seeing snow in various shades of red, green, and even black. Theorists quickly seized on this as evidence that pollen was wafting from a verdant interior world to stain the snow around the portals.

But more exciting was the publication, in 1908, of a book by Willis George Emerson called *The Smoky God, or, a Voyage to the Inner World*. It was the story of a ninety-five-year-old Norwegian sailor, Olaf Jansen, who claimed that as a boy he and his father sailed to Franz Josef Land in search of ivory tusks—and, driven off course by a terrible storm, found themselves in an inner world lit by a smoky sun. The pair remained for more than two years among a race of giants who lived in golden cities and feasted like gods. Sadly, on their return to the exterior world through the south polar opening, their sloop was crushed by an iceberg, the father drowned, and the son was rescued by a passing whaler. But why did Jansen wait until the end of his life to tell his tale? When he first described the wonders of the inner world, Jansen said, he was locked away in an insane asylum for twenty-eight years.

Emerson was not the only writer who was inspired by a vision of a hollow earth. Edgar Allen Poe was so influenced by Symmes's theory—and the championing of it by Reynolds—that he wrote a short story, "Ms. Found in a Bottle," about a ship-swallowing hole at the South Pole. He later took a different approach to the same theme in his longest work of fiction, *The Narrative of Arthur Gordon Pym*. Curiously, as Poe lay dying in a Baltimore hospital in 1849, he repeatedly called for Reynolds in his delirium. Although some scholars think he was calling for a family friend, others believe he was asking for the South Seas explorer.

Jules Verne, the prophetic French science-fiction writer, was almost certainly influenced by Symmes and other nineteenth-century theorists, and the result was one of his most popular novels, *Journey to the Center of the Earth*, published in 1864. In it, the narrator and his uncle, an eccentric professor, descend into the cone of a volcano in Iceland and follow a trail of clues left by their intrepid predecessor, a sixteenth-century alchemist named Arne Saknussemm. Along the way they find a vast ocean, prehistoric monsters, and the bones of a race of giants. Their adventure, however, fails to fulfill the promise of Verne's title: the intrepid, if fictional, travelers descend less than a hundred miles into the earth.

Edward Bulwer-Lytton, a Victorian novelist and member of Parliament, imagined an underground civilization of superhumans in *The Coming Race*, which was published posthumously in 1873.

Lord Lytton, whose best-known work is the historical novel *The Last Days of Pompeii*, describes an apparent utopia populated by a race of giants who have mastered a liquid substance called Vril, making them the lords of all forms of matter. The motto of this society of supermen is, "No happiness without order, no order without authority, no authority without unity." Although the novel is clearly a cautionary tale—the narrator recognizes this supposed utopia for what it really is and eventually escapes to warn the world—some groups found comfort in its vision of an advanced authoritarian society. The novel became part of the unofficial canon of turn-of-the-century occult lore.

In 1933, James Hilton (and later, movie director Frank Capra) offered a variation of the Shamballah myth in *Lost Horizon*, which told of a paradise of eternal youth and refuge from war called Shangri-la in a hidden valley somewhere in the Himalayas. From 1925 to 1928, a Russian artist named Nicholas Roerich led an expedition that

scoured Tibet looking for the real (and allegedly subterranean) Agartha. Although Roerich did not find a
physical entrance to the hidden kingdom, he apparently
found a spiritual one, which he discussed in his 1930 book,
Shamballah: In Search of the New Era. Roerich also produced a number of striking paintings inspired by his
Tibetan adventure, became a leading peace activist, and
returned to Tibet in 1935 to resume his search.

Nazis and the Occult

Pop culture to the contrary, we will probably never
know to what extent Adolf Hitler and the Nazi party were
influenced by the occult. Much is a matter of interpreta-
tion, and what may seem to one person a healthy interest
in folklore—a pagan ceremony in celebration of Nordic
ancestry, for example—may strike others as a morbid
interest in magic.

There was, however, both a Thule Society and a Luminous Lodge of the Vril, much as described in *Indiana
Jones and the Hollow Earth*. From the Thule Society came
the German Workers Party, which Hitler reorganized as
the Nazis.

The Thule group was named for a mythical island in the
North Atlantic that, in folklore, was the center of an
Atlantis-like lost civilization. After World War I, the Thule
Society evolved as a sort of anti-Communist, anti-Semitic,
nationalist study group. Some of its members were also
deeply involved in the occult movement, which had
spread from England and the turn-of-the-century Theo-
sophical Society.

It is often reported that Hitler and other Nazi leaders
took seriously hollow-earth theories and reports of secret
underground kingdoms. Hitler, so the story goes, dis-

patched squads to the deepest mines in Europe and to the Himalayas in search of the entrance to Agartha, and at one point during World War II had top German scientists testing Koreshian theories of a concave earth. Such tales have become the apocrypha of World War II, repeated from one popular writer to the next. Even if true, the layers of secondhand information that surround them would make substantiation maddeningly difficult even for the most dedicated of scholars.

It is uncertain as well whether Hitler was a member of the Thule group—or what he truly believed in regard to the occult—but some leading Nazis, such as Deputy Führer Rudolf Hess, were members. Hess was also a devotee of astrology, but astrology's most potent contribution to World War II was not in predicting the future, but in people's belief that it could. Both the Axis and the Allies used bogus astrological forecasts to influence public opinion at home and abroad.

Heinrich Himmler, the head of Hitler's secret police, sought to imbue the SS with a mystical pagan tradition better suited to the Middle Ages than the twentieth century. Even if Himmler was not a practitioner of black magic, as some claim, his deeds could hardly be considered any less diabolical: as the chief enforcer of the concentration-camp system, he was ultimately responsible for the executions of eleven million people.

Also, it is important to remember that not all—or even most—Germans during this period were Nazis. The Nazis existed as a minority party for years before coming to power through a complex chain of events, and even at the height of their power failed to gain as much as fifty percent of the popular vote. Because of the lack of news and information available to people living under a dictatorship, many Germans never knew the extent of human suffering caused by many Nazi policies.

E. B. Baldwin

Evelyn Briggs Baldwin was born in 1862, during the Civil War, and grew up near Edna, in Southeast Kansas. After graduating from North-Western College at Naperville, Illinois, in 1885, he toured Europe by bicycle and returned to Kansas two years later to become principal of Oswego High School. His adventurous spirit refused to be tied down for long, however; in 1891, according to an *Oswego Independent* report of the time, Baldwin made a night ascent of Pike's Peak—during a thunderstorm.

In 1892 he became an observer of the U.S. Weather Bureau, and his skill with meteorological instruments earned him a spot in the North Greenland Expedition of Robert E. Peary a year later. Having received an impressive endorsement from Peary for perseverance and resourcefulness, Baldwin began to lecture about the Arctic. His goal was to raise enough funds to mount his own expedition in search of the North Pole.

So bitten was Baldwin by the arctic bug that in 1897 he raced to Spitsbergen Island, hoping to convince Salomon Andree to give him a berth on an intended balloon exploration of the pole. Lucky for Baldwin that he arrived late; neither the balloon nor Andree was seen again for the next thirty-three years. Andree's body, and those of his two companions, were found in 1930.

In 1898, Baldwin was the second in command of the Wellman expedition, during which he established Fort McKinley in Franz Josef Land. On the same expedition, he discovered Graham Bell Land.

Baldwin's dreams of his own polar expedition were realized through the generosity of William Ziegler, a retired Brooklyn businessman who had made a fortune in baking powder and real estate. In 1901, Ziegler announced his commitment to plant the American flag at the North Pole. He backed his boast with a quarter of a million dollars for an expedition, to be led by Baldwin.

The Baldwin-Ziegler expedition was reportedly one of the most lavish ever mounted, with forty-two men, fifteen Siberian ponies, and four hundred dogs. Despite careful planning, it failed when a supply ship didn't arrive on time, and Baldwin's stock of supplies began to run low. One of the balloon messages Baldwin sent during June 1902 was found by Russian fishermen in 1949. It read: "Five ponies and 150 dogs remaining. Desire hay, fish, and 30 sledges." Rather than tempt disaster, Baldwin returned to Norway—and brought with him the first motion pictures shot in the Arctic.

Disappointed with the expedition's failure to reach the pole, and because of differences Baldwin had with the expedition's sailing master, Ziegler refused to fund Baldwin a second time. He did, however, bankroll a 1903 expedition led by one of Baldwin's subordinates, Anthony Fiala. Ziegler died in 1905, before learning that Fiala had failed as well.

Baldwin continued to lecture and campaign for funds, and on at least one occasion tried to stir interest by claiming the aurora borealis could be harnessed to provide the world with a never-ending supply of electrical energy. But if he discovered the secret to this (or any other) arctic mystery, he kept it to himself.

Baldwin never again received the funding necessary for another expedition. His ambition was thwarted for good when his old commander, Robert E. Peary, reached the North Pole in 1909. From then on, history relegated the flamboyant adventurer and self-promoter to obscurity.

After World War I, Baldwin took a series of minor government appointments until he lost his last position under the New Deal. In poverty and living on the generosity of his friends, he died in October 1933 of a fractured skull after being struck by an automobile on a busy street in Washington, D.C.

Baldwin never married. His closest surviving relative, a niece by the name of Geraldine Pinsor, died in Oswego in the 1980s. She should not be confused with the entirely fictional niece, Zoë Baldwin. And unlike the portrayal of this event in *Indiana Jones and the Hollow Earth*, foul play was not suspected in the automobile accident that caused the explorer's death.

Such liberties will be forgiven, it is hoped, in the name of adventure.

ABOUT THE AUTHOR

Max McCoy is an award-winning journalist and author whose Bantam novels include *The Sixth Rider* and *Sons of Fire*. He lives in Pittsburg, Kansas, where he is currently at work on the next Indiana Jones novel.

Don't miss
INDIANA JONES
AND THE
SECRET OF THE SPHINX

Coming Soon
from Bantam Books

⊰ **INDIANA JONES** ⊱

Bold adventurer, swashbuckling explorer, Indy unravels the mysteries of the past at a time when dreams could still come true. Now, in a series officially licensed from Lucasfilm, we learn what shaped Indiana Jones into the hero he is today!

THE PERIL AT DELPHI by Rob MacGregor
_____ 28931-4 $4.99/$5.99 in Canada

THE DANCE OF THE GIANTS by Rob MacGregor
_____ 29035-5 $4.99/$5.99 in Canada

THE SEVEN VEILS by Rob MacGregor
_____ 29334-6 $4.99/$5.99 in Canada

THE GENESIS DELUGE by Rob MacGregor
_____ 29502-0 $4.99/$5.99 in Canada

THE UNICORN'S LEGACY by Rob MacGregor
_____ 29666-3 $4.99/$5.99 in Canada

THE INTERIOR WORLD by Rob MacGregor
_____ 29966-2 $4.99/$5.99 in Canada

THE SKY PIRATES by Martin Caidin
_____ 56192-8 $4.99/$5.99 in Canada

THE WHITE WITCH by Martin Caidin
_____ 56194-4 $4.99/$5.99 in Canada

PHILOSOPHER'S STONE by Max McCoy
_____ 56196-0 $4.99/$5.99 in Canada

THE DINOSAUR EGGS by Max McCoy
_____ 56193-6 $4.99/$6.99 in Canada

Ask for these books at your local bookstore or use this page to order.

Please send me the books I have checked above. I am enclosing $_____ (add $2.50 to cover postage and handling). Send check or money order, no cash or C.O.D.'s, please.

Name _____

Address _____

City/State/Zip _____

Send order to: Bantam Books, Dept. FL 7, 2451 S. Wolf Rd., Des Plaines, IL 60018
Allow four to six weeks for delivery.
Prices and availability subject to change without notice.   FL 7 3/97